—————• THE SEEKERS | BOOK TWO •—————

THE STUFF OF STARS

DAVID LITWACK

FIRST EDITION SOFTCOVER
ISBN: 1622534360
ISBN-13: 9781622534364

Content Editor: John Anthony Allen
Senior/Line Editor: Lane Diamond
Interior layout & design by Mallory Rock

Printed in the U.S.A.
www.EvolvedPub.com
Evolved Publishing LLC
Cartersville, Georgia

Other Books by David Litwack

Along the Watchtower

The Daughter of the Sea and the Sky

The Children of Darkness – The Seekers Book 1

www.DavidLitwack.com

For Mary Anne, who always knew I would write again.

Part One

THE MASTERS OF MACHINES

"I will tell you a great secret, Captain, perhaps the greatest of all time. The molecules of your body are the same molecules that make up this station, and the nebula outside — that burn inside the stars themselves. We are star stuff. We are the Universe made manifest, trying to figure itself out."

- Delenn, Babylon 5

Chapter 1

The Shining City

I startled awake to the touch of a ragamuffin boy with long hair tangled into knots. He wore a threadbare shirt and leggings with holes at the knees, and seemed no more than nine years old. I blinked at him three times to drive the cobwebs from my mind.

The boy stared back with eyes too big for his head.

After a moment, he reached out a finger and brushed something coarse from my cheek. Wet sand caked on my skin. I must have been lying face down.

I rolled over and sniffed. The air bore the brackish odor of low tide, thank the light. Had the tide been higher, I'd have drowned. I inhaled more deeply. Low tide for sure, a stale smell of tides gone by, of half-conscious sailors who had crashed on the reefs before me. The air still reeked of their fear at finding themselves, as I did, alone in a new land.

Well, not entirely alone.

"Who... are you?" My voice sounded scratchy like the sand. *How long have I been lying here?*

The boy stayed silent as my memories trickled back in. My name, Orah Weber. My birthplace, Little Pond. The discovery of the long-lost keep. The building of the boat, the first of its kind in hundreds of years. Its once unthinkable launch from the far side of the granite mountains. The endless days at sea. The storm.

Nathaniel!

I raised up on one elbow and scanned my surroundings. "Do you know where my friend is?"

The boy shook his head. Still no sound from his lips.

A clamor from behind, and I twisted around to catch a gaggle of children approaching from the dunes above the beach. Arms were raised, fingers pointed, and the younger ones squealed with delight. Then a cry of relief from a deeper voice, one I knew so well.

I turned to thank the boy for leading Nathaniel to me but saw only his back as he raced off down the beach, leaving a trail of bare footprints in the sand.

I shook off the crick in my neck and sat up to greet the newcomers.

These new children were different, cleaner and better kempt than the silent boy. Their hair was short and razor cut, like the hair of all who had come of age in Little Pond.

A girl marched at their lead, barking out orders for the younger children to stay in line. She strode down the dunes, flush with the fragile self-assurance of early adulthood, so much like me when I first set out to seek the keep. She wore tight-fitting pants that reached midway down her calves, and a tunic with no visible belt or button to hold it in place. Her clothing was made of a material like none I'd ever seen, gleaming almost metallic in the sunlight.

The fog in my mind continued to clear as an onshore breeze kicked up, making the girl's tunic billow.

I scrambled to my feet, checking for injuries as I stood—nothing but bumps and bruises. Then I limped off to meet Nathaniel as he sprinted toward me like the winner of a race at festival. Neither of us slowed until we were wrapped in each other's arms.

Nathaniel. My best friend. My husband.

I held him close, consumed by the same fear that had haunted me after our escape from Temple City—that one day we'd be separated forever. But now, like then, I had little time to savor the moment. I pulled away to assess his wellbeing. Sand mottled his hair and beard, and a purple welt blossomed on his right forearm where the sleeve of his tunic had torn, but no other wound showed.

As I breathed a sigh of relief, he glanced over his shoulder.

The girl had whirled on her troop, quelling their excitement with a wave of her hand and urging them to retreat up the dunes, as if coming to the beach had trespassed on enemy territory.

I questioned Nathaniel with my eyes, but he answered without a word, reaching out a hand and beckoning me to follow.

I did my best to keep up with the children on legs unsteady from the weeks at sea. As I staggered along, I studied them.

Each wore a hand-sized black box in a pouch at their hip, and carried a sack filled with fresh fish. Some of the older boys brandished sticks with sharpened points. Spears for fishing, or weapons for defense?

At the top of the dunes, their leader stopped before a series of stone benches. "Rest here," she said. "We mustn't stay long, but you'll need to get your legs under you before you make the trek uphill."

"What if more IBs come?" the youngest boy whispered.

"Hush, Timmy. Can't you see how tired they are? Besides, we have time. The IBs don't worship till sunset."

My legs throbbed too much to be concerned with sunset or IBs, whoever they might be. I collapsed with Nathaniel on the nearest bench.

"Who... are you?" I struggled to form the words through parched lips.

"I am Kara. You sound as if you need a drink." She reached into her pocket and withdrew a soft-skinned bottle, like a Little Pond goatskin, but made from the same shiny material as her tunic. "Have some of mine. Take as much as you want. The streams on the lower mountain have all gone foul, but the desals make all the water we need from the sea. At least when they function."

I took a sip from the bottle. The water tasted sweet with a hint of apple.

Kara hovered over me as I drank. Her eyes shone with a forced pride, like someone filled with doubt trying to look confident. She blinked and turned her attention to Nathaniel, who sprawled on the bench beside me, then lowered her voice and spoke in the way people back home addressed a vicar. "Are you from the ancient land?"

"If you mean the land across the sea, then yes." His voice sounded raspy like mine.

I passed him the water skin.

"We learned about you in our lessons," Kara said. "The mentor taught us that people lived on the far side of the ocean, but they'd forgotten how to think. One day, he said, they'd remember and sail here." Her smile broadened. "And now you have come."

3

The boy who had asked about the bench stepped forward and tugged at Kara's thumb. "Could they be dreamers?"

"No, Timmy."

"They might be."

"You mustn't pretend. It's unseemly. Use your brain. We have no reason to believe they're dreamers."

Undeterred, the boy huddled with the other children and whispered.

I picked up snippets of his words. "... might be... what if... the dreamers returned."

"Who are the dreamers?" I said.

The children stopped their chatter and stared at their shoe tops.

After an awkward moment, Kara stepped forward. "The mentor prefers we call them machine masters."

"But—"

"You must be hungry. We've caught fish to cook, and hopefully, the synthesizers will work today and make something tasty to go with them. Come now. We need to leave this place before the grown-up IBs come for their sunset nonsense. Come with us to the city."

I scanned the woods bordering the beach, hoping to catch sight of the shimmering towers I'd seen from our boat before the storm struck. Nothing. We sat too near the slope, and tall trees blocked our view.

I looked to Kara instead. "Is the city where your elders live?"

She eyed me. "What are elders?"

"I'm sorry. I don't know the words you use. We're seeking the descendants of those who first came here, the kin of the keepmasters."

The girl stared open-mouthed.

"The ones who built the city," I said.

More chatter from the younger children, and Kara hissed at them to be quiet.

I overheard the same phrase as before: *the dreamers.*

At last Kara turned back to me. "Those who built the city have gone to a higher place. The mentor can tell you more. We'll take you to him."

I took one final swig of the sweet water and forced myself to stand. My muscles groaned, but my mind churned. *Desals and synthesizers, machine masters and dreamers?* We had lots to learn.

The children hoisted their sacks and led us along a muddy road that straddled the rim of the cliffs. Breakers from the storm still pounded the rocks and sent an angry spray across our path. Clouds of squawking gulls wheeled overhead, eyeing the catch of fish.

After a while, we left the gulls behind and entered a well-trodden trail cut through the woods. The scent of the sea dwindled with the offshore breeze, replaced by the welcome smells of land — pine resin and moist earth, growing plants and animals with fur instead of scales. How good to leave the tumultuous sea behind, even if its waters represented our last link to home.

The line of children rambled along without speaking. What must they think of us, these strangers who'd crashed so unceremoniously on their shore?

A rustling in the trees distracted me.

Not far from the start of the inland path, the silent boy peeked at us between the branches. The other children ignored him.

I caught up to Kara. "Who is that boy, and why do you pretend he's not there?"

Kara shrugged. "He's an IB."

"What's an IB?"

"They call themselves people of the earth, but we call them greenies, just as they call us technos. The younger children prefer IB, short for ishkabibblers. The mentor teaches us that their thoughts are nothing but babble. That's why we started calling them ishkabibblers."

I gaped at her, my mind too tired to comprehend.

Her mouth spread into a grin. "You know, the sound you make by running your fingers over your lips while humming."

She demonstrated, making the silly sound, and the other children joined in.

I had to laugh despite the cramps in my legs, and she laughed with me. I glanced over my shoulder, taking in the last glimpse of the ocean. *How different this new land is from our side of the sea.*

Nathaniel smiled and squeezed my hand, and I squeezed back. Then I looked past him into the woods, searching for the young IB, but the boy had vanished, devoured by the trees.

***

We followed the techno children on a serpentine path steep enough to challenge our breathing. In places where the footing turned treacherous, with slick roots and loose scree, some craftsman had embedded stone steps to ease the way. After too many weeks on the waves, Nathaniel and I tottered along, clinging to each other for support as we fought the lingering sense of the ground undulating underfoot.

I swallowed to wet my throat. The water Kara had shared had been insufficient to quench my thirst, but my stomach growled as well. How long had I lain asleep on the sand? To the west, the sun sank low on the horizon, heralding the advent of twilight. Our boat had crashed before dawn. A whole day lost.

Our last week at sea, we'd rationed both food and water. Now hunger and thirst conspired to muddle my mind, and the usual fire in Nathaniel's eyes had dimmed as well. I willed myself to keep up with the children, driven by a new hope — that any second the shining city I'd seen from the boat would appear. I prayed it was no illusion.

After a while, we emerged from the woods into a rounded knoll, its edges too perfect to be natural. The clearing marked the start of a paved road with the blackened surface I'd viewed on screens in the keep. This road, however, had buckled from weather, leaving cracks and hollows. Recent damage, I prayed, for these descendants of the keepmasters would never tolerate imperfection. Then I glanced up, and my doubts evaporated.

The shining city was no illusion, no trick of the dark or the storm. The road led to a hilltop adorned with beams of light streaming to the sky, more glorious than anything in the keepmasters' city, even before it fell into ruin. These rays glimmered in the impending dusk, bringing joy to the heavens, the first row as high as I could see, but then the next, farther back and even higher, and then another and another.

The keep had opened my eyes to the past, but my people had shunned what we'd found, wary of a return to the darkness. After centuries of stagnation, their vision had narrowed, and their sense of adventure had dulled. We'd crossed the ocean to prove the possible, to show what a boldness of spirit could achieve. We'd hoped to discover the future.

Now we'd done it. We'd found the kin of the keepmasters. How far had these people advanced in the past thousand years? What wonders awaited?

Nathaniel threw an arm around my waist and pulled me tight. "You see it too, don't you? It's all real."

I clutched him closer as we stared up. "Your dream come true."

"*Our* dream."

The city had been cut into a sheer rock face that girded the midsection of the mountain. Higher up, a second cliff loomed, with another man-made structure carved into it. I strained to distinguish its features, but mist from a nearby waterfall veiled its lines. To be visible from so far away, the place must be a fortress for giants.

Far above both, a snow-covered peak lorded over the land, as if to remind its citizens that, despite their genius, a greater power ruled their world.

As we drew closer, I had to cup a hand over my eyes to see through the glare. An arched gate straddled the road ahead, providing the only access to the city or the mountain beyond. The wall of light combined with the rock face to create an impassible barrier, seemingly built to keep out the most powerful of enemies.

When we rounded the final curve, the road straightened, letting me grasp the details more clearly. The arch was made not of light like the wall, but of sandstone, with carvings etched across its top, faded images I could recognize only by squinting and using my imagination—men and women, it seemed, clutching scrolls and instruments in their hands, with tiny wings on their shoulders. On either side of the opening stood a statue of a stone warrior, four times Nathaniel's height and twice his girth. Each carried two swords crossed on their armored chests, and their eyes glowed red and unblinking.

Through the arch, I was surprised to find not a glorious city, but a cluster of dwellings cobbled from sheets of metal and covered with gray slate roofs. These appeared humbler than a Little Pond cottage and crammed together to fill every inch of space. Neither land nor trees separated the dwellings; no vegetable garden or flower box added color to the gray.

Behind the dwellings, a sturdier structure dominated, more substantial than the others. It was capped with a dome that seemed to mimic the mountain, a place where the interior might meet my lofty expectations. Yet even at this distance, I sensed something wrong. The walls of light blazed too brightly for the dwellings inside, too magnificent even for the austere dome. And a sadness pervaded the place, as if some tragedy had happened there and left its mark in the bones of the city.

A flutter unsettled my stomach, different from hunger. *What if these aren't the visionaries we'd come all this way to find?*

A rush of feathers churned the air as a flock of blackbirds startled and took flight, a foreboding cloud darkening the already dim sky. They squawked and swirled and flew off toward the distant cliffs, as if the fortress that loomed higher up was their resting place. In an instant the sky had cleared and all was silent again.

7

With the birds announcing our approach, the dwellings came alive. More techno children poured forth from the gate to greet us, all bearing the same hand-sized black box carried by our companions

Two red-haired girls raced to the front, one about eight and the other ten—they might have been sisters—jostling each other to reach us first. They unlatched the pouch as they ran and pulled out their boxes. Each tried to point hers at us, but the other kept swatting it away.

"Let me," the older one said. "Yours is broken."

"You promised we'd pretend," the younger girl cried.

Kara stepped in between. "Behave, Marissa, and you too Maisha. Remember the rule: those with goodies mustn't gloat. There someday will go all of us."

"What are they doing?" I said.

"Our way of greeting. Like all our machines since the day of ascension, many have failed beyond our skill to repair." She studied her toe digging a hole in the sand. "Some of the children pretend they work to keep up the tradition."

More people poured out to greet us, dozens of them. Mostly children, they swarmed, a few reaching out to touch our clothing, and others waving their black boxes at us. The younger ones asked the familiar questions. "Who are these strangers? Where are they from?"

And the same phrase repeated—*the dreamers*.

In this way, they swept us along until suddenly, all conversation stopped. We'd reached the archway, the entrance to the city.

Kara stepped in front and held up a hand.

"Wait here." She gestured to the stone statues with the glowing eyes. "The guards won't let you through. Not yet. I'll ask the mentor to grant you access."

She ran through the archway, dodged among the hovels, and vanished into the dome.

We waited before the silent crowd, shuffling our tired feet and eyeing the guards.

Moments later, Kara reemerged, smiling and relieved. She turned sideways and waved us through.

I grasped Nathaniel's hand, and together we stepped into this new world.

Then, as we strolled through the gate of the city, basking in the glow, the wall of light surrounding it shimmered one last time, rippled, and winked out as if it had never existed.

Chapter 2

The Mentor

After the wall of light winked out, my eyes flitted everywhere trying to adjust to the suddenly drab surroundings. In my more innocent youth, I'd gone to Temple City expecting virtue, but found corruption. Then I'd sought the keep anticipating magic, but found knowledge. Here, I'd hoped for wonders, but found fantasy.

This place was not as it seemed from the sea.

After the long weeks on the waves, buoyed by the hope of discovering a better future, I'd found a city in ruins. The shimmering light was nothing but a mask, but what lurked behind?

I spun around to Kara. "The wall? What happened?"

She shrugged. "The lights stayed on all the time when I was younger. Now that the mentor is alone, he rations the power of his mind, showing the city walls only as needed. In that way, he saves strength for the desals, synthesizers and other machines."

No, not yet in ruins. Not like the abandoned city of the keepmasters. People still lived here, but the place reeked of decay.

I glanced up at the underside of the archway and took a deep breath. "Well, I suppose the keep wasn't what we expected either."

Nathaniel's mouth twisted into a wry grin. "And we have nowhere else to go."

I grasped his hand, and we passed through the gate, ready to share whatever trials might come, as we had since childhood.

With the shimmering lights gone, the city lay bare. A clutter of makeshift hovels lined a narrow street, with little space in between except where a building had fallen. What passed for windows were covered with a clouded material, and neither curtains nor flowers graced their sills. It had the look of a deserted village recently ravaged by a storm. A few more impressive structures still towered over the rest, but even these were remnants of their former selves, with cracked roofs and surfaces bearing holes where material had been plundered for repairs.

Strangely, a series of shoulder-high, insect-like machines flitted about on treads, clicking a series of grippers and pincers, and flashing a red-hot welding beam as they patched the hovel walls.

A well-beaten path led to the largest structure, a village commons of sorts. A warm man-made breeze wafted from its entrance, warding off the night chill. Capped by a marble dome, a grand hall awaited inside, a vestige of prior glory. At its rear, twins of the two stone statues guarded a second arch leading to a tunnel up the mountain, making the building a way station on the road.

"Who has access through there?" I whispered to Kara as we marched in."

"None but the mentor."

Inside, the dome was shrouded in its own dusk. A pyramid of oval windows, set into the rear wall, gave a view of the fortress higher up, but now cloaked in the mountain's shadow, they yielded little light. Cables had been strung through the rafters overhead, leading to a dozen naked bulbs. The rest of the lighting came from torches set in sconces along the circular wall—not unlike those that lit the chambers of the vicars.

Their smoky glow flickered off the expectant faces of a few hundred people, a handful of older men and women, but mostly the children who had accompanied us. Their silver garb reflected the flames and made them seem ablaze.

No one spoke up to welcome us. They merely gaped as we approached, our footsteps echoing off the dome overhead. The only other sound was a low humming like the one I'd heard in the keep, a heartbeat of sorts that provided power to the lights and warmth to the air.

Nathaniel strode in front and faced the gathering. "Are you the descendants of those who crossed the ocean, kinsmen of the keepmasters?"

No reply. Some turned away and huddled closer together.

The tiny hairs on the back of my neck stood on end. These people seemed worlds away from what I'd imagined.

"Where are your mothers and fathers?" I said.

I expected them to point to the village outside or to the many doors lining the walls, but instead, they raised their arms and pointed through the oval windows.

I followed their fingers to the columned fortress carved high up in the rock face. It looked much like the Temple of Truth, but I feared we'd find something more forbidding than truth there — a resting place for the dead.

The girl, Kara, gestured to a mark in the center of the floor. "Wait here."

I accompanied Nathaniel to the spot, while Kara cracked open a door in the back wall and whispered a few words before returning.

"The mentor needs a minute," she said.

While we waited, the chamber became so still I could count each breath.

Kara fiddled with her hair, pulling it back behind her ears, and chewed on her lower lip.

A moment later, the door swung wide, and the man who must have been the mentor emerged, rolling on large brass wheels that bracketed an elaborate chair. He moved not a muscle, yet the chair whirred along as if with a mind of its own.

The mentor was much older than the others, with a long face, partially obscured by a hat angled low over his brow. The hat was unlike any I'd seen, high-crowned with a broad brim all the way around, a hat made more for shade than warmth. Stray locks of white hair slipped out from beneath its rim, framing a face marked by a prominent nose with a bump in the middle. His crystal blue eyes belied his age.

He glanced around the room, tossing a friendly nod to the smattering of adults and waving to the children, acting more like a father than leader.

Though seated, he seemed the tallest person I'd ever known, perhaps due to the respect the children gave him. As he rolled closer, I realized why. His knees rose nearly to his chest, all bones and legs. I wondered how he'd be able to rise from the throne.

The chair came alive again with no apparent effort from the mentor and stopped an arm's length from Kara. He smiled and motioned for her to approach.

11

She paused in front of him, and lowered her head in what seemed almost a bow.

He placed a huge hand behind her neck and pulled her close, giving a kiss on her forehead. Then the chair rolled forward until it rested in the center of the circle.

Kara signaled to one of the children to untie a rope secured to a stanchion on the wall, and a bar dropped from the ceiling toward the throne.

When it was level with his chest, he slid his arms around it and four children tugged at the rope. The mentor rose, more unfolding than standing, until he reached his full height, a head taller than Nathaniel.

The children bowed, and I struggled to keep from bowing as well.

The mentor shuffled toward us in obvious pain, his feet hardly lifting off the floor. Despite his infirmity, he straightened his back and held his chin high, a picture of grace and dignity.

Nathaniel and I stepped forward to meet him halfway.

He extended his right hand and grasped mine in his. His hand was large and knobby, with long, slender fingers, except where the knuckles were swollen. He added his left to his right, so the shake became more of a hand embrace. All the while, his blue eyes stayed focused on mine, as if we'd known each other before—not just known but liked each other, if not in this life then in another.

"Welcome," he said, "to our side of the world. You must be brimming with questions, and we have many of our own. Though we knew you'd come eventually, you're the first contact since our ancestors fled. I'm eager to share stories like long lost brothers, reunited after a lifetime apart. But I can tell you're weary." He turned to Kara. "Have you offered them something to eat?"

She shook her head.

He gestured toward the far wall. "Some of the synthesizers still work, some of the time. Kara, please show them the way."

Kara brought us to the north side, grinning like a child about to show a friend a new toy. She waved her hand over a panel attached to a table and, at once, a sumptuous feast danced in the air before us, and with it, smells like those of the festivals of my youth.

But these were only temptations. I could see right through them to the wall behind.

"Is this... what you eat?" I asked Kara.

"No, these are just holos." When I furrowed my brow, she said, "Pictures to choose from. This is the main menu—meats, fish, fruits and vegetables, breads and cakes. Touch one, and more choices will appear."

I reached out a doubting hand and touched the air in front of a plate with fruits.

A message appeared. "Error. Selection not found."

"Oh dear," Kara said. "Bad luck. You've chosen a broken one. Try another."

I smiled, hoping to soothe her disappointment. We'd seen such failures before in the keep. I thought of the machines outside, dashing about making repairs. The keep had repaired itself for a thousand years.

"It'll be fixed soon," I said.

"Perhaps, but more stop working every day. Some the mentor can fix. Most only the dreamers can repair."

At her urging, I touched another, and this time a selection of plates with meats appeared. I sniffed at one and caught the distinct aroma of lamb.

"Go ahead. Touch it."

I did. To my delight, a bright light flooded the table before us and seconds later, a dish of steaming lamb appeared.

"They've done it," I whispered to Nathaniel. "Gone beyond the keepmasters. No more dusty powder revived by hot water."

Nathaniel gaped at the meal, seemingly freshly cooked on the table, and turned to Kara. "Real food, conjured out of air. How could you possibly...?"

"The synthesizers do it all." Kara smiled, but her smile quickly turned into a frown. "How does it work? Only the dreamers know."

"If your machines make all your food," I said, "why do you bother to catch fish?"

"We need to learn, the mentor says, because someday the machines will fail, and we'll be on our own."

The two of us proceeded through the menu, touching holos of carrots, yams, and braided rolls. We made choices until the smells were so enticing, we could no longer resist.

Like good hosts, the children waited until their guests were settled in with their meals. Then the mentor reached up and rang a bell overhead, swinging it until the peals filled the hall and echoed to the rafters. At this signal, the assembled formed an orderly line at the food wall to partake in the feast.

At the mentor's invitation, Nathaniel and I joined him and Kara at one of the metal tables. With little strength to ask the many questions rattling around in my head, I focused instead on filling my stomach. The food, though better than the paste of the keep, lacked the taste of a home-cooked meal. Still, after the past week on beef jerky and flatbread — and not much of either — I found it more than enough to satisfy my hunger. I watched relieved as the color returned to Nathaniel's cheeks.

The mentor ate little, mostly poking at his dish as he waited for us to finish. After we had eaten our fill, he folded his hands on the table, leaned in and fixed us with his blue eyes.

"I'm curious about you," he said, "and I'm sure you'd like to know more about us, but you're tired from your journey. As a good host, I'll contain my curiosity until tomorrow, after you've had a chance to rest. I'll be happy, however, to answer whatever questions you have that can't wait."

I straightened in my chair and assumed the demeanor of the scholar Nathaniel knew so well. "Can you tell us why the children were waving around those black boxes when we first arrived?"

The mentor wiped his mouth and hands with a cloth napkin, refolded it and set it back down.

"These are devices from the time before." His voice was kindly but remote, as if speaking from the past. "Like all our machines, they are failing bit by bit. Once they performed many tasks to make our lives easier — taking pictures, playing music, providing answers to our questions. They let us speak to each other from far away and showed us the way if we were lost. We few elders have given up on them, frustrated with their lack of reliability, but the children insist on using them — or pretending to do so. A new tradition perhaps... or a morbid memory."

"Can't they be fixed," Nathaniel said.

"You don't understand. These machines are unlike any you may have known. They're... thinking machines, with a simplistic intelligence of their own that thrives only when connected with the minds of their creators. Without that connection they become like lost children, and over time cease to function, unless the creators return or the minds of our next generation grow strong enough to take their place."

14

Then he closed his eyes as if praying, a remembrance of times gone by.

"The mentor is always sad," Kara said, "because the others like him have flown and now he's alone. Yet he teaches us to have hope."

The mentor's body shook with a tremor and he glanced up. His big hand patted Kara's head and smoothed down her hair. "Our children are the hope for the future. Ah, before I forget, we must give them the medicine so their brains will grow, and they can master their lessons tomorrow."

He sent Kara off, and a few seconds later, the children lined up before the mentor to wait as he placed a small tablet on their tongues. After they finished, he urged them to go to bed and get ample rest in preparation for another day of learning.

As soon as the chamber had cleared, I asked the question I'd been saving until the children were gone.

"These creators... are they the same as the dreamers?"

The mentor cast a questioning glance at Kara, who flushed and turned away. He tilted his head back and gazed out the oval windows to the darkened mountain beyond, as if waiting for permission to speak.

At last, he drew in a long breath and blew out the air like a silent whistle. "I try to tell them they're not dreamers, but their little minds can't comprehend. Those they call the dreamers should be properly called machine masters. They're the ones who built this city and learned to merge their minds with the machines. They did all the research and hard work, while the rest sat back and reaped the benefits."

I thought of the scholars isolated in the keep, with a thousand years of learning added on. "What happened to them?"

"They've risen beyond themselves, ascended to a higher plane, a concept too lofty for the children. I don't blame them. Sometimes I have trouble understanding it myself. Perhaps I should give in and call them dreamers too."

Machine masters, whose minds were one with their machines? I found the concept too lofty as well, but of one thing I was certain: if anyone could help my people back home, it was the dreamers. They seemed so much more than the keepmasters, the reason Nathaniel and I had risked our lives to cross the ocean.

I opened my mouth to ask the next question, but Kara waved me to silence. The mentor was beginning to nod off, and she asked our help to shift him into his wheeled chair.

I waited until the last minute, after he was settled and preparing to roll away. Only then did my words rush out. "May we speak with these dreamers?"

"Why would you want to speak with them?"

"Because they're the wisest ever, wiser than the keepmasters. We all need their wisdom. They can repair your machines. They can help our scholars in their struggle to learn. They can teach us wonders beyond what we found in the keep." I paused, checked with Nathaniel and took a deep breath. "And they can help us build a new boat so we can return home."

The mentor's eyelids drooped again. I feared he'd fallen asleep, but an instant later, the blue eyes startled open and alert, though tinged with sadness.

"You're tired now, your minds unclear. Let's save talk of the dreamers for another day."

Then without a gesture or twitch of his hand, the wheeled chair spun about and rolled him back to his chamber.

Chapter 3

A Safe and Dry Place

Kara led us along a curved hall that circled the rear of the commons, with a smooth outer wall broken by a series of stark doors. I suppressed a shudder—too much like the passageway to our cells in Temple City. But this seemed no prison, with a polished floor and gleaming metal doors so spaced that each chamber appeared as broad as a Little Pond cottage.

A featureless, glass box hung at eye level beside each door. I stopped to examine one, thinking it like the box with numbered stars that unlocked the entrance to the keep. I reached out to one and let my fingertips glide over its surface. Nothing. Perhaps a form of decoration or another failed machine.

Kara raced ahead and stopped several doors down. When we caught up, she pressed lightly, and the door swung wide. The room inside was simple but well kept, not too different from the inns we'd stayed at in our travels to the keep. After all we'd been through—those weeks in cramped quarters being tossed by the waves, waking in the middle of the night to stand solitary watch, getting buffeted by the storm and shipwrecked on the shore, and now, bearing the disappointment of this ramshackle city—this chamber seemed the best I could hope for, a safe and dry place where Nathaniel and I could be alone.

Foam-like tiles checkered the ceiling in alternating squares of white and gray, and seemed to muffle all sound. My boot steps muted as I ventured onto the cushioned floor, and Kara's words emerged hushed.

"This was once a dwelling of dreamers," she said.

Like a newly freed prisoner, I wandered about the room, sliding my fingers along the dust-free top of the bureau and pausing to gawk at myself in the mirror above it. How awful the reflection that stared back, like flotsam washed ashore. My hair hung limp as seaweed, and my skin looked rough as driftwood. Nathaniel hovered behind me looking no better—a pair of vagabonds discarded by the sea.

At the far wall stood the largest bed I'd ever seen, far bigger than the one in my night chamber in Little Pond. It was backed by a birdseye maple headboard and covered with a flowered quilt mixing the purple of lilacs and the bright yellow of daffodils. I lifted a corner of the quilt and examined its stitching.

"The handiwork of the greenies," Kara said. "Before the day of ascension, many of the dreamers favored greenie crafts, those made by hand with quirky designs, unlike what our machines produce. This quilt is an example."

Nathaniel sat on the bed and bounced to test the mattress, which met with his approval.

Two flat doors made up the right wall, similar to the automatic kind we'd found in the keep, but when I approached them, they failed to open. I waited, puzzled and dazed, until Kara pulled out a hidden latch and slid the left one sideways into the wall. Inside, fresh clothing hung from a wooden rod, similar to the silver garments worn by the children but sized for adults.

"Something for you to change into." Kara knelt down and withdrew a pair of shoes for each of us. "I had to guess your size. Please tell me if they don't fit. We have plenty of clothing for grownups like you."

I grabbed mine, settled on the bed, and tried them on, peeling away my own boots, which had been handmade by the fourth keeper, the shoemaker's daughter. The leather had become waterlogged after so long at sea and had likely shrunk. I slipped my bare feet into these dry ones and let out a sigh.

Kara opened the second door to reveal a sink and a tub for bathing.

I was accustomed to washing with hard brown soap made of beeswax and lye, with cold water fetched from a stream. To my delight, the water from these spigots ran hot. On a shelf built into the wall sat several jars in a row. I twisted off the cover of one and sniffed. The powder within had a rose-petal fragrance. Above the bath was a rack with towels as soft as clouds and big enough to wear as a robe.

"We can't stay here," I said. "It wouldn't be right, when you have so little."

"It's the wish of the mentor. No one has slept here since...." Her eyes glistened as she glanced about the room, but then she steadied, straightening like a child who'd just finished a growth spurt and remembered her true height. She raised her chin and stood confident once more. "Since the day they ascended. I knew the dreamers who lived here. They favored the crafts of the IBs and traded food and medicine from the machines for towels, quilts, and handmade soaps — anything to make their chamber special. The mentor insisted on keeping this room as it was, as much as we're able. He honors you by letting you stay here, our special guests."

I flushed. What had we done to be so deserving? I thanked Kara for her hospitality, for the food and drink, for the shoes and fresh clothing, and bid her goodnight.

Nathaniel collapsed back on the bed as soon as we were alone, no longer needing to pretend to be a living legend from the across the sea.

I settled next to him and rested my head on his chest. "Not like the quest for the keep."

He nodded, then shook his head. "Well, a bit like it. We weren't what the keepmasters expected either."

A moving picture formed in my mind: Nathaniel and I, along with Thomas, stumbling upon the keepers' clues, following the trail of riddles left so many centuries before, solving the rhyme, and discovering the keep. How I had rejoiced when the ancient gears groaned, and the golden doors swung wide.

Then, we listened to the recorded greeting of the keepmasters, explaining how they expected the seekers to be leaders of a revolution, fresh from overthrowing the power of the vicars. And the three of us, little more than bumbling children, huddled together at the front of the near empty hall to ponder our fate.

"What poor seekers we are," I said. "Whatever we seek turns out to be different from that which we sought."

Nathaniel rolled toward me and touched my cheek, gently brushing aside matted curls. "Yet we managed to change the world."

"Changed it, yes, but to what end."

"The story's not over. The end hasn't been written."

How simple it had all seemed then. We'd open the eyes of our people, show them the wonders of the keep, and reveal the truth about

19

the darkness. After the revolution, Nathaniel and I would retire to a life of peaceful study with no more risky adventures. Others would do the rest, take the knowledge we'd discovered and build a new world.

Now, older and wiser, we'd crossed the ocean not for adventure but out of necessity. The revolution was going poorly. The keepmasters had overestimated their descendants. Their treasure store of knowledge proved too complex for a people kept simple for so long. Yes, we'd change for the better, but it would take generations. In the meantime, those fearful of change agitated for a return to traditional ways, swayed by disgruntled vicars whispering in their ears.

To keep the revolution alive, we had to cross the sea, to find people for whom the knowledge was current and real, those who might return with us and teach the new ways. But what had we found?

The denizens of this city had problems of their own, searching for their lost past and struggling to survive. Most were children, and their wise ones were nowhere to be found.

A myriad of questions swirled in my mind, a tangle of knots I could pick at for hours and never unravel. Who were these children, and where were their parents? Why did they cower behind walls of light? What was their mentor hiding from us? Who were the greenies? And how would we get back home?

I'd assumed we'd meet wise ones who'd help us return, people who'd traveled to the stars. How much simpler to cross the sea.

But now our boat was destroyed.

I lifted my head from Nathaniel's chest and stared into his eyes. "Technos and greenies. Thinking machines with the brain of a lost child. Who can we turn to?"

He looked at me, a hint of a twinkle showing beneath eyelids heavy with sleep. "The mysterious dreamers, of course."

The arch vicar had accused Nathaniel of being a dreamer of dreams—a crime punishable by death. Dreaming led to unrest, chaos, and a return to the darkness, something to be strangled in the cradle. The very purpose of a teaching was to kill dreams.

Yet here the people revered dreamers as gods. Perhaps a good sign.

So now a new quest—to seek the dreamers. But what if these dreamers were as unreachable as a dream?

"How will we find them?" I said.

"The light knows, but one thing's for certain: it won't be tonight."

Before I could respond, he gave me a long kiss and bid me goodnight.

Chapter 4

A New Adventure

I lay on my back while Nathaniel dozed, his mouth closed, breathing quietly through his nose so that his breath grazed my shoulder at regular intervals. Unable to sleep, I dragged myself to my feet and grabbed the waterproof sack that had thankfully survived the crash. From it, I withdrew my log. With the pad of my thumb, I flipped through to the first entry I'd written on our now destroyed boat, needing to review what had brought us to this point.

***

Dawn heralds our second sunrise at sea, another day to cross off my calendar. Thirty-four remain, if I trust the keepmasters' calculations. As the red glow lights up the rim of the sky, I'm forced to admit the truth — my homeland is gone. No glimpse remains of my neighbors gathered on the shore, no sign of my mother waving goodbye. Not so much as a reassuring hint of the tips of the granite mountains peeking above the horizon.

At least Nathaniel and I will be together throughout this voyage — my fondest wish — but we'll be apart for long stretches as each of us sleeps while the other stands watch. I take some good from this.

Today is the third anniversary of the enlightenment, and looking back, all has not gone as expected. Now at last, after our frenzied rush to depart, I have time to update this log, to chronicle the events leading up to this day.

In the beginning, my people flocked to the keep like children to festival, curious to discover the wonders preserved from the past, but after several months, many returned home. Despite the challenges foisted upon us by the vicars, they found the keep's knowledge too hard to master, the work on the farm more familiar, and they missed the beauty of our world. They wondered how the keepmasters had survived all those years cooped up in such sterile chambers. Some speculated they had gone mad.

The life of study suited only a few. After a while, those of us who persisted — the scholars, they called us — began to settle in and create our own identity. We were idealistic, eager to find ideas that would change the world, but we struggled to translate the keep's knowledge into action. We had some successes — medicines beyond what the vicars provided, a more efficient way to harvest wheat, machines to automate the spinning of yarn — but these were infrequent and rare.

With so much effort and so few results, Nathaniel grew restless. The other scholars urged him to join their meetings, but he'd had enough of talk. When they voted him a hero of the revolution, he walked out. A hero by sitting in a chair and talking? Not my Nathaniel. I worried he might return to Little Pond without me.

I set out to find us a common purpose. While I searched, I calmed myself by listening to the keepmasters' stories, not only the ones read by helpers from the screens, but those presented in what they called videos, tales told in moving pictures. People (actors, as I later learned, those pretending to be others) roamed beautiful places pursuing adventures to the strains of stirring music. Like Nathaniel, I became especially fond of videos about explorers. One about a hero named Jeremiah played a song as he rode a horse across snow-covered mountains. The words stuck in my head, because they reminded me of Nathaniel: "Sunshine and thunder, a man will always wonder where the fair wind blows."

Where had that longing gone among my people? Why did it beat so strongly in the one man I loved? Perhaps, despite all my caution, it was the reason I loved him.

Then, true to his nature, Nathaniel conceived of a new idea. He'd talk about it whenever we were together. What else in the world was left to do?

To cross the great ocean, of course.

At first, I raged at him. We knew little of oceans and boats, and less about what awaited us on the far side. Such a quest was madness, but Nathaniel was never one to let a notion go. His twentieth birthday came and went, an age when the elders claim a person should accept who they are. There'd be no acceptance for Nathaniel. I was prepared to choose a life of learning, centered on the keepmasters' wisdom, but he paced the keep from anteroom to anteroom as if

trying to master all subjects at once and none at all. I knew where his heart lay,
so I chose for myself and for him — for we were one now — the study of boats,
how to build them and, once complete, how to guide them across the sea.

To my delight, we studied together every day, obsessed by the ocean and
the means to cross it. Most of the methods we found were too complex. Others
relied on sources of power beyond our reach. Only one kind of boat lay within
our grasp — a vessel with a tall mast and white sheets that billowed like clouds,
one that ran on the waves before the wind.

The notion progressed from dream to reality as Nathaniel worked on the
design of the boat and the materials needed. He drew diagrams, built models
and tested them on a nearby pond. He learned how to set the sails to best ride
the wind.

My challenge was to figure out how to guide our boat to a safe harbor on
the far side of the world.

First, I needed to learn how to chart our course. The answer lay in the
magic of numbers and the laws of mathematics that held them together. These
had once led the keepmasters to the stars; they could certainly guide me across
the sea.

When I asked how to track our speed and location, the helpers proposed
complex thinking machines and trackers talking to ships in the sky. I had no
more chance of constructing these than of building one of their flying machines.
Then I realized people had been sailing the ocean since ancient times, long
before the keepmasters, so I focused instead on older methods.

I learned to determine speed by casting a log off the stern attached to a
rope with knots tied at regular intervals. By counting the knots as they slipped
through my fingers, I could calculate how fast we went.

For direction, I rediscovered the compass. As children, Nathaniel and I
used to play with magnets — despite the vicar's prohibition — making a toy with
a floating needle that pointed to the same place no matter how we spun it
around. From the helper, I learned the needle always pointed north, a reliable
way to tell direction.

The next problem was location. I hoped to record our progress on a map as
I had from Bradford to Riverbend, but no landmarks existed on the vast and
featureless sea. I printed charts and drew a black circle around our departure
point. From there, using direction from the compass and speed from the log, I
could track where we sailed, a technique the old mariners called dead reckoning.

Still, over such long distances, the smallest of errors would leave us lost
forever at sea. I asked for a more precise way to validate our position. The helper
told me every location on Earth was specified by two numbers called latitude
and longitude. To measure these required a pair of devices — a chronometer for
the exact time and a sextant for the angle of the sun. Thankfully, these and

other inventions had been preserved in the museum, an obscure room in the depths of the keep. With these wonders in hand, I set to work, learning to master their use.

Once Nathaniel and I gained sufficient confidence in our new quest, we badgered the elders for support — the undertaking was too complex for the two of us alone. We needed woodsmen to cut down trees and slice them into boards, coopers to curve the staves, and carpenters to saw the planks and hammer them into place; then roofers to boil the tar, caulk the cracks, and make the wood waterproof, and seamstresses to sew the canvas into sails. Most of all, we needed strong backs to lug the sails and wood, the barrels filled with water and tar, and sacks of provisions up and over the treacherous trail to the shore.

Once the boat was built, we spent months practicing within sight of land, testing the accuracy of my instruments and getting a feel for the currents and the winds. Soon all that was left was to stock the hold with provisions and sail away.

Only one obstacle remained. The elders and vicars refused to give their blessing unless we married.

The whole village of Little Pond came to the ceremony, performed on the near side of the mountain so those too old for the climb could attend. Our former enemy, the recently named Grand Vicar, traveled from Temple City in a fast wagon to give us our vows. Yes, he bore this responsibility as the human embodiment of the light on earth, but despite the changes we'd forced on the Temple of Light, I liked to believe he'd developed an affection for us. I couldn't help but smile when this grim leader, who'd once threatened to sunder us apart, joined us forever.

After toasts with freshly brewed wassail made from the autumn's crop of apples, the townsfolk placed wreaths of flax upon our heads though our race had not yet been run. All those able-bodied enough to climb the newly constructed path over the mountains came to see us off. The grand vicar demurred, too old for the trek, and perhaps reluctant to acknowledge the forbidden ocean whose existence he'd once denied.

Our neighbors stocked the boat with fruits that would last but a few days, and smoked meats and grain that would sustain us much longer. Strong young men hauled casks of fresh water over the mountain trail and secured them to the deck with thick ropes. I lovingly placed my charts and notes, my new instruments, and an ample supply of paper and quill pens into a pouch my mother had stitched from otter skin treated with oil — waterproof to survive the storms at sea.

The time had come to set off.

When Thomas, Nathaniel and I first left Little Pond to seek the keep, I worried we'd never return. I suspected danger but, blinded by my youth and the lure of adventure, I was unfazed. Now, as we sailed away, I had no such illusions, yet I was unprepared for the sight of land receding into the distance. Soon all I'd ever known had vanished – no elders to guide me, no vicars to offer spiritual guidance or threaten to split us apart, no pursuing deacons, no hope of finding the keep. Only the green water, the lapping of the waves on our hull, and the dome of the sky overhead, the universe so much larger than what I'd viewed from the keep's observatory.

As I finish this, my first log entry at sea, daylight flickers on the horizon. With the shoreline a memory, I'll use my newfound skills to guide our ship by the sun. If the day turns overcast, I'll navigate by dead reckoning and faith, calling on the light for guidance to lead us to the distant shore.

The new day dawns at last, and I'm struck by my new reality. Everything I've known is gone, leaving Nathaniel and I afloat on an endless sea. Our newest adventure has begun.

***

I flipped through and skimmed the rest. How enamored I'd become with my knots and compass, with my chronometer and sextant, and the numbers that combined to mark off another day's progress on the charts. I'd grown excited as the days sailed became greater than the estimated days remaining, but once my countdown reached zero with no land in sight, my mood had darkened and my words bemoaned my fate.

***

By dead reckoning, we should have arrived by now. By the readings on the sextant and the time on the chronometer, we still should be close. Yet no land appears.

Did I err in my calculations? Or did some demon from the darkness lead me astray?

Some days, a stinging spray breaks over the bow and surges along the deck. I tie the waterproof pouch more tightly about my waist and cling to the rail, staring into the teeth of a northwest wind, and trying to penetrate the mist. I feel seasick occasionally, especially when the sea breeze is up and the ship plunges heavily over the crests of the waves.

Then Nathaniel tells me his vision to keep my spirits up, how one day soon we'll spot the shining city rising from the mist. He speaks as if he's already been there, promising a place grander than the keep. I bask in his energy and forget my queasiness for a time. But still the sea goes on, and the endless waves break across our bow.

Oh, where is the land?

Or is the shining city I viewed on the screen just another of the keepmasters' tales?

***

Enough! I clapped the log closed and pressed down on its cover with my thumbs, as if afraid it might spring back open on its own. What a fool I'd been. How simple-minded my planning, all my calculations for naught.

I tucked away the log in its waterproof pouch, my eyes too heavy to read more. Then I lay down beside Nathaniel and drifted off toward sleep.

***

I dreamed I floated alone on the sea. Not on the deck of a boat but on my back, arms extended out to the sides. Above me spread an infinite sky, the kind I remembered from the keep's observatory – stars so dense they massed in clouds, and planets of unimaginable brightness. The sky was so clear I believed I could count the millions of suns in the galaxy, one at a time.

I scanned the stars and picked out the many constellations I'd learned. I found the hunter, Orion, with his sword and bow, and the three stars in a row forming his belt. I followed the belt to the dog star, Sirius, brightest in the sky. I located the big dipper and tracked the stars at the end of the ladle to Polaris, the north star that had helped guide my way on our voyage. Perhaps it would guide me now.

Suddenly, I needed to calculate my exact longitude and latitude, the magic numbers signifying my position on this earth. I splashed about in the water, groping for my chronometer and sextant, but they were nowhere to be found.

Then something changed. I felt myself – or the essence of myself – begin to expand. I became no longer merely Orah but the sea itself, and more – the whole world and all of the people upon it.

I relished the feeling of weightlessness, the sense of being pure mind. No need for chronometer or sextant now, or any other device. As I gazed at the sky, I saw not just stars but a myriad of numbers. I knew the speed of the wind, the direction of the currents I floated in. No moon? No problem. I sensed it on the far side of the world, its precise angle and location. I knew the speed at which it orbited around the Earth, my precise position on this planet without need to calculate, and my place in the universe as well. I knew all the answers to the hardest questions I'd ever asked. I just... knew.

26

***

As I emerged from my dream, I considered that if the dreamers had ascended to a higher state of consciousness as the mentor claimed, perhaps I might speak to them now by reaching out with my mind.

I paused to listen.

I heard Nathaniel's measured breathing beside me, the beating of my own heart, but nothing more.

Then my breathing slowed to match Nathaniel's, and the images faded away.

Chapter 5

A Cry in the Night

I awoke before daylight and stared at the ceiling, trying to see through the foamed panels to the stars of my dreams. After the long weeks at sea, I needed more sleep, but no sleep came. Beside me, Nathaniel snored softly. Afraid to disturb him, I slipped out of bed, wrapped a blanket around my shoulders, and went to check outside. Yesterday had been a fuzzy day, swaddled in scrim, muddled by exhaustion, hunger and thirst. Would the world look better today?

I hesitated at the door. After months confined to a cell in Temple City, I'd developed a fear of being locked away and worried we might be prisoners now. I tested the latch, pressing the handle so lightly it made no sound. The door swung wide.

I padded through the assembly hall, now dark except for a few bulbs hung from wires in the rafters, and went out the front entrance. Once outdoors, I inhaled the cool night air. Overhead, the stars blazed brightly across the dome of the sky, and a crescent moon prepared to set on the horizon. I connected the points of light into my favorite constellations. Pictures appeared in my mind—hunters and bears and a flying horse, old friends I'd learned to love in the keep's observatory. Thankfully, the night sky had stayed the same.

Even in this strange new land, stars remained stars, nothing more.

An onshore breeze blew across the shantytown, bringing a hint of salt air. As it traveled inland, it mingled with other familiar smells—pine trees and moist earth, and the smoke of smoldering fires burning low.

Comforted that earth, sea and sky had returned to normal, with no whiff of dreamers in the air, I turned to head back inside, but before I reentered the commons, a cry disturbed the night. I followed the sound to a nearby shanty, where candlelight flickered through an open door.

Inside, Kara held the little boy Timmy in her arms, rocking him back and forth and whispering soothing words. When she recognized me, she motioned to join her.

"Is he all right?" I whispered.

"Just frightened. He's afraid to fall asleep."

"Why?"

"He worries that if he dreams, he'll never awaken. Like the dreamers."

I squatted on the ground next to the boy and stroked his arm. "When I was little, about the same age as you, my father died. Like you, I was afraid to sleep, worried I'd never wake up."

Timmy became still. His eyes grew larger. "What did you do?"

"My mother sang me a magic song that made me feel better. Would you like to hear it?"

He nodded.

"There's one thing I ask: the magic only works if you come so near you can listen to the beating of my heart."

The little boy shimmied over and sat on my knee, but hesitated to get closer. I stayed silent until he snuggled in, his ear to my breast. He stared up at me, his eyes as bright as the hooded kerosene lamp that glowed each night as I stood watch on our boat.

Then I sang the song my mother had taught me, with words that calmed when I was most afraid. Like the day I stood in the vicars' chamber, facing the teaching alone, or that morning I pressed my cheek to the pine needle floor and prayed the deacons wouldn't find me. After the arch vicar threatened to split us apart, I sang this song to Nathaniel through the peephole separating our cells—a way to comfort us both.

Hush my child, don't you cry
I'll be here with you
Though light may fade and darkness fall
My love will still be true
~~~

So close your eyes and trust in sleep
And dream of a better day
Though night may fall, the morn will come
The light will show the way
~~~

Though you may roam to far off lands
And trouble comes your way
You'll still be here within my heart
I won't be far away

~~~

So when you fear the darkness
Sing this simple rhyme
This song and I will never die
If you dream of a better time

As my voice trailed off, the child fell asleep in my arms.

After I carried the boy back to his bed and tucked a blanket around him, Kara thanked me for my help and turned to leave.

I followed her out and grasped her arm. "I'm still thirsty from yesterday, and chilled as well. Is there a place I could get a warm drink?"

"Yes, from the synthesizers, if I can get them to work."

"Will you show me how?"

She led me back into the domed commons, where she navigated the aisles of tables to the holos. Quicker than I could follow, her hand flicked among the menus until two steaming hot chocolates appeared, one for each of us.

"First try," she said. "You bring good luck."

I settled down at a table and waited for my drink to cool. "Are all the children afraid like Timmy?"

"Not all, but most. There aren't enough adults left to comfort them, so I do my part. I'm the oldest of the techno children, one of the few who remembers clearly the day the dreamers left. It was a happy day for us, a time of celebration, blessed with a perfect blue sky. The synthesizers were programmed to serve us special food, a big feast. Those we now call dreamers were dressed in white as they paraded up the mountain path from the city. Everyone fit enough to make the climb went with them.

"We were given an examination once we turned thirteen, and only those who passed were deemed strong enough to enter the mountain. I was two weeks shy of that birthday, but I was the smartest in my class. Passing the exam was never an issue, but they refused to let me take it early—rules were rules. I wanted so badly to go with them that I cried and fussed. 'Not yet,' they said. 'Your time will come.'"

A soft sadness blanketed her features from the pain of times gone by. She took a sip of her drink, a ploy to calm herself and make sure her nearly adult eyes stayed dry.

"At least I had a chance to say goodbye. For children like Timmy, the dreamers are nothing more than a story... and not a pleasant one. So they imagine the worst."

I calculated. Kara was on the threshold of womanhood, perhaps sixteen. That meant the dreamers had left... ascended... three years before. Was it possible...?

I took a deep breath. "Are the dreamers still alive?"

"Oh, yes," Kara said, though her eyes didn't agree. "Alive of sorts. I find it hard to explain. Even the mentor doesn't know for sure. Now he gives us medicine to grow our brains, and we study hard so someday we might merge our minds with the machines like them."

"Will you succeed?"

She shrugged. "The mentor says we have to try because without us, the machines will one day fail. The greenies think we're fools. Even before the day of ascension, they were suspicious of the machines. They learned a different way, to live without them, except when they need what only the machines can provide. Then we trade with them."

"Do the greenie children have trouble sleeping as well?"

"No. The ragged lady claims they sleep well at night because their labor with the land gives them peace."

"The ragged lady?"

"She's like the mentor, but for the greenies. We call her that, but they know her as the earth mother."

A thought struck me, a glimmer of hope. "Do either technos or greenies have the skill to build a boat?"

Kara shook her head, her hair flying about her eyes. "Not that I know of. I've learned nothing about boats, and the greenies stick to the land."

I took a chance. "Would the dreamers know?"

"Yes, of course. The dreamers know about everything, but we children can only listen to recordings of them in the classroom. Nothing in the lessons so far has ever mentioned a boat."

"Is there a way to speak to them directly?"

Kara's hands flew to her face. Her fingers widened so she looked at me only through the spaces in between.

"If only.... I'd give anything to speak with them, to say what I should have said on that day. I've begged the mentor to let me try, even for a few seconds, but he says my mind's not strong enough yet, and I'm needed here. Maybe in a few years...."

I recalled the long hours I'd spent in the keep, listening to recordings of the ancient keepmasters. Was speaking to the dreamers like communing with the helpers? If so, would my mind be strong enough to learn from them?

Curiously, Kara's eyes began to fill, hinting that the dreamers meant more to her than helpers on a screen.

"Why do you want to speak to them so much?" I said.

"Because on that day, I was an ungrateful child, demanding they let me go with them, caring only for myself. If I'd known I was seeing them for the last time, I would have told them...."

The last time. Last times were horrible things: like the last time I spoke to my father; or fearing I'd seen Nathanial for the last time. And now, with our boat destroyed, another awful truth emerged—the parting on the shore may have been the last time I embraced my mother. Last times carried a finality about them, like death.

I grasped Kara's hands, forcing her to face me. "What would you have told them?"

"That I loved them," she said. "My mother and father. My very own dreamers."

Chapter 6

Seekers Once More

Still restless after my encounter with Kara, I drew a hot bath while Nathaniel slept. When finished, I wrapped myself in one of the lush towels and dried my hair with another. As I stepped back into the bed chamber, the lights brightened.

Nathaniel stirred, sensing morning had come, but he seemed loath to confront the day. Was he dreaming of the children dressed in silver, rushing to help us on the shore? Did he wonder as I did if the memory had been real? I recalled my panic when I scanned the shoreline, littered with shards from our shattered boat, and discovered he was nowhere to be found. I knew at once it was real—no dream could be so painful.

He groped at his side, eyes still closed, scratching the fabric of the bed and searching for me.

I lowered my voice to sound like a man. "She's not there."

He forced his eyes open and blinked at the light. "Orah?" In his half-awake state, my name sounded more plea than cry.

He looked so forlorn I curled up next to him and crooned my mother's song, just as I'd done during those dreadful days imprisoned in Temple City:

Hush my child, don't you cry
I'll be here with you
Though light may fade and darkness fall
My love will still be true

33

He stretched his arms overhead in a yawn, and then gave me a lingering kiss. "How long have you been awake?"

"Too long. I couldn't sleep, but my time hasn't been wasted. I learned a lot while you were snoring away."

He glared at me sideways, knowing me too well. "What have you been up to?"

"I wandered outside for fresh air and found the girl, Kara, comforting one of the younger children. She told me more about the dreamers. She's one of the few old enough to recall the day they left, and she remembers some especially well, the two she cared about most in this world."

I flashed my I-have-the-answer-and-you-don't smile, knowing it would annoy him while he waited for his mind to clear.

"Do you mean... the dreamers were the missing adults, the mothers and fathers of these children?"

I nodded. "About three years ago, they went off to some kind of festival, a celebration of knowledge. Only those thirteen and older were allowed to go, and then only if they'd passed some kind of test. The festival was high up on the mountain, inside the fortress built into the rock face."

"Like the keepmasters taking their knowledge to the keep." He dragged his fingers through his hair and ruffled his beard, prodding his tired brain to grasp what I'd been saying. "Three years ago? These are the wise ones who made food out of air. They should still be alive."

"I pray it's so. These are the ones we crossed the ocean to meet, people like the keepmasters but more advanced, and not mere recordings on screens."

"But if they're alive, why would they leave their children alone all this time?"

I fumbled in the closet for clothing, flipping through one, two, three choices and plopping the third on the bed. "That's the riddle. Kara expected them to return soon, if not the same day. She's devastated they're gone, yet she believes she'll speak to them again someday. In the meantime, the techno children meet them only in their lessons."

"On screens like in the keep?"

"Or a similar device. The children are taught daily by the dreamers. The mentor insists on it, but they're unable to speak with them."

Nathaniel scrunched his face as if he'd eaten something sour. "Did we cross the ocean to find more screens? What good are these lessons?"

34

"None, unless we can meet with the dreamers themselves."

His eyes widened. At once, he was awake and alert. "Yes, of course. After a thousand years of growing beyond the keepmasters, they must be a little less than gods. We need to find a way to speak with them directly. Is that possible?"

I finished dressing. Now that I was freshly bathed and clothed in the silver tunic, my confidence rose. "Kara's eyes misted when she talked about them. She's desperate to have a chance to say a final goodbye, but the mentor's forbidden the children from going into the mountain fortress until they're grown—something about their brains not being strong enough." I came closer, wrapped my arms around his neck, and whispered in his ear. "But you and I are fully grown, aren't we?"

He stared past me to the back wall as if trying to see through it to the columned fortress beyond. "So we're seekers again but with a new goal—to find a way to speak to the dreamers."

***

By the time we marched into the domed commons, I felt like a seeker once more.

Nathaniel, with his long hair brushed back and his beard groomed, looked like one of the explorers in the videos from the keep that he loved so much.

As we glided along with our shiny new clothing flickering in the torchlight, I wondered: would the younger children take us for dreamers or upstart invaders from across the sea?

Neither, it seemed. We'd slept too late and the common room was nearly empty. Only one of the technos remained—Kara.

The girl stood when she noticed us enter and made almost a curtsy. "I hope you slept well and have recovered from your travels. The mentor asked me to wait for you and be your guide for the day."

I glanced around the domed room. "Where is he?"

"Some days, when he's not well, he takes his food in his work chamber. The mentor's old and is often sad. I help as much as I can. You must be hungry."

She led us to the synthesizers and, after taking our orders, produced a passable meal, with only a few fits and starts. Nathaniel and I wolfed down our food while she laid out her plans.

"With the dreamers gone and much of their knowledge with them, the mentor insists we learn everything we can. In our lessons, we study holos the dreamers left behind, hoping to strengthen our minds so someday we may command the machines as they did. Sometimes, we even exchange ideas with the greenies, when their minds are not too muddled. In these hard times, we forgive their transgressions, because we need each other. They need us for our medicine and fresh water. We need them for their craft and their skill in finding food from the land.

"Now, thanks to you, we can discover what the ancient world has to offer, but first, you must learn something of our ways. The mentor wants you to attend our lessons, to compare what you know with what the children are taught."

"When do the lessons begin?" I said.

"They've already started. I've missed more than an hour." She glanced out the oval windows in the dome as if trying to gauge the time by the daylight. "You slept late, but the mentor said not to wake you."

"We're sorry to have kept you from your lessons."

"Not a problem," she said. "I'm the oldest of the children and have a knack for study. A few hours missed won't hurt. I'll still be ahead of the others."

She raised her chin and smiled with an arrogance I'd once possessed as the smartest in my class, though those days were long gone. Now I dwelled more on how little I knew.

After we finished eating, Kara led us past the many side chambers lining the circular wall of the commons. Most, she explained, had been living quarters before the day of ascension. She'd lived in one herself as a child with her parents. Others were work areas, laboratories where the dreamers worked their wonders with the machines. Now, by order of the mentor, they left these untouched, keeping them as they'd been on that fateful day.

At the front stood classrooms where the children took their lessons. Kara stopped at one and waved her hand across a glass box by the side of the door. A screen above it brightened and a helper appeared, but unlike the friendly helpers in the keep, this man seemed almost angry.

"Step forward and hold for a security scan."

"It's all right," Kara whispered to Nathaniel. "The mentor has added you to the access list. Just step to the line."

Nathaniel shuffled forward until his toes touched a red line that had appeared on the floor. Immediately, a thumb-wide ray of light emanated from the screen and scanned him up and down and back again, making him wince as it passed before his eyes.

I held my breath, realizing the dreamers were testing him, judging him to see if he deserved their wisdom. Would he pass? And if he failed, what would be the punishment?

After a few seconds, the scanning ceased, and to my relief, the helper said, "Approved."

I was next. Nathaniel nodded encouragement as I stepped to the line. If he could pass the test, I should be safe. Throughout our childhood, I'd scored better than him in school.

At last, the helper passed both of us and the door slid open.

Inside, the room was not so different from the many rooms we'd visited in the keep, with white walls, a low ceiling, and tiles on the floor. The youngest children from the day before sat at desks in a half-circle facing in, organized in three orderly rows sorted by size, the shortest in front and tallest in back. All appeared solemn but eager, beautiful as only the young can be, not unlike the students in a Little Pond classroom. Instead of a teacher standing in front, a screen was embedded into the surface of each desk.

A thought struck me: why start us with lessons for the youngest?

Of course. Much like the keepmasters, they'd assume these primitives from across the sea would know little and need to start with the simplest lessons.

I surveyed the room and recognized Timmy, the little boy I'd comforted the night before. He smiled up at me, and I smiled back.

So young; just a baby when his parents went off to the mountain, too innocent to understand.

Who were they, his dreamers? Had his mother come to his crib when thunder frightened him at night? Did she sing songs of comfort as I had, then tuck his blanket more tightly about him and tell him to have no fear because she'd stay nearby?

On that fateful day, had his father picked him up in his arms, brushed away his tears and smothered him with kisses? Had he lifted him high upon his shoulders and said, "Look, Timmy boy, the great mountain. Wait here while we go off to become gods. We'll be back in no time."

Now Timmy beckoned to us, strangers from across the sea, to take the two desks beside him.

Nathaniel chose the larger of the two, but even so the desk was too low for his knees. He twisted sideways in the chair, and sat as upright as possible. He'd been out of school for several years and had never been as comfortable a student as me, but he appeared confident now as we towered above the children, adults among babes.

No sooner had I settled in my chair than my screen came alive. A helper began to speak and holos like the menu in the dining area whirled and spun above the desktop. I glanced at the students around me, hoping to discover what was expected.

The nearby children were infants when their parents had gone off. Now they appeared no more than seven years old.

I grimaced as I stared at the dancing numbers and letters, taunting me to make sense of them. I recognized some, what the helpers had called equations, mathematical formulas I'd encountered only recently after years of study in the keep.

Nathaniel turned to me and shrugged, hoping I'd fare better than him.

I reached out to touch the holos but my hand wavered in midair. My fellow students played with the symbols like toys, their tiny fingers flying as they rearranged the glowing numbers and symbols. I sat back with hands folded and mouth agape. These were the youngest children, yet here I struggled in their classroom, trying to comprehend a lesson for babes.

Chapter 7

The Welcome Feast

That evening, the mentor invited us to a welcome feast. Once we'd freshened up from the long day, Kara came to our door, cradling a bundle in her arms.

"Ceremonial dress last worn by the dreamers," she said. "The mentor insisted, a great honor. I'll be waiting outside to take you to his chamber when you're ready."

We changed out of our silver tunics and into silken robes all in white. I stood before the mirror and preened, but Nathaniel fidgeted uncomfortably, making me laugh. In his formal attire, with his tall bearing and freshly groomed beard, he looked like an ancient god who'd stumbled into a ritual from the wrong religion.

Kara marched us to the mentor's chamber, but when we arrived, the room was empty. His quarters mirrored our own but for a stout wooden cane resting against the wall, and a night table covered with medicine bottles. Prominent at its front, someone had placed a glass of water with a fresh spray of heather in it, the only attempt to enhance the space. The water, apparently from a fouled spring, had evaporated down a finger's width, leaving a nasty brown ring. The only other glaring difference lay at the back wall—an extra door with a screen above it like the one at the entrance to the classroom.

Kara asked us to wait, and then stepped to the screen. The same angry helper we'd confronted that morning appeared. After a quick scan, the door slid open, and she passed through.

A moment later, she emerged with the mentor rolling beside her. He acknowledged us with a wave, but remained focused on the door and the commons beyond, as if practicing his welcome speech in his mind.

Kara had added one accessory for the ceremony, a striking white bonnet with flowers embroidered on the front. Pointed flaps rose up from its sides like little wings, and it seemed too big for her head

"Such a pretty hat," I said. "Was that also made by the greenies?"

She raised both hands and wiggled the hat until it fit tight. "Yes, the mentor asked them to decorate it, offering more than the usual amount of food and sweet water. Then he added... his own touch. He gave it to me for my fifteenth birthday."

I stretched out a hand. "May I see it?"

She drew back a step and shook her head. "This hat is special. No one may touch it but me. Now, wait here until I return for you. The mentor wants your entrance to fit the occasion."

She accompanied him outside, leaving us alone.

Curious as always, I eyed the door from where the mentor had emerged. Nathanial cast a warning glance, knowing me too well, but I approached the entrance anyway.

The screen lit up. "Step up and hold for a security scan."

I stepped forward as requested and toed the red line, just as I'd done that morning. The blinding light flashed, scanning me from head to foot, but this time, the result was different.

"Access denied." The helper seemed more upset than before.

Afraid to risk some unknown punishment, I backed away just as Kara returned.

She froze in the doorway, the blood draining from her face. "What were you doing?"

"You tell us so little. I hoped to find out what's behind that door."

She jumped in front to block me. "That door goes to the work area, where the mentor speaks to the dreamers. I'm the only other person allowed in, and only when he teaches me my... more advanced lessons. Now, please, I know you're guests, but try to obey our rules. The mentor is standing by his table to honor you, despite the pain in his legs, and everyone's waiting. Come with me."

After exchanging puzzled glances with Nathaniel, I grasped his arm and paraded three paces behind Kara, trying to mimic her solemn stride, like a king and queen from the keepmasters' tales, following our page into court. As soon as we appeared in the commons, all eyes fell upon us.

The tables had been embellished in a way, covered with what seemed to be sheets from the sleeping quarters, with a sprinkling of flowers in a jar on top.

In the center of the commons, a fire pit burned. Sad-faced women and bowed old men—presumably those too frail to have gone into the dream—gathered around it, turning metal racks filled to capacity with the children's daily catch of fish. Smoke swirled around the glowing embers as the fish oil dripped down, most rising through a grated opening at the peak of the dome, but some stayed inside, leaving a haze throughout the chamber.

The mouthwatering smell of sizzling fish pervaded the room, reminding me of my mother's cooking. Despite the number of days recorded in my log, Little Pond seemed a lifetime away. My eyes misted, and I wondered if I'd ever see home again.

The few adults not busy with the fish went from table to table, filling cups with the sweet water. When all were full, the mentor raised his goblet above his head, and the assembled did the same.

"To our new guests," he said. "May their arrival portend a better future."

"A better future," the others repeated, though their chorus lacked conviction.

As the mentor lowered the goblet and took a sip, a quiet expectation filled the room.

He raised his drink a second time, higher than before, and his voice rang out, each word spoken clearly and echoing off the rafters. "To the return of the dreamers."

"To the dreamers," the others said, sounding like the people of Little Pond repeating the vicar's words during the blessing of light—by rote and without passion. The mentor drained his cup, his bulging Adam's apple bobbing as he swallowed, and at this signal, everyone emptied their cups as well. Their version of a blessing was followed by the clatter of cups on metal.

How often had they performed this ritual since the dreamers left? Did any of them still believe the dreamers would return?

With the ceremony ended, the mentor grasped the edge of the table and grimaced as he lowered himself into his chair. Once settled, he invited us to join him, Nathaniel to his left and me on his right.

41

The few adults served the fish, first to their guests and then to the children.

I devoured my meal, the first real, hot food I'd had in weeks. While I ate, the mentor repeated his hope that our arrival would be beneficial and proceeded to pepper us with questions, which Nathaniel and I took turns answering between bites.

What was our boat like? How did we learn to navigate across the sea? How long was our voyage? In what way had our homeland changed since the separation? What had we expected to find?

After our plates were cleared, the adults brought out brightly-colored bowls, orange and yellow and green, made of the same kiln-hardened clay the people of Little Pond crafted back home. To my delight, each bowl contained freshly picked blueberries with warm goat milk poured on top. But the colors of the bowls were too cheerful, the pictures of animals painted on them too whimsical for the somber technos.

I cast a questioning glance at Kara.

"Food and dishes from the IBs," she said. When the mentor glared at her, she looked away embarrassed. "I mean the greenies. They've learned to raise goats for milk and to harvest these berries from the wild."

"We call them greenies," the mentor said, "because they believe in the land. They call us technos, because we believe in machines and in our ability to someday relearn the science behind them."

"Is that what's driven a wedge between you?" Nathaniel said.

"No, we're more reasonable than that. The greenies started their movement decades ago, and we've always accepted our differences." He held up his painted bowl. "And we value many of their crafts."

"So what caused the rift?" I said.

The mentor's long features hardened. "Their conduct following the day of ascension, behavior we'll never forgive. And some still lurk among them who wish to do us harm. For now, we need each other, so we co-exist uncomfortably and barter what successes we have."

As I chewed a few berries, his words fueled the bonfire of questions burning in my mind. Time for my turn. "Kara tells us you speak to the dreamers, but no one else can."

The mentor slowed his chewing and swallowed. His lips pressed into a thin and pale line. "Kara is a good child, but a child nevertheless. There's a great deal she does not understand."

"But do you speak to the dreamers?"

"In a way, yes." His words came out one at a time as if he were picking them with care. "But the dreamers do not speak as you and I are speaking now. They've moved to a higher plane."

I ground my teeth and held back my response. I was the mentor's guest, and my mother had raised me to believe in manners.

Before I could give voice to my thoughts, Nathaniel blurted them out. "When may *we* speak to the dreamers?"

"Speak to the dreamers?" The blue eyes crinkled at the corners, the lines around them deepening as his voice rose. "Only the mentor speaks to the dreamers."

I leaned in, my hand pressing on the arm of the mentor's chair. "Our boat is gone. The people of our world have a desperate need for the dreamers' wisdom. You must let us speak to them."

The mentor pushed his lower lip upward so it covered the upper, and his head bobbed from side to side as if on a spring. With no gesture on his part, the chair came alive and jerked away, leaving my hand hanging in midair.

His blue eyes blazed. "You may never speak to the dreamers."

"Never?" Nathaniel and I said together. "Why?"

His brow knitted into a thundercloud. "Do you think the mentor doesn't know how you performed in the lessons today? Someday, if the children work hard enough, they may be worthy to speak to the dreamers. As for you from your primitive world, you are as simple-minded as greenies. Your brains will never be strong enough to open the gateway to the dreamers. Never."

***

After the meal was finished and the cleanup done, the children lined up to pay respect to their guests and bid us goodnight. With so little sleep and after a tiring day, I longed to go to bed, but once the crowd dispersed, I lingered in the common hall.

The air beneath the dome had grown steamy from the crush of people and the heat from the smoldering embers, and I was steamy as well. The mentor had lied to us, I was sure of it. But to what end?

Too restless to sleep, I urged Nathaniel to join me outside to take some fresh air. We walked arm in arm, pausing to watch the clacking and crackling of the repair machines as they patched the metal of the children's dwellings, making the walls glow red in the dark. I wondered who controlled them, and what other talents they might offer. Might they possess the skill to build a new boat? I studied their mechanisms until my eyes watered, but their workings were beyond me.

Once we'd wandered past the sandstone arch, I turned to stare back at the city lights, still bright for now, perhaps in tribute to the newly arrived guests. I tried to analyze what they were made of. Memories and dreams, I suspected, like so much else in the techno city.

The lights had caused my vision to narrow and when I glanced down, I had trouble piercing the dark. I sensed the children in their shelters readying for bed, and wondered how different the evening must be in the homes of the greenies.

I glanced up to the night sky for guidance, as I'd done for so many weeks at sea. The crisp air carried little moisture, and a crescent moon shed its pale rays on the jumble of ragtag shelters, but not so brightly as to obscure the stars. At sea, on a night like this, the stars would sparkle like jewels in the blackened sky, but here the lights of the city overwhelmed them.

I turned to Nathaniel and studied his profile as he gazed up as well. His chin was raised, his jaw jutted out. His eyes burned as if he too were boiling inside.

Was this how our quest would end, far from home, unable to help our family and friends? Was this what our search for truth had wrought, a land of brilliant children sustained by failing machines and fantasies and lies?

Nathaniel caught me staring and reached out, tracing the line of my cheek with his thumb. Then he drew me beyond the children's village, leaving the shining lights of the techno city behind. How well he knew me. He was leading me to the shadows where I could better view the sky.

At the edge of the trees, he spun me away from the city so I faced the woods, pulled me close and held me tight, two strangers alone in a world we did not understand.

As I focused over his shoulder at the darkened tree line, my pupils widened, and I sensed a presence nearby. I squinted, trying to tell real shapes from imagined, then moved closer for a better look.

At the start of a narrow path stood a lone figure—the silent boy from the beach, half hidden behind a spruce. He separated from the trees when he saw me, but not far, wary of the techno city. As I closed the distance between us, he signaled for me to bend low and stroked my cheek with the tip of his finger, a memory we both shared.

Yes, I nodded. *I've cleaned up, and the moist sand is gone.*

Apparently comfortable I was as human as him, he reached into his pocket. Still without a word, he handed me a crumpled scrap of paper, so worn it seemed to have been erased and reused many times. I unfolded the message, smoothed out the wrinkles on my palm, and read the words, barely visible in the light of the crescent moon.

The earth mother says to come in the morning. Step into the trees, and this boy will show you the way.

PART TWO

THE PEOPLE OF THE EARTH

"The great enemy of truth is very often not the lie—deliberate, contrived and dishonest—but the myth—persistent, persuasive and unrealistic. Too often we hold fast to the clichés of our forbearers. We subject all facts to a prefabricated set of interpretations. We enjoy the comfort of opinion without the discomfort of thought."

- John F. Kennedy

Chapter 8

Greenies

"Sorry, Kara, no lessons today."

"But...." Kara's polite morning smile rounded into an O.

"We need time to ourselves," I said. "Today's a special holiday where we come from, the festival of the light. It's our tradition to go off into the woods and reflect for the day."

Nathaniel and I had stayed up late concocting this story. Afterwards, for the first time in weeks, I slept soundly, dreaming of blueberries and flowers—no midnight watch, no cries in the night. The bruises from the shipwreck had begun to heal, and I had a new quest to look forward to.

As soon as I awoke, I located the crumpled piece of paper the silent boy had given me and reread the message. Not my imagination. The invitation was real, and I was eager to accept it. All we needed was a way to slip from Kara's watchful eye.

"The mentor says you should—"

"He's *your* mentor, not ours," Nathaniel said.

Kara flushed and pressed toward him, but I slipped in between. "We're grateful for your hospitality, but I'm sure the mentor also teaches respect for the customs of guests."

"But the mentor insists I escort you everywhere, and I mustn't miss any more of my lessons. I have so much to learn from the dreamers."

"You go along to your lesson. I'm sure we'll find our way without you."

When the girl refused to move, I signaled to Nathaniel who brushed her gently aside.

After we'd cleared the doorway, I turned. "Forgive us, but we're bound to do what we must."

Kara chased us across the large hall, shouting after us. "The mentor still sleeps, but when he wakes, I'll tell him what you've done."

"That sounds like a fine idea," I said on my way out the door.

We wasted no time leaving the techno city behind. Once we reached the path through the woods, I ducked behind a thick oak and peered around it back toward the gate.

Seconds later, a flustered Kara rushed out accompanied by several of the older boys, each bearing one of the sharpened sticks we'd seen on the beach.

We may not be prisoners, but the technos and greenies were enemies, and as newcomers, our loyalties were unknown. Best to keep our destination hidden. I grasped Nathaniel's arm and drew him deeper into the woods.

Finding our way was no problem. The techno city had been built on a plateau on the shoulder of the mountain. The terrain above it was steep and rocky, a poor home for those wishing to live off the land, so we headed downhill, following troughs made by the runoff of rainfall and bushwhacking through brush where none could be found—an approach I'd taken years before when we'd fled the deacons outside Little Pond. I prayed this new adventure would end as well. Still, I paused every two minutes to glance over my shoulder, trusting nothing to chance in this strange land.

Partway down the slope, a rustling came from the bush below, too loud to be a bird. Moments later, the silent boy emerged from the trees.

I blew out a long stream of air, knelt down, and waved him closer.

After a moment's hesitation, he rushed forward and gave me a hug.

From there, we followed the silent boy to a meager path, only wide enough for one of us at a time. The trail seemed infrequently used, but was at least free of the prickly burrs of the woods.

The silent boy pranced ahead, but every few steps came running back. He seemed to have taken a liking to me. After his third foray, he stuck by my side.

At the first glade, he motioned for us to stop. He pulled a hand carved flute from his pocket and blew five notes—one long, one short, and three long, like the woody call of a mourning dove. Hoo-ah, hoo

hoo hoo. The same notes answered back, but too far off to be an echo—a response from downslope.

In a matter of seconds, two dozen men and women surrounded us, more adults than I'd seen in the entire techno city. Like the silent boy, they had long tangled locks and wore tattered tunics patched with animal skins. Every stitch of their clothing was brown or grey, as if anything brighter had been dulled by the sun to the color of dust.

Despite their clothing, they looked more like my neighbors in Little Pond than the technos, a proper mix of ages, with thickened arms and bronzed skin, people accustomed to hard work outdoors. Several carried skimpy baskets, but most bore crude spades and pruning knives, the tools of a poor farmer.

Such a strange world—small children who'd mastered mathematics more complex than anything I'd learned in the keep, machines that synthesized food out of air. Yet before me stood adults with clothing and tools more primitive than any back home. Where were their craftsmen, their blacksmiths and carpenters, spinners and weavers? Or had they relied on their machines for too long?

The greenies gathered in a circle, evenly spaced around us in what seemed a well-practiced formation. A fair-haired woman, not much older than me, stepped forward and made a formal bow, then laid her stone axe at my feet.

A sign of peace, I presumed.

"Welcome to our home," she said. "My name is Devorah. The earth mother sent me to bring you to her. I see you've made a new friend." She ruffled the silent boy's hair. "You've done well, Zachariah."

The silent boy nodded and beamed back at her.

"Come with us," she said. "We're out for our daily chores, so we'll need to gather food on the way. I'll show you what we've learned of berries, how we tell which are safe to eat and which will make us ill. We have much to learn about finding food from the land, and there are many plants we haven't tried. Perhaps you'll recognize some from your homeland and teach us about them."

Zachariah grasped me with one hand and Nathaniel with the other, as if to show the others we were friends. Then the whole band resumed hiking downhill. Several of the stoutest lagged behind, a rear guard, I presumed.

As we walked, I breathed in the scent of sap and pine needles from the trees lining our way, and the aroma of the rich brown earth giving gently beneath my feet, a fertile land any farmer in Little Pond would be happy to till. On the surrounding hillside, I caught a familiar growth, a field of flax in bloom. Their pale blue flowers brightened my day.

Soon the trail widened and side paths spiraled up a steep embankment to my right. The greenies spread out and put their tools to work, clearing and widening the access to what they hoped would be a rich crop of berries.

Devorah handed me and Nathaniel spare baskets she'd brought, so we could help in the gathering.

As we strolled along, stopping occasionally to poke through the brush, I studied my basket, a flimsy, shallow thing woven from straw, unlikely to survive a hard rain. Every child in Little Pond made baskets better than these, not of straw but of willow or oak or ash, with a tighter weave, braided or coiled, crafts practiced and perfected across generations. All carried more weight and would last for years—a skill I could teach them.

The slope steepened. After a ten minute climb, we came to the edge of the scree, where the trees thinned and turned to bramble. Scattered throughout were low bushes of what I instantly recognized as blueberries.

The greenies split up, each of them seeking their own spot apart from the others. At once, they began to fill baskets with fistfuls of plump berries.

"These are the same as we pick back home," I said. "Do you eat them often?"

"It's much of what we eat this time of year," Devorah said, "along with the fish we catch, now that we get so little food from the technos. It's that or starve. But taking food from the land is new for us. The earth mother teaches us to proceed cautiously. Some of the berries can make us sick or even kill us. So we test new berries by feeding them to our animals. It's a cruel trial, and we use it sparingly. The earth mother teaches us to treat our animals with kindness, harming them only out of necessity. Mostly, we stick to what's proven to be safe."

I wandered deeper into the berry patch, in search of fertile bushes still unpicked, as I'd done so often with Nathaniel and Thomas in childhood. At the far edge, I caught a pleasant surprise—raspberries. I reached in to pick some, but my attempt was stayed by the grasp of a small hand. I looked up to find the silent boy frantically shaking his head.

Devorah and the others were immediately upon us. "Not those berries. The earth mother teaches us to avoid them."

"Have you tested them?" I said.

The greenies shook their heads and eyed the raspberries fearfully.

"Then what makes you think they're dangerous?"

Devorah glanced back at the others and fidgeted, suddenly less sure of herself. "The earth mother tested a number similar to those. She believes the safest berries are blue with a smooth skin. She teaches us to shun the blacks or reds, or ones with clusters of droplets like these."

I suppressed a grin. A little less than gods, but afraid of a raspberries. I reached in and popped one into my mouth.

The greenies gasped and held their breath, but I only smiled.

"Delicious," I said, "and they make a lovely jam."

"What is jam?" Devorah said.

I started to answer, but stopped when I noticed the greenies hanging on my every word. All I'd learned in the keep, the science and mathematics, were of no use here. I could do more good by teaching what my mother had taught me as a child.

I finished filling my basket with raspberries while the skeptical greenies looked on, and then followed them down the path to their village, staying close enough to eavesdrop on their chatter. "No earth mother" I heard them say, "but a lord and lady in silver, perhaps sent by the dreamers."

Innocent as babes, makers of flimsy baskets, frightened by raspberries, and ignorant of jam. What else might Nathaniel and I teach them? How to pick flax and shear sheep? How to spin the harvest into thread and weave the thread into cloth? How to till the land?

I was no dreamer, but here in this world I could teach them so much. I hoped I could learn as well.

***

With baskets filled, our troop resumed its trek down the slope. After an hour, the scenery changed from wild growth to land with a more human touch, the prelude to the home of the greenies.

I took in every detail, hoping to better understand these people the mentor so mistrusted. Their village differed from the city of the technos, and not just because of the absence of machines. Here, someone had made an effort to beautify the place. White rocks lined a path groomed with crushed shells from the beach. Though the land was not as well tilled as Little Pond—with its fields of wheat in rows and apple orchards dotting the hillsides—cleared plots began to appear, kitchen gardens with tomatoes, peppers and cucumbers, and green beans spiraling around poles. In between grew a welcome display of color, beds of daffodils and lilies, with tiny snowdrops and blue forget-me-nots, and here and there, a splash of daisies.

I'd gone so long without seeing flowers in bloom that I stepped off the path to inhale their perfume.

Soon after, I sighted the tops of modest huts, the first sign of the village. These were round in form, with roofs made of thatched branches rising to a peak with a smoke hole in the middle. They reminded me of our NOT tree, the play shelter Nathaniel's father had built for us as children—called NOT for the three inseparable friends: Nathaniel, Orah and Thomas. At the start of winter, before the annual festival of light, we'd gather to dress it with freshly cut balsam boughs, not mere decoration but a covering to block out the wind and the cold. These dwellings seemed not much sturdier.

Thoughts of my childhood distracted me, and the village loomed. Soon, the crunch of shells underfoot announced our arrival. Several children ventured out of the huts to greet us, all dressed like Zachariah, their feet bare, their shirts and leggings worn and tattered. A few sheep and goats wandered freely among them.

I turned to Devorah. "Why do you dress your children like this?"

Devorah stared at the ground, watching her sandal dig a hole in the soil. "Before the day of reckoning, we received all our clothing from the technos. No more. We wear what's left, and stitch the pieces together with bits of animal skin. But the earth mother forbids us to harm the animals unnecessarily. We take their skins only after the rare times they've been killed for food or died of natural causes."

I eyed the greenie children. No parent in Little Pond would dress their child so poorly. With so much flax in the surrounding hills and sheep bulging with unshorn wool, they must know nothing of weaving and spinning. Yet these children seemed happy, and Kara said they slept well at night, without the nightmares that cursed the technos.

Who was the better off? The greenies living their crude, uncomfortable lives with their belief in the land, or the technos placing their faith in brain-building drugs and failing machines? Had Nathaniel and I come so far across the ocean to find people worse off than our own?

54

The children held back, gawking from a distance. What must they make of us, me with my auburn hair, and my tall, bearded companion, both dressed in the silver garments of the technos. Then the silent boy, Zachariah, raised his hands over his head, still grasping ours, like an elder declaring a winner at festival, and the children rushed forward, wanting to be part of the celebration, reaching out and touching us as if to make sure we were real.

"So much like Little Pond," Nathaniel said.

"And so different."

Devorah broke into a wide grin. "Everyone's glad you came. We need a glimmer of hope. The earth mother will be pleased."

The huts were arranged in circles, with eighty or more on the outer rim, and lesser groupings inside. As Devorah escorted us down one of the paths radiating from the heart of the village, I counted the circles — six deep, dwellings for several hundred families.

At the very center, an ancient beech tree sprawled, its broad arms extending in all directions as if to protect the village. At its base lay a single hut, no different from the others, yet it had an aura about it — perhaps the way the greenies gathered round it and hushed in awe.

"Wait here a moment," Devorah said. "I'll tell the earth mother you've arrived." Then she entered the hut.

I strained to listen, but caught only murmurings.

A few seconds later, Devorah emerged.

"The earth mother will see you now."

Chapter 9

The Ragged Lady

Nathaniel bent at the waist to clear the entrance, but I had only to duck my head. Inside, I needed a few seconds for my eyes to adjust.

The round room was low and ill lit, with a dirt floor and a single wooden bench to one side, no bigger than my cell in temple city. But where the vicars' prison reeked of mold, these branch-covered walls gave off a scent of pine. A small fire smoldered within a ring of stones, providing warmth and a little light without much smoke. Against the back wall lay a heap of rags I took for bedding.

No, not bedding. As my vision brightened, I recognized a rumpled old woman seated crossed-legged on a bed of straw.

I stifled a shiver. Before me squatted the revered earth mother. No wonder the technos called her the ragged lady.

The woman's silver hair hung in half-formed ringlets as if cut with a dull knife rather than scissors. A few stray locks grew long on either side, and these were bound in braids dangling down to her breasts. The braids framed a square face with sharp angles and a strong chin, as if her features had been chiseled out of stone. She regarded me with striking green eyes, the color of a newly sprouted leaf in spring with the sun shining through it. After a moment, the lines around her eyes crinkled, and her mouth widened until her teeth showed.

"Welcome to our home," the ragged lady said in a voice too deep for a woman. "Devorah tells me you bring wisdom to our shores."

I made an awkward bow. "More longing than wisdom. Longing to learn more than we know."

"Ah. That, my child, is the beginning of wisdom. She tells me you come from a world with no machines and are familiar with the ways of the land."

I nodded, and then cast a glance at Nathaniel. We'd risked a voyage across the ocean to find advantage for our beleaguered people, but here everyone looked to us for help.

The ragged lady flashed a warm but vulnerable smile. "My people tell me you're staying with the technos. What lies has William been filling your heads with?"

"William?" Nathaniel said.

"You'd know him as the mentor. The children started calling him that, but he's never discouraged it. I think he likes it."

"Yet here they call you the earth mother."

The ragged lady let out a full-bodied laugh that started in her belly and rose to her chest, before escaping through her lips as a howl.

How could one not like a woman with such a laugh?

"An unfortunate term, but it's hard to get them to change. You may call me by my given name if you prefer. Annabel."

"Why, Annabel, do you believe the mentor lies?"

"Because I know him so well. William and I are old friends—we used to play together as children, even though the stubborn fool speaks poorly of me now. No matter. His time will come, like mine, probably sooner rather than later. He puts on a brave front, the wise mentor, but I bet he wishes he'd died with his so-called dreamers."

A shudder ran through me. The dreamers dead? They were the last of the keepmasters' kin. "He said the dreamers still lived. Why would he tell such a lie?"

"He uses the myth of their return to inspire the children so they'll study harder, become as wise as the dreamers someday, and regain control over the machines, but since the day of reckoning, too much has been lost. Over time, like us, they'll need to learn to live off the land—a harder life, but we're all headed that way."

Live off the land—the life of every family in Little Pond. A harder life, yes, but my mind filled with memories of childhood, and my heart ached for home. Yet I'd learned such a life led to stagnation and dreams unfulfilled. We were meant to strive and grow.

But what of the technos with their city in decay? Had they taken a wrong turn in their quest for knowledge? Or was theirs the fate of all knowledge seekers, as the vicars had claimed—a path leading back to the darkness?

An agreed upon silence settled between us, the ragged lady letting her words sink in, and me needing time to accept them. I felt Nathaniel's gentle touch massaging the small of my back.

He finally broke the silence. "The mentor claims he speaks to the dreamers. Is that a lie too?"

"Not exactly. The dreamers did not die in the way you know, but they do not live either. Perhaps he can speak to them... after a fashion."

Nathaniel bent low so he could peer into the ragged ladies eyes. "Enlighten us, Annabel, though we may not be as wise as the earth mother. How is it possible to not die but not live? Are the dreamers gone or not?"

"Believe me, they're gone."

"To where?"

The ragged lady motioned upward, where the smoke from her small fire danced and swirled before sneaking through the hole in the roof to the sky. "They dissipated like the smoke. Nowhere. Or everywhere, if only old William would open the vent and let them go."

"What does that mean?"

"It means they shine not as if they were burning from within but as if sunlight shined upon them, even in the dark of night. It means they are flaming souls yearning to be set free."

Ishkabibble. I recalled the sound Kara made with her mouth. No wonder the techno children called them by such a name.

Nathaniel saw no humor. His hands clenched, and the color rose in his cheeks.

I pressed between him and the ragged lady to give him time to settle down. "In our homeland, we're called the seekers of truth. Don't muddle your answer with riddles or speak falsely to us. Tell us only what is true. "

The ragged lady laughed again, this time with an unpleasant cackle, more like someone who'd been offended.

"They seek the truth, these people from the land of the past, but what kind of truth? The dreamers sought only a truth they could prove through experiments. Where has it led them? Here, we believe in a different truth. Where you're from, do you have legends, stories of the past?"

I nodded. "Such stories were frowned upon by our leaders, because they were from the darkness and fantasies, but our mothers told them to us anyway."

"Yes, yes," the ragged lady said. "So they should. We need such legends. We need to pass them on to our children, as our mothers told them to us and their mothers to them. Our children need more than science and knowledge and things they can see and touch. They need to learn about things not of this world, of the magic that dwells in our hearts, of angels that fly in the heavens and demons that dwell in the dark. They need to experience the mystery of this life and the awe we feel for this world, not just that the stars shine on a clear night, but that we ourselves are made of stardust."

"Why make up angels and demons," I said, "when your ancestors visited the stars? What good to teach such things? They bring no knowledge nor do they create a better world."

"You asked me for truth, and I told what I believe. All is not knowledge. There must be mystery as well. Each child must create their own secret world to live in, and they must believe in things unseen, so when their suffering becomes too great, they may seek refuge in a kinder place.

"Even at my age, I need to find wonder in little things, because unlike the dreamers, I accept I'll pass from this earth one day. Despite all their science, I've learned more than they did. Not what makes the wind blow, but that it feels so good on my cheeks. Not what makes the grass grow, but that it tickles my palms and the soles of my feet. Not how the Earth came into being, but that we would have no life without her and should give thanks. You've stayed with the technos, and now you've come to us. It's for you to decide which truth you believe."

This ragged lady was no dreamer. No light shone upon her in the dimness of her hut, but as she recalled places she'd never been and visions not of this world, a light burned within, making her face glow.

Might she be like our dotty old neighbor back in Little Pond, who believed in ghosts and fairies and all things of the shadows? That lady brewed potions if you were ill and afraid to ask the vicars for medicine, and produced charms for sickness of the spirit—a woman who would have been sent for a harsh teaching if the vicars knew. Everyone in Little Pond believed she was mad, but they protected her from the Temple of Light, just in case there was something to her charms.

The ragged lady had finished speaking, and now stared up at the smoke leaving the hut, as if communing with the dreamers.

I crumpled my brow, and a great puzzlement slowed my heartbeat and made me still.

A flash of orange streaked past. A tabby cat with black stripes had slipped into the hut and was winding its way between the ragged lady's legs, oblivious to demons or angels.

Devorah dashed in after her, clapping her hands. "Here, Bella, leave the earth mother alone. She has important visitors and no time for your foolishness."

The earth mother reached down and stroked the cat behind the ears. "Oh, leave her be, Devorah. She's no bother to me."

Devorah glared at the cat, now with its eyes closed and its satisfied purr filling the room. "Bother or not, you need the time. You only have a few minutes left."

With that pronouncement, she scooped up the unwilling cat and hurried her outside.

"A few minutes?" Nathaniel said.

"Each day, after we've gathered our berries and caught our fish, and finished our labor at weaving our baskets, mending clothes and doing other chores, we take a few minutes to meet and reflect on what we've learned. Then, before we eat the evening meal, we give thanks for the bounty of the earth."

"Like a prayer?" I said.

"Oh no. Just a meeting, nothing more."

Just then, a distant bell began to peel, ringing once, twice, a dozen times, like the bell at the top of the Little Pond commons announcing the arrival of the vicar.

Devorah returned, clutching the cat in her arms and petting it, apparently having made her peace. "The people are gathering, earth mother. Time for your blessing."

"Fetch me my walking stick," the ragged lady said. "You, my strong young man, lend me your arm."

Annabel, the ragged lady and earth mother, tucked her legs beneath her, grabbed Nathaniel's arm, and unfolded herself until she stood upright. Then she grasped her walking stick, lifted her chin as the mentor had done, and followed Devorah outside while Nathaniel and I gaped after her.

Chapter 10

The Hall of Winds

We followed the ragged lady beyond the circle of huts to a well-groomed path through the woods—another procession like our grand entrance into the technos' welcome feast—but this time we weren't the guests of honor. The trail was lined with adoring greenies who whispered as we passed, "Bless you, earth mother," and then fell into a solemn step behind her.

The earth mother—protector of the land, purveyor of wisdom—sauntered unfazed, waving to her people as if she'd done this many times before. Along the way, she gave us a lesson on their progress. "You've probably observed the crudeness of our skills."

I nodded, careful to hide my disdain.

"The machines produced tools with precision, and we still have a few, but as they wear down, we're learning to make our own. We started with stone, chipping away to shape them, a long and arduous process with poor results. Now, we've learned to take metal from the ground, heat it in a flame and pound it on a hardened stone platform. Though we're not yet able to match the quality of blades produced by the machines, we improve daily."

The ragged lady rambled on, boasting of their accomplishments, their fashioning of dwellings from wood and their coaxing of food from the land. None filled me with awe. Little Pond was a tiny village at the edge of the Earth, yet its meanest inhabitants possessed greater skill than these people. Beyond Little Pond, blacksmiths and carpenters,

61

coopers, shoemakers and others labored at their crafts, all more advanced than any I'd seen here.

The greenies were like children snatched from their cradles and left to fend for themselves without parent or past. They'd learned enough to survive, but their path to mastery had been clumsy and flawed. The village of the greenies contrasted with the keep, not a leap forward, but a step back. Not a past rediscovered, but a past lost.

The ragged lady curled her lips and snorted. "You're unimpressed, I see. No wonder. You come from a people who have benefited from the resourcefulness of their forbearers. Our forbearers yielded their resourcefulness to the machines in exchange for a life of pampered leisure. All but the dreamers. In the nearly three years since the day of reckoning, the machines have gradually failed, and we've had to grope our way forward in the dark. You may belittle our accomplishments, but we're pleased with the progress we've made. Now, Devorah tells me you can teach us which plants to eat and show us a better way to weave baskets. What other skills do you bring to our shores?"

I glanced at Nathaniel, asking without words who should respond first. A tilt of his head sufficed, the language of friends since birth.

"In our world," I said, "I was raised as a weaver, a craft that produced cloth for the garments we wore. You have a rich crop of flax on the hills surrounding your village. Its fiber can be spun into thread, which in turn can be woven and stitched to make clothing better than what your people wear. You can do all of this with simple machines, spinning wheels and looms, powered by nothing more than your hands and feet. I can teach you to build them."

I nodded for Nathaniel to take his turn.

"My family has always been farmers," he said. "The soil of this land is ripe for planting. I can teach you to grow more than these few vegetables, crops you can bake into bread, grains you can store to eat long after the season for growing has ended."

The column of greenies paused as the ragged lady stopped to gaze up at the treetops swaying in the breeze. At last, she looked down and fixed us with her green eyes.

"If what you say is true, you must abandon William and come live with us. You can teach us your ways, and we would make you most welcome."

"We could teach you more," I said, "if you'd help us return to our land. We could bring back others with skills beyond our own. Those who know how to make bricks and cut granite from the mountain, to forge metal and make better tools, to build hardened dwellings protected from the weather, to cobble shoes for your children, to till the land, to sow seeds of wheat and corn and reap their harvest, to plant trees that bear fruit, and much more."

The ragged lady began walking again, but slower this time.

Nathaniel cut in front. "To do so, we need your help to build a new boat."

"A boat? What do we know of boats?"

"The dreamers would know," I said. "They know more than all of us together, even more than the keepmasters. Help us with your friend, William. Convince him to let us speak with the dreamers."

The ragged lady all but spat out the words. "I have no desire for the knowledge of the dreamers."

"Why?" I said. "Don't you want to be more than you are?"

"Oh yes," she said. "I believe we were meant to be much more than we are. We were meant to aspire to the divine, but how can the way to the divine be through machines?"

Before I could respond, we rounded the next curve and our destination came into view. Like so much in the greenie world, this gathering place seemed tossed together, far less crafted than the great halls of Temple City or the domed commons of the technos.

Its walls consisted of odd-shaped stones, marbled gray and flecked with rust, stacked one on top of the other with no mortar in between. Straw and mud filled the cracks but imperfectly, so rain and wind could blow through—a building that would need repair after every storm.

Overgrown holly bushes framed its entrance, with their spiny-toothed, shiny leaves and red berries—probably why the greenies feared such fruit—an easy mistake. When I was little, I'd watched the birds nibbling at the holly berries and assumed them safe to eat. My mother stopped me after I'd swallowed a few, but I still had a dreadful night.

Three stairs, bracketed on either side by log railings, led up to a modest doorway. Above the door, unvarnished wooden beams sloped to a peak, topped by an arched steeple. An ancient, brass bell hung in the hole in the arch, so much like the bell atop the Little Pond commons. The bell's curved lines were so perfectly formed it seemed beyond the skill of the greenies.

The ragged lady caught me eyeing it. "We came upon that bell buried in the ground when we tilled one of our gardens. A relic of the past, from a time before the machines, proof our forbearers had a sense of wonder. It became our inspiration to build this communal hall. We chose a style to contrast with the cathedral of the dreamers, built into the rock face of the mountain. For them, no setting was grand enough, so they had to keep moving to ever higher ground. Their minds had exceeded their humility, and they began to view themselves as gods. Now their cathedral has become their tomb. Here, on this humble flatland, we dug out every stone and set it in place by hand. We built this hall with honest sweat and without the aid of machines—a tribute to our humanity."

I followed the lines of the building, from stairs to door, to the sloped roof and steeple framing the bell. The structure was simple, not like the monuments of the vicars or the miracles of the keepmasters—not even as well made as our village commons back home. Yet it possessed a raw beauty, and based on how the greenies gazed up to its steeple, they had imbued it with meaning.

At its base stood a formation of men, positioned on either side of the door. Unlike the others, they had arrived before us. They aligned in two perfect rows, backs straight, feet wide and chins jutted out, looking grim as deacons. Their apparent leader towered over them from behind, a man of middle years with wild black hair tempered by gray at its edges, as tall as Nathaniel but half again as wide. While the rest of the greenies had left their tools behind, these men carried axes and pruning knives on their shoulders, high up and threatening.

"Who are they?" I whispered to the ragged lady.

She waved a hand at them. "Oh, that's Caleb and his men. They're among my most zealous followers and the hardest workers. Caleb insists someone should guard us while we gather, as if the technos might attack. An unnecessary step, but it does no harm."

To the right of the stairs, behind the men, a white cornerstone had been set into the wall, with words chiseled into its polished face. I stepped closer and read them aloud.

The Hall of Winds

In remembrance of the Day of Reckoning

"Why the hall of winds?"

"To mark the difference between us and the dreamers. They sought to control nature but could never master the winds. Here, we don't try to take charge of the Earth. We accept our mortality and know our limits."

The column of greenies had assembled in a half circle outside the entrance. Apparently, by tradition, the ragged lady was to enter first. She offered Nathaniel and I the honor of accompanying her.

We passed one at a time through the narrow doorway, its frame arched so low Nathaniel had to duck his head to clear. Inside, an altar built of flagstone stood at the front, much like the altar the visiting vicar used during the seasonal blessing back home. The ragged lady shuffled ahead and took her place behind it, as her people filled the wooden benches on either side. High above her on the back wall, a circular window loomed — the hall's sole concession to grandeur — with fragments of colored glass pieced together to form rays of blue spiraling out from a golden center. The window was situated so the afternoon rays streamed through in slanting columns, warming the faces of the congregants and making rainbow flecks of light dance across the ragged lady's cheeks.

I could almost picture the vicar's sun icon glowing beside her.

Two of Caleb's men marched behind the altar and unfurled a banner depicting a scene more frightening than the mural that graced the vicars' teaching chamber. That image showed the mythical battle of darkness and light — a storm cloud, signifying the darkness, pitted against a legion of vicars in prayer.

This greenie banner bore a painting of four horsemen, their steeds caught in full gallop, one white, one black, one red, and one pale. Steam burst from their nostrils, and their eyes blazed, but the riders burned most in my mind, demons all, each inspiring fear in their own way. The first with a flaming sword; the second, a caped creature, with a skull for a head; the next, a cloaked fiend whose features were hidden by a cowl; and the last a woman with serpents for hair. Across the bottom in red letters three words shouted out: *Beware the machines.*

The ragged lady caught me staring. "Caleb's idea — the riders symbolize desolation, destitution, destruction and death."

I recalled a game Nathaniel, Thomas and I used to play as children in the NOT tree, where we'd pretend to be besieged by demons from the darkness. We'd take turns being spies, each venturing out of the shelter and then returning with a made-up tale, trying to frighten the others. Thomas always told the scariest stories, tales of dark riders with faces like skulls and flames flaring through their empty sockets. He'd scare me so much I'd have nightmares, until I grew old enough to understand. Demons were nothing but stories made up to put a face on ideas, a trick to frighten people into embracing beliefs.

The ragged lady waited, hunched over the altar until Caleb and his men took their seats in the last two rows, and the scuffling of footsteps had stilled. Only then did she begin.

"Today is a special day, as we welcome guests from across the sea. Like us, they are children of the great cataclysm, but unlike our people, their forbearers chose a different path. Not the pursuit of science or the drive to master nature, but a simpler life. And so they bring with them not our meager few years of struggling to live off the land, but many generations of accepting their place in the world."

I twisted around to check the expressions of the assembled, not so different from my Little Pond neighbors at the blessing of the light. I flushed when I realized most eyes were on me. If the ragged lady was right, our quest for the keep had been wrong.

She droned on, like the grand vicar recounting the events of the day: the number of baskets of berries they'd harvested; how many fish they'd caught; the birth of a baby goat; an impending marriage, whose ceremony she would preside over that night. Then she urged her people to embrace Nathanial and I, and the renewed hope we brought when we sailed in on the tide—neglecting to mention that our boat had crashed.

Finally, she told everyone to grasp their neighbor's hand, close their eyes and bow their heads.

"Today," she said, her voice rising, "our labor has yielded food enough to sustain us. We thank the earth for its bounty."

"Thank the earth," the people repeated.

"May the day come soon that brings peace to the dreamers."

"Peace to the dreamers," the assembled chanted as one.

"Earth mother?"

I opened my eyes and looked back. Caleb had risen from his seat.

"Each day we wish peace to the dreamers," he said, "those poor souls left to wander for eternity. When will we act on our beliefs and finally set them free?"

She sighed as if she'd heard this question before. "It's not our place to change the fate of the dreamers."

"Was it the place of the technos to challenge the heavens, to raise themselves up as gods?"

"No. No more than it's for you to judge them."

Eyes turned. A murmur filled the hall. Only a few voices sounded on Caleb's side.

He blanched and took his seat.

I recalled the blessing of my childhood, how I'd been awed by the voice of the grand vicar resounding from the sun icon. I remembered the sense of calm and wellbeing that came over my people—all the goodness that came with devotion to the light. Then a vision of the future spiraled forward out of the mists of my mind. What if the earth mother and her people were of the light, the true light and not the light of the temple? One day, would some of their descendants become vicars, and would their symbols and rituals harden into law? Would any who opposed them be punished? I recalled my own few hours in the teaching cell and shuddered.

When the hall of winds had settled again to silence, the ragged lady motioned to the front row.

"Come now, Zachariah, and honor our guests with a song. The one about the ship on the tide."

The silent boy approached the front, as the ragged lady took her seat beside me.

"But he has no voice," I whispered.

"Oh, Zachariah has a voice. He just chooses to use it only in song. Hush now and listen."

The silent boy stood before the altar with a wholesome, doe-eyed innocence, not like the arrogance of the helpers in the keep, who had never seen the light of day, or the pale stares of the techno children manipulating the holos in their lessons. More like my friends in Little Pond who had lived most of their lives outdoors.

The boy raised his eyes to the topmost rafters of the hall of winds, so the blue and gold light streaming through the window flickered off his tangled locks. Then he lifted his absent voice into song.

The wise ones climbed up to the mount
A place so very high
They reach so far beyond themselves
They tried to touch the sky

His song soared like that of an angel, bouncing off the stone walls and echoing like a celestial chorus singing in harmony.

The earth roared its displeasure
What would become their fate?
The mountain shrugged and cast them off
into their dreamer state

~~~

"How long the dream?" their loved ones cried

67

DAVID LITWACK

When will they wake once more?
Not until the stars wink out
And the ocean leaves the shore
~~~
*The people left unto themselves*
*Made peace with mother earth*
*And now live one day to the next*
*Searching for their worth*
~~~
Until a sailing ship arrives
From the ocean's farthest side
It comes to us upon the wind
Bringing hope with the morning tide
~~~
The ship sails in upon the waves
With those who'll show the way
And all the children of mother earth
At last learn how to pray

As the boy sang, a breeze blew in through cracks in the walls, and the sweet-smelling air moved gently in my hair. I folded my hands on the bench in front of me and laid my chin on them, gazing up at the colored glass as I once had gazed up at the million suns in the keep's observatory.

After the song finished, the greenies filed out, Caleb's men with a grumble, but most as respectful as when they'd entered.

I waited by the altar with Nathaniel and the ragged lady. No. No longer would I call her the ragged lady, but the earth mother, a name she'd earned.

"Earth mother," I said. "What happened to the boy? Why does he choose to hide such a beautiful voice?"

"He was only six years old on the day of reckoning. For two days while the technos dug with their hands through the rubble, he was a forgotten child, left alone in his chamber. For two days, until my people took pity and came with their strong backs and tools to help. Only then did the frantic technos take time to comfort the younger children. Zachariah was an oversight, they said, a victim of an epic disaster. When they found him, he had ceased to speak, and he has never spoken since."

"How did he come to be with you?"

"The technos nurtured him for five months, healing his body but not his soul. They fed him meals and brought him to lessons each day,

68

but he refused to learn, sitting silently and staring at the walls. Finally, they sent him to us."

"But why?"

She shrugged. "Why? It's what they've always done, these so-called machine masters. They cast off children who fail in their lessons or are unable to pass the exam. They exile all who don't measure up, whose minds will never be strong enough to control the machines. They told this beautiful child he was not worthy, and their loss is our gain. He's lived with us ever since. "

I pictured a six-year-old Zachariah left alone and frightened in the sterile techno room. "Is he an orphan then?"

The earth mother gazed up at the rafters as if I'd asked a question too hard to answer. When she looked back, her lips bore a crooked smile.

"What is an orphan? A child whose parents have died? Then he's no orphan."

I opened my mouth to speak but no words emerged. The final question stuck in my throat.

Nathaniel gave voice to it instead. "His parents were dreamers?"

"Dreamers, yes," the earth mother said, "though he shall never see them again."

Chapter 11

A Dread from the Past

Nathaniel and I trudged up the narrow path back to the techno city, but now with a slower stride. So much to take in, so little of it understood. I longed to approach one of the screens in the keep and consult a helper.

"Help," I'd say. "Tell me who the dreamers are. Explain how it's possible to be alive but not live. Most of all, find a way for me to speak with them."

Perhaps the dreamers could dispel my confusion. What *should* I believe?

Was righteousness on the side of those who worshipped the sun or the earth, or those who sought knowledge instead? Should I have heeded the keepmasters and dreamers, who found cures for disease, built wondrous machines, and traveled to the stars? Or should I have trusted the vicars and greenies, who branded such efforts a treacherous slope and chose a simpler life, even at the cost of stunting their growth and robbing every child of their potential for greatness?

The arch vicar had once told me there was no such thing as absolute truth. Now the earth mother had said much the same. Perhaps, they were right.

We reached the knoll where the trees opened up, and I had a clear view of the techno city. The wall of lights blazed as if the mentor had left a beacon to guide our way home.

Unwilling to face the technos so soon, I swept clean a flat rock at the edge of the knoll and sank down upon it. My legs were still wobbly from our time at sea, and the trek uphill had drained me more than expected.

Nathaniel collapsed beside me on the makeshift bench and took from his pack a goatskin flask and pouch of berries, gifts from the greenies to sustain us on the trail.

Once we'd quenched our thirst and ate our fill, Nathaniel draped one arm around me and stretched out the other, pointing above the tree line. "There, high up on the mountain, awaits what our new friend, Annabel, calls the cathedral of the dreamers."

I followed his gesture and squinted, trying to peer past the rock façade to the dreamers inside. Through the mist kicked up by the falls, I beheld a gate fronted by stone columns with forbidding black doors behind. Would we ever be allowed in, and if so, what would we find?

"Such a long journey," I said.

"Which? This trek back from the greenie village, or the path we'll travel one day, through the city and beyond to the dreamers?"

"Neither. I meant the journey we've been on since first leaving Little Pond. I mean searching for the keepers and finding the keep, then starting the revolution against the vicars. I mean living with the peephole in the cells of Temple City and worrying if each day would be our last together. I mean winning the support of the people, only to lose most of it when they discovered what the keep had to offer. I mean our voyage across the ocean, our boat floundering in the storm and crashing on the rocks. After four years, where has our striving left us? Stranded and bewildered on a distant shore. The more we discover, the less I understand."

He pulled me closer. "But always, we've had each other."

I rested my head on his chest and snuggled in, listening to his heartbeat, calm as always despite the turmoil swirling around us.

After a minute, he glanced up at the graying sky. "Alive or dead, the dreamers lay safe in their fortress, but we're exposed on this ridge. Soon, the sun will set behind the mountain and twilight will fall."

A cooling breeze swept in from the ocean as if to confirm his words. I hugged myself and rubbed my bare arms to ward off the chill, then returned the flask to him, brushed the dirt off my silver clothing, and stood. "We best get going before the trail turns dark."

A half hour later, we reached the outskirts of the techno city. I paused to catch my breath, only to be startled by a rustling in the trees on either side.

Kara jumped out, accompanied by a dozen of the older boys, each brandishing a sharpened stick.

"What now, Kara?" I said. "Do you mean to do us harm?"

Kara flushed and looked away. "Not harm, but you need to come with me to speak to the mentor."

"Now?"

"Now."

"What if we're too weary and wish otherwise."

Kara lowered her eyes. "Please, you've been kind to me, and I have no desire to harm one who can sing as you did to poor Timmy, but you've been with the ragged lady. She and her people have caused injury to us in the sad days following ascension, something we can never forgive. You must come with us now."

Several of the boys circled behind us and lowered the tips of their sticks. All were slightly built, lacking the thickened muscles of someone like Nathaniel who'd grown up on a farm. Out of the corner of my eye, I saw his jaw tighten and his fists clench.

He glared at the boys, who shuffled their feet and fell back a step.

I placed a restraining hand on Nathaniel and extended an arm to Kara, palm outward. "We'll go with you to the mentor. Perhaps he'll shed light on what we've learned. Lead on. We trust ourselves in your care."

***

Kara paused at the door to the mentor's quarters. A glass plate was attached to the wall above her shoulder, identical to the one outside our bed chamber, though this one blinked red. She ordered the boys to wait in the hall, explaining that only she and the newcomers were allowed in. Then she pressed her palm to the plate. The blinking stopped, and the door clicked open.

I squinted inside, trying to pierce the darkness, expecting to find the mentor in bed. As the lights detected our presence and brightened, I found him slumped in his wheeled chair. The wide-brimmed hat still rested on his head, tipped low to cover his eyes. Apparently, he'd drifted off while waiting for us.

Kara rubbed his arm to wake him. "Mentor, we found them. They're here."

The mentor stirred, stretching his long arms high in a yawn, and then straightened his hat in a grandfatherly gesture, but as the light filled the room, the shadows crossing his face refused to leave.

His features hardened. "Where have you been?"

I tensed as I did when the arch vicar interrogated me, trying to learn the location of the keep, but this time I was proud to answer. "You already know. We've been to visit the earth mother."

"My friend, Annabel. What lies did she tell you?"

Nathaniel stepped forward and towered over the old man. "That's the same question she asked us. She said you lied as well."

The mentor laughed, but it was not a kindly laugh. "Ah. Did she also preach to you about the evils of machines? Did she explain how they intended to survive without them? And did she share her fanciful notion of what happened to the dreamers?"

I nodded, then shook my head. "She spoke of the day when the dreamers left, a time she called the day of reckoning, but like everyone here, she told us only enough to confuse. We don't know what to believe. Perhaps you can enlighten us."

"Only if you're minds are open to enlightenment."

"Try us." I waited, hands folded in front, holding my breath. I prayed to hear the truth at last.

The mentor blew out a long stream of air, as if to expel his displeasure. Then, though he made no motion, no touch of his hand or twitch of his legs, the chair rolled toward us. He stopped so close I could feel the heat of his eyes on my cheeks.

"What Annabel calls the day of reckoning, we call the day of ascension. It's an annual festival we've celebrated for many years, the one day a year when the wisest among us, the ones who created and controlled the machines, had the chance to indulge their brilliance, to meld their minds together. Ascension is a... wondrous event, but not without risk, a time when mortals ascend to the edge of the infinite. Out of such days our greatest innovations have emerged, our finest ideas.

"On this one day, nearly three years ago, a disaster occurred. Not an act of some angry god or the reckoning of a vengeful earth as Annabel preaches, but a natural phenomenon with the worst of timing. The mountain which had lain dormant for millennia chose that moment to erupt—an event even our brightest could not have foreseen. Yet they'd planned for such an unpredictable occurrence. All would have gone well if not for the ignorance of Annabel and her people."

His voice cracked at the last words, and his fingers tightened on the arms of the chair until his knuckles whitened. He stared past us as if reliving that day, and a thin sheet of sadness veiled his long face like the viewing gauze covering a coffin.

I waited for him to continue. When the silence dragged on, I prompted him. "If it was a natural phenomenon, what fault could the greenies bear?"

His blue eyes turned back to me, burning with rage. "Ascension is science, not malice or magic as their feeble minds imagined. It requires an enormous output of power. For centuries, we've received our power from the waterfall cascading down the mountain, but on this day of ascension, the mountain sent debris flowing down to divert the water that fed the falls.

"My colleagues in their wisdom had planned for such a disaster, reinforcing their mountain fortress and adding several layers of backup. Throughout the disruption of power, their plans worked perfectly, leaving their chambers intact and them safely suspended in the dreamer state. But no one had ever dwelled in the dream for so long. Time was of the essence. We needed labor to clear the debris and restore power. Our repair machines helped, but without the minds of their masters to guide them, they functioned poorly.

"So for once, after years of sustaining their people with nothing in return, we begged the so-called greenies for aid. Annabel and her ilk had started the earth movement a generation before, a bunch of the disgruntled too incompetent or lazy to pass their exams. For the day of ascension, they'd organized a peaceful protest based on a silly superstition, as if some jealous god had placed limits on mankind.

"Our adults helped, those too old like me to go into the mountain. The rest of our people were children, little more than babes. All did their best, working day and night without sleep, but we were unaccustomed to physical labor and lacked the tools. For two days the greenies refused to help despite our pleas, until selfishly they realized the consequences of their actions. They'd get no more free bounty from the machines if we failed. Those two days might have made the difference.

"We created a better world for them, despite how little they contributed. How did they repay us? They turned their backs in our time of need. Now you've betrayed my trust by befriending them."

I waited until the mentor's breathing had calmed, then dared a small step toward him.

Without any apparent gesture on his part, his chair recoiled.

"We take no sides," I said. "We're only trying to learn your ways."

"Our ways are clear for all to see. Theirs are devious. They preach of peace and the good earth, but they plot the murder of the dreamers. Did my good friend, Annabel, tell you that?"

I stayed silent, recalling the earth mother's prayer—to one day bring peace to the dreamers.

When I failed to answer, the mentor's eyes narrowed. "And if she *did* tell you, would you reveal their plans to me?"

Nathaniel grasped my hand and squeezed, as he had that day in the arch vicar's chamber.

I licked my lips and swallowed to moisten my throat. "Please, sir, we're innocents who sailed into your world. The greenies are struggling to live off the land. We bring skills from our side of the ocean that can ease their way. As for you, we may not match your science, but we come with fresh eyes and good intentions. We're not your enemy. Let us help both sides."

The chair whirred suddenly, an angry, grinding sound. It backed away and whirled in a circle, finally resting with its back to me.

"Help us? You with your primitive minds? I waited all day while you communed with my enemy. If you're truly innocents with fresh eyes, you'd be able to distinguish right from the obvious wrong. I've listened, hoping to hear some hint of remorse or regret. I have no more use for you now, and I'm tired." He motioned to Kara with a flip of his wrist. "Take them out of my sight."

***

As soon as we exited the mentor's chamber, the boys with the sharpened sticks surrounded us. At Kara's direction, they escorted us back to our room.

By the entrance, I noted our glass box now also glowed red.

Kara touched the box. A sharp click sounded as before, and the door snapped open.

A frustrated Nathaniel lurched inside and collapsed on the bed, but I waited, glaring at the door. As it swung shut behind us, the walls of the room seemed to close in, and the air became musty and thick. A tremor passed through me, a familiar dread from the past. I shuffled to the door in tiny steps and brushed my fingertips over its metal surface. Then I tested the latch as I had on our first night.

The door was locked. We were prisoners once again.

Chapter 12

The Gilded Prison

For three days, we stayed locked in our quarters, but this troubled me less than the dank cells of Temple City—no grim deacons lurking about, no stench of stale air, no wall to separate Nathaniel and me, no peephole needed here.

Each day, Kara provided us three good meals, the same as she and the others ate, and when she was able to barter for fresh berries from the greenies, she brought us an ample portion. I suspect she added her own share to ours to make up for our treatment.

Just as in the keep, our space stayed protected from the elements, never too warm or too cold. The bath water ran hot. The towels felt plush, the sheets silken, and the bed soft. We had everything we needed... except our freedom.

Kara seemed to fare worse than us. The shadows beneath her eyes deepened daily, as if she'd slept poorly at night with the burden of being our jailor resting heavily on her. If I asked for help or insight into our fate, she'd bite her tongue and decline. Her loyalty to the mentor remained absolute.

When I made a simpler request, to bring a supply of paper and pens, she was pleased to agree for a change and happily complied.

At last, I could resume my log to chronicle the events in this new land. I did so thankfully, with no rocking of the boat to muddle my script and no splashing of the waves to smudge my words.

THE STUFF OF STARS

***

What to make of this world?

We risked this journey believing some of the keepmasters' kin must have fled to the far side of the sea. Not all would have chosen the keepmasters' sacrifice, to be locked away for the rest of their lives while recording their knowledge. Some must have preferred to flee. These refugees had the means to make such a voyage, and the confidence they'd find safety here. We expected their descendants to be wise people, like those we'd met in the keep, but advanced by a thousand years. What timid souls we'd be to forgo such a quest.

Were we fools to think we'd find what we sought, that we might discover miracles to improve the lives of our people? No. We were no more fools than when we set out to seek the keep or chose to tell our neighbors the truth about the darkness.

Nathaniel and I need to follow our nature, and that nature is to strive for a better world.

What drives the potential for greatness? Is it learning and knowledge, or faith and passion? Neither is sufficient by itself, unless mixed with a willingness to view the world anew, to see possibilities rather than barriers.

That's what drove us to cross the sea and brought us to these shores.

But what have we found?

Both greenies and technos are mired in their own myths, each with customs cast in stone. What Nathaniel and I do best is bring about change, but only if they'll let us. How can we help from behind these walls?

***

I stopped writing, my pen poised in midair. Though locked away, I held in my hand the most powerful weapon—along with the paper, my thoughts and my stubborn will, strengths that can never be imprisoned.

I set down the log, withdrew a fresh sheet of paper, and smoothed it on the table. After a long and cleansing breath, I grasped the pen and started a new stream of words.

***

To the mentor, honored leader of the machine masters:

I write to you today in the spirit of respect for all you have accomplished. Yet this land we've sailed into lies in a state of sorrow. I make no claim to understand all that has happened—neither you nor the earth mother have shared enough — but whatever name you give to that tragic day, ascension or reckoning, it has cast this land into turmoil.

The greenies would be as children on our side of the sea, trying to live off the earth for the first time in generations. They mean well but are struggling. We possess skills to help them along.

Where we're from, there are those who believe in the sun, giver of light, kindred spirits who would sympathize with the aspirations of the greenies. Yes, some, like the greenie zealots, opposed the pursuit of new ideas, but Nathaniel and I convinced them to change. Many in our land now yearn for knowledge, to understand the ways of the keep, but we have so much to learn. Your children could speed up our learning, teach us the wisdom of the past, and move us beyond it.

So we can help the greenies and you can help us. What is it we can do for you?

You are a wonderful leader but will not live forever. The other adults we've seen in your city are elderly as well. The children are so young, you may never see them mature.

We can be your ally. Help us understand what needs to be done. Though we lack the knowledge of your children, we're not without abilities. We've already brought astonishing change to one land fixed in its ways. Our minds are open, and we're willing to risk our lives if need be.

You claim to be a reasonable people, yet you keep us as prisoners when we've done you no harm. We are not your enemy. Let us speak with you. We may not be as learned as you, but we come from a different world. Let us understand more fully your dilemma. Perhaps with fresh eyes, we can find a better way.

You call us primitives, but who is the more primitive? We who risked so much to become more than we are, or you, who out of fear have locked us away?

Please, sir, do not leave us to languish in our gilded prison. We can help. Give us the chance.

Yours hopefully,
Orah Weber

Chapter 13

A Tapping on the Door

After penning my letter to the mentor, I slept well, hopeful he'd respond, but when no response came, my mood darkened. The next night, I tossed in bed for hours until exhaustion let me nod off.

Then I was visited by a vision, a memory long buried in my mind.

***

A week before my father died, he came to me as I slept and woke me with a finger to my lips, a warning to stay quiet. Then he beckoned for me to follow.

Once we were far enough from our cottage, beyond earshot of any villager, he bent low and whispered in my ear. "I have a secret, Orah, something even your mother doesn't know. Take me to the special place where you and your friends play, and I'll show you."

I loved him so much, I had no hesitation. I took his hand and led him down the path through the darkness to our newly built shelter, the NOT tree.

At the clearing in the woods, he sat on the flat rock and lit three candles, his face gaunt and drawn in their flickering light.

Even as a seven-year-old, I could tell he was ill.

He took out a velvet pouch and from inside withdrew a gold piece, round like a coin but three times the size and thicker, with the head of a king engraved upon its front. He held the piece before my widening eyes.

"What is it?" I said.

"A device to make music. After years of trying, I've learned how to make it work, but it's a remnant of the darkness, so I've never shown it to anyone before. Now I'm more afraid its secret will die with me."

Only much later did I learn he'd been subjected to the Temple's teaching. Like Thomas, he must have been terrified of being discovered by the vicars and dragged back to the cramped cell. But at that moment, the urge to show this remnant from the darkness to his daughter was stronger than his fear.

"Behold, Orah, something more wonderful than temple magic."

Though his hand shook, he flipped open the case and inside lay a fantastic mechanism. He sat on the flat stone before the NOT tree and worked by candlelight, removing prongs and a wheel, and a drum and tines. He let me touch each, and then lovingly set them back into place. A remnant of the darkness? The darkness be damned.

"Can you play it for me," I said.

He waited, staring out, not saying a word.

I watched the face of my dying father as he tried to decide.

"Very well," he said. "Just this once. A secret for only you and me."

He placed his fingertip on the tiny lever, closed his eyes, and pressed. The candlelight reflected off his moist cheeks as the device began to make a sound like angels flying.

After he died, I searched our cottage but never found the gold box in the velvet pouch. Perhaps my mother, for fear of the vicars, had buried the blasphemy with him. As time passed, the pain of his death drove the memory deeper into my mind, until this night when it returned to me in a dream.

But then, the dream kept on. After the music stopped, the box broke apart, the parts grew in size and became houses, and the houses became temples, and the temples became a fortress carved into a mountain, all gold and gleaming with detailed etchings and turrets. The front gate opened, and inside stood my father, alive again and beckoning.

"What awaits me," I said.

"You must enter to find out." His voice trailed off into an echo of a whisper. A gust of wind kicked up, and my father turned into a wisp of smoke and blew away.

I ran after, not wanting to let him go.

Inside, at the center of a vast chamber, sat the mentor in his wheeled chair. He glared at me from beneath the brim of his hat and said, "Once you've entered, you may never leave."

The gate slammed shut behind me, locking me in.

***

When I awoke, my forehead was clammy with sweat.

My eyelids fluttered and closed as old memories swirled through my mind.

In the wee hours of the morning on the day of my father's funeral, I'd snuck off while the village slept. Only seven years old, I'd hoped to view the casket lying open in the commons.

The large chamber, with its gabled roof, exposed beams, and pew-like seats, stood empty awaiting the mourners. In the naked rafters above me, the shadows had lengthened and seemed to dance and jiggle like ghouls. At the far end, the casket awaited, surrounded by flowers. Their scent failed to hide a stale odor that repelled me.

I thought of all the villagers who had died before him, those men and women welcomed to the light. The thought gave me no solace.

I crept closer to the casket and touched my fingertips to the copper pennies the elders had placed over his eyes. After a moment's hesitation, I removed them, wanting him to see me one last time.

Beneath the pennies, his eyes were glassy and vacant.

I stared into them, hoping to see the father I loved, as I'd stare into the ice on the pond in winter, trying to pierce the blackness to the water below. "No," I cried at last, and flung the pennies away. This was not my father. My father was gone... but to where?

The morning of the funeral, I awoke to the dawn leaking beneath the window shade, and the reality of his death surged into my thoughts. Tears flowed, soaking my pillowcase.

My mother heard me sobbing and rushed into my room.

"Will you die too," I asked.

"All of us must pass to the Light in our time." She wrapped her arms around me and drew me to her breast. "It's in the nature of things."

***

I may have buried that memory, but now I could picture the gold box spinning in the air before me. I could almost hear its magical sound.

81

I woke Nathaniel and told him my dream.

He listened patiently and said he'd dreamed as well, but refused to share his with me.

When morning finally came, I arose and stomped about our chamber, each footstep landing on the padded floor with a thud. We'd survived the deacons and the arch vicar's threats, found the keep and rallied our people, crossed the sea and survived the storm. Yet now we sat, well fed and helpless, like pets in a gilded cage.

With so much time on my hands, I composed a fantasy in my mind: Thomas would rally the people of the Ponds, build a second boat, and come to our rescue. I never wrote down a single word. What a waste of paper to pen a work of fiction no one would ever read.

As I circled the walls, I heard a tapping on the door. *What now?*

Never before had Kara knocked. Why should she? Like the deacon guards before her, she possessed the key. Always she'd entered unannounced, bringing us our meals with four armed boys in tow, but this was far from mealtime.

I again imagined Thomas to the rescue. *What a fool I am.*

Nathaniel strode to the door and pressed his palms against its surface, as if to prevent the caller from entering. "What do you want?"

"It's Kara, bearing a message. I didn't want to surprise you."

Nathaniel glanced at me and stepped away from the door.

"Come in," I said.

The door creaked open, an inch at a time, and Kara peeked through, her face pale and drawn. She thrust a sealed envelope toward me with both hands. "The mentor asked me to give you this. He said to keep its contents to yourself. Knock when you're ready. I'll be waiting outside."

Once she closed the door, I broke the seal and unfolded the paper. Unlike the handwritten note from the earth mother, this one was printed in the block lettering I used to call Temple magic before I discovered printing in the keep.

With Nathaniel looking over my shoulder, I read the message aloud.

***

We are a reasonable people, but we've become fearful for our future. Perhaps you are right, that your courage may be of more value than our knowledge. I am alone with what's left of the dreamers, and I grow old. Perhaps you can help, especially if, as you claim, you are willing to risk your lives.

Tell Kara nothing. I have instructed her to bring you to me. Come to my chamber, and I'll reveal to you what I've been afraid to tell the children — the truth about the dreamers.

Chapter 14

Truth at Last

After the mentor dismissed a disappointed Kara from his chamber, he wheeled his chair around and regarded us for what seemed like an eternity. At last, the blood drained from his face, and he slouched in his wheeled chair as if the years of supporting the weight of his people had finally worn him down. "Ask me, and I'll answer as simply as I can. I'll explain what has brought us to this day."

Nathaniel and I glanced at each other. So many questions. A blink of my eye, a tilt of his head — he yielded to me.

Where should I begin? At the beginning, of course. "A thousand years ago, a cataclysm occurred, what our vicars call the darkness. Both you and the earth mother mentioned it as well. Perhaps you know more about what happened than we do, but on these points we agree: our ancestors overreached, a horrible war ensued, and many died. The few who survived tried to recover in different ways. The Temple of Light dragged us back to a simpler time, banning all technology save what they kept for themselves to control the people. The keepmasters dedicated their lives to preserve their knowledge for the future, hoping a more responsible generation would emerge someday and use it for good. And your forbearers fled to this side of the ocean."

I paused, waiting for the mentor to respond.

He chewed on his lower lip before answering, as if considering his words. "Yes, you're right, as far as it goes. This ground you stand on had been the epicenter of the destruction. My ancestors fled here to be free from the persecution of the Temple of Light, committed not only to preserving their knowledge but advancing it. They vowed to leave your misguided vicars behind and shun your part of the world until more open minds prevailed. We've waited a long time for an expedition to arrive, though I have to admit, I expected a delegation more substantial than the two of you."

I sighed. Were we forever fated to underwhelm? I pictured the recording of the keepmasters welcoming us to the keep, greeting us as revolutionaries that had overthrown the Temple, though we'd done no such thing. Yet in the end, we managed to change our world.

Now, the mentor expected a more substantial delegation. Might we still change his world as well?

He continued. "When they arrived on these shores, they found an uninhabited wasteland and struggled for decades, but just as the land recovered, so did my people. We rebuilt what we once had and vowed to move beyond it. Over time, we asserted our mastery over nature to provide for all of our needs.

"Perhaps we succeeded too well. As we mastered our machines, we also became dependent on them, no longer needing to work to survive. Many became too self-absorbed to raise families, and our population diminished. As our technology advanced, the science behind it grew more complex, requiring years of hard work to master. Fewer and fewer tried. For most, the machines became like gods, providing for all their needs but taken on faith, their inner workings akin to magic. Despite the brilliance of our age, we stagnated, all except for the elite.

"We became a society of classes—those who lived off the fruits of the machines and those who studied the science behind them. The few of us willing to continue the research became revered as high priests, and each new feature was hailed as a revelation. But the worship of everyday people wasn't enough. Our thirst for knowledge remained unbounded. So we took on a new challenge, what would become the breakthrough of our age."

The mentor stared out as if trying to envision both past and future at once.

I recognized that look, one I'd seen so often in Nathaniel—the gaze of one discontented with the world as it was and yearning to discover what might be. "The dreamers?" I said.

A laugh rose up from the mentor's throat, almost a chortle. "Those who the children call dreamers were as mortal as you or I, albeit brilliant, curious, and some might say arrogant. Though the machines they'd invented provided for all their needs, they wanted more—to make their machines not just servants, but partners in their quest for knowledge. They enhanced them to be faster and more capable, but to complete them they had to make them smarter. Yet despite years of research, endowing them with true intelligence remained beyond their grasp. The machines lacked that all-too-human knack for stumbling on serendipity through trial and error, for being able to see the world anew. So the researchers changed their approach. They turned inward to study the untapped potential of their own minds."

The mentor paused to take a sip of sweet water from a cup in a holder on the arm of his chair.

"I don't understand," I said.

His eyes bore into mine. "Have you ever awoken from a dream to find you remembered something long forgotten from your childhood? Have you ever been struck by a flash of insight that solved a problem you'd been grappling with for days?"

I nodded, thinking of the previous night's dream of my father, or the moment in the keep when I first heard my recorded voice and knew at once how to overthrow the vicars. At the time, I considered such inspirations a gift of the light.

The mentor rolled his chair closer. "Where do such insights come from? From a place with more power than we know. The brightest among us discovered their minds—what in your world you might call their souls—were nothing but impulses, billions of bits of lightning flashing in their brains. That led to the breakthrough I spoke of. They learned to channel these impulses, to share them beyond their physical bodies with the brains of the machines so they could control them with the power of thought."

He must have read my disbelief, because a wry smile spread across his face. "Ah, you need proof, but you've already witnessed an example."

With no movement on his part, without the twitch of a muscle, his wheeled chair backed up, spun about and returned, as we'd seen before.

"I also control the food synthesizers, the desals, and the healing machines. I can turn the lights of the city on and off or grant you access past the stone guards with a thought. All these machines are conditioned to respond to my brain waves. I ask in my thoughts, and they comply."

"Then why," Nathaniel said, "do the machines fail."

The smile vanished from the mentor's lips. "Because I am failing, and I'm the only one left who can control them."

He went silent.

I cleared my throat as if afraid my voice had gone silent as well. When I spoke, my words sounded unnaturally loud. "What happened to the others? Where did they go?"

"After they'd mastered the machines, my curious young colleagues posed the next logical question. Was there a way to move past the limits of our minds? Throughout history, people have tried to preserve their thoughts beyond their physical being, first on the walls of caves, later in paintings, sculpture, and books. We too sought a way to store our thoughts, the impulses that define who we are, outside of these frail bodies.

"We built a prototype storage device, and one among us volunteered to be the first. We preserved his body with artificial life support, and then transferred his consciousness to the device, but only for an instant before we transferred him back.

"When his eyes opened, they shone with an ethereal glow. For that one instant, he'd surpassed the limits of the flesh and accessed the full capacity of his brain. Others followed, carefully at first, and later for longer trials. Of course, we had some failures as all pioneers do—like those brave souls who gave their lives in the early days of space exploration—but we pressed on. After much research and hard work, the technology matured and our doubts vanished. Each time someone went under what we began to call the dream, they awoke with a greater grasp of themselves and the universe.

"Then came the final step: connected machines, communal consciousness—the minds of more than one, severed from the constraints of our physical selves and joined with the others. With the help of such advanced insight, the pace of the project accelerated. We built a chamber inside the mountain, a protected place where we could maintain our bodies while our minds melded with the infinite.

"As time went on, the dream came to dominate our waking lives. The more we dreamed, the more we wanted to dream. In ancient times, the time you call the darkness, people took chemicals to alter their consciousness for brief periods, but these chemicals became addictive, often preventing them from living their lives. The dream state became addictive as well.

"We sensed the danger. Even in its infancy, the technology had been intoxicating. For those brief moments, we became more than mere dreamers. We imagined ourselves as gods. Throughout history, power has always corrupted, so we instituted a strict set of controls. Yes, the dream was good for our people. Out of the collective mind came wonderful innovations, but we limited the event to a single day each year.

"None wanted to be left out, so we built more machines, enough to meet the needs of all those strong enough to withstand the rigors of the dream. We established a festival to celebrate the wonders of the human mind — the day of ascension. But this festival became an abomination to the greenies, who believed we'd gone too far."

"Why?" I said. "What you created benefited them as well."

"You've missed the point. By storing our thoughts in the machines, we'd opened the possibility of maintaining our consciousness forever."

I let out a gasp. "The dreamers became immortal?"

The mentor smiled, seemingly pleased he impressed me. "Immortal? That depends on your point of view. Had we become immortal men or lifeless machines? Technos and greenies disagreed on the answer. We saw the dream as ascension, aspiring to be more than we are. They viewed it as transgression, why they call what happened the day of reckoning, our punishment for trying to become gods." He shrugged. "It hardly matters, because all are gone now but me, and the machines built to depend on their masters' minds are dying too."

A weariness overcame him, and he sighed deeply. "As the oldest, I'd been left out of the dream, with a small crew to monitor the event. When the mountain erupted blocking the waterfall, we worked night and day to free up the flow. Eventually, even the greenies felt sorry for us and came to our aid. Backup generators maintained limited power while the rescue went on, keeping those inside the protected fortress alive. Eventually, full power was restored, but my friends had dwelled in the dream longer than ever before. Our emergency measures had preserved their bodies, but when I tried to restore their consciousness, nothing happened. I was unable to awaken them."

The mentor took a wheezing breath and paused as if waiting to see if we could surmise on our own.

"Did they die?" I said at last.

"There's the rub," he said. "I don't know. All I can be certain of is that they remain in their mountain fortress, still lost in the dream."

He spun his chair around and rolled silently toward the entrance of his inner sanctum. "Come, let me show you."

Chapter 15

Images on the Wall

I shuffled to the back wall, grimacing at the thought of confronting the angry helper again, but this time, after scanning the length of my body and nearly blinding me, he approved. The door slid open, and Nathaniel and I were allowed to enter the chamber where the mentor worked his wonders.

And what wonders they were.

No sooner did we pass through the doorway than my eyes were flooded with light. Every wall was a screen, but unlike in the keep, no helpers awaited. Instead, myriad images flickered across too fast to follow — glimpses of diagrams and faces and formulas flashing by faster than I could fathom. My nostrils tingled from a sharp odor, like the smell of air freshly cleansed by lightning in a storm.

"Are these the dreamers," I said.

"Yes... and no. These are the thoughts of the dreamers stored in the machines."

"Is this how you speak to them?" I waited breathlessly for his answer, but no answer came.

He turned away and stared at the images on one wall, then another, anywhere but at me. The hum of the fans that blew air through the commons grew unbearably loud.

An empty feeling filled the pit of my stomach. "The earth mother was right. You lied to us, and you lie to the children as well. You can't speak with the dreamers any more than we could speak to the helpers in the keep. These aren't the dreamers. They're nothing but recordings."

The mentor's back stiffened. "No, not recordings. What appears on these walls are living thoughts, the impulses flashing through the dreamers' minds at this instant, images not so different from what *our* thoughts would look like if we could project them on this wall. For nearly three years, I've watched with fascination and horror as their drama unfolded, a community of geniuses trapped outside their bodies, desperately planning, designing, conceiving, but unable to alter the physical world.

"How was I to explain that to the children? I lied to them to keep up their hope for the future, to encourage them to work hard. Perhaps one day, one of them will succeed where I've failed, and find a way to actually speak to the dreamers."

Nathaniel had been silent, staring at the four walls. Now he inched forward and brushed the tips of his fingers to the images. Here, a diagram like the ones he'd drawn of our boat in the keep but far more complex. There, a girl twirling in the sunlight, but tinged with the color of sadness, all glimpsed for an instant and then gone.

"These children," he said at last. "They're so young, many younger than any we've seen. What we're watching are their parents' memories, showing them as they once were, but with no eyes to see the present, these images are frozen in time. Now I understand what Annabel meant—to be alive but not live. "

My mind raced in a different direction. Before me were the finest minds of the machine masters, enhanced beyond imagining. What might they not accomplish? If we were to find a way out of our dilemma, they were the ones to know how.

"Is there no hope?" I said. "No way to talk with them, if not to bring them back to life?"

The mentor's chair whirred and moved up beside Nathaniel. He scanned the wall as if searching for an answer.

"From here, I cannot speak with them. I can only monitor their thoughts. Occasionally, as an image flashes by, I make sense of what they're trying to say. There—" He pointed to an image that flashed briefly in a corner. "That's an enhancement to a new machine we'd been working on, and here—" He pointed to where Nathaniel had been staring. "Do you recognize that child?"

I gaped at the image. The girl seemed familiar, but I had trouble placing her. Then I recalled what Nathaniel had said—children frozen in time. I squinted, redrawing the face to add three more years, and gasped when the realization struck.

The mentor caught my flash of insight. "That's right. My dearest Kara." His voice became choked with tears. "You're watching the thoughts of her father... my son. What I'd give to speak to him now."

Nathaniel came up behind me and rested his hands on my shoulders as we viewed the moving images with fresh eyes. I recalled Kara the night I sang Timmy to sleep, how she'd longed to tell her parents goodbye.

After a while, Nathaniel gave voice to my thoughts. "If their minds are alive, there must be a way to speak with them."

The mentor shook his head. "I tried everything I dare. Unless I can restore their consciousness to their bodies, I know of only one way. One of the living must join them in the dream. I would gladly volunteer, but the dream challenges not only the mind but the body. As one enters the dream-like state, the expanded mind needs more blood flowing through it. The breathing quickens and the heart beats faster. The body does not easily let go of the mind. My frail flesh would never survive the rigors of the dream. And what would become of the children if I die?"

"What of the children?" I said. "You insist they study to make their minds stronger. Are none of them ready?"

"A few, perhaps, but I'm loath to test them. How can I know what it's like to be trapped in a machine for all these years? What if I thrust a child into the dream among a group of mad minds, and I'm unable to wake him again."

The mentor's chin slumped to his chest, and he stared at the floor.

I came closer and knelt before him to regain his attention. "But for a chance to meet the dreamers? Think of the miracles that might await us all."

His shoulders heaved in a sigh and his deep blue eyes rose to meet mine. "You don't understand. In the early days, we had failures, those who returned to the living, but as a shadow of themselves, no longer able to speak or relate to the physical world. These few poor souls stared out through vacant eyes, giving no inkling whether a mind lay behind or not. After several agonizing weeks, we made the painful decision to send them to the disintegration chamber and end their misery, a decision that haunts me to this day. But these were adults, heroic volunteers aware of the risk they took." He waved at the wall. "Which of the children should I send into the mountain and risk condemning to such a fate? What right do I have to ask? Kara pleads with me to let her go. She's the best of them, the oldest and the brightest. She begs me as once she begged her parents, but how can I send my only granddaughter into the mountain alone? What if I were to lose her as well, my last link to my family?"

His chair whirred and he retreated to the corner of the room. "I have no good choice. I'm no mentor but a desperate old fool whose past faces extinction in a mere thirty days."

Thirty days. The phrase set my heart racing. "What happens in thirty days?"

The chair crept closer, its lack of energy perhaps reflecting its master's turmoil.

He stopped an arm's length away. "Thirty days from now, we commemorate the third anniversary of what the greenies call the day of reckoning. Some among them plan a reckoning of their own that will end all hope for the dreamers."

I recalled Caleb's outcry in the Hall of Winds, and the earth mother's harsh response. "The earth mother would never allow such a thing."

The mentor cast me the look of a weary teacher about to explain an obvious truth to a slow student. "Did you know my good friend, Annabel, was once a brilliant scientist? She turned against us when we began to delve into the dream, believing we'd gone too far. She knows perfectly well the damage wanton violence would cause, but she harbors among her followers those who would do the dreamers harm."

"How do you know this," Nathaniel said.

"I have ways of listening, but the leader of these zealots is devious. He conceals the details of his plot from my listening devices and speaks only in code, but I know this man, and his bitterness knows no bounds. He speaks of a reckoning, but I know what he means. Each day my sensors pick up the battering of hammers on stone, growing closer by the hour, yet I'm powerless to stop them. What good are my children scholars against these hardened laborers? What good are these machines I control, when I'm confined to this accursed chair?

"These zealots believe the dreamers wander, lost in shadows, and it's their duty to set them free. For them, the upcoming anniversary offers the ideal time to act, to end what they perceive to be an unholy state. Their misguided attempt to grant the dreamers peace would be like the vicars destroying your keep, only worse. We'd lose everything, not just all the knowledge of the dreamers but their lives as well."

I sensed a stirring behind me, a tremor in Nathaniel's hands. No need to ask why. We'd been friends since before we knew how to speak. Like the dreamers, we shared our thoughts, but without machines.

We were so different, Nathaniel and I. He was rash; I was cautious. Where he'd rush in, I'd deliberate for days before taking the first step. Yet somehow we always arrived at the same place. I'd never have left Little Pond without him; he'd never have discovered the keep without me. I'd never have sailed away from the shore; he'd never have found his way across the sea.

Now we stood at another crossroads, and I knew what choice he'd make. As he stepped toward the mentor, I grasped his elbow and tried to drag him back from the precipice.

He turned and took me in his arms, fixing me with his eyes. "We risked the arch vicar imprisoning us for life. We dared to face the stoning. Why? For the chance to be more than we are. Now the fruits of that dream lie within our grasp. How can we risk anything less?"

I wanted to damn the dream, just as I'd wanted to run from the vicars. Even after the slow drag of years, I remembered how that morning's fear had made my mouth dry. Yet I'd marched into Little Pond as the sun rose and the arch vicar urged our neighbors to cast their stones. At Nathaniel's side, I'd found the strength to go on.

Now before us loomed our greatest challenge, our most dangerous step into the unknown. How could we turn back when we'd already come so far?

A vision filled my mind—the first day of spring in Little Pond with the locust trees in bloom, sending their blossoms down like tiny sailboats to float on the water. If I was too fearful to take this step, I might never see home again.

My eyes welled, but I blinked back the tears and nodded.

Nathaniel turned to the mentor. "Teach us, and we'll go."

The mentor winced as if in pain. "Didn't you hear what I told you? You might lose your lives or worse. You might become lost forever in the dream."

"We heard you," Nathaniel said, "but we left our family, our friends and everything we hold dear to cross the sea. Why? To go beyond recordings on screens. To seek out the keepmasters' kin and bring back their knowledge to our people." He waved at the moving images on the wall. "And here they wait, so near."

The mentor squeezed his eyes shut, concentrating until beads of sweat formed on his brow. The images on the walls flickered and winked out like the lights of the city. With only their faint afterglow, the room turned dim.

He opened his eyes. "When you wrote how you'd risked your lives for a cause, I selfishly hoped you'd do the same for us, but now that you stand before me, how can I accept? How can I dishonor myself and the dreamers, to abandon the values they believed in? Take back your offer before I give in to its temptation. Take back your offer and live."

Nathaniel glanced at me, pleading for my approval.

Slowly, I began to nod, but then I thought of the silent boy, Zachariah, with the voice of an angel, and of the others with their flimsy baskets, scrabbling to find food in the brush.

"We're willing to risk our lives," I said. "But what if we fail? If the fanatics destroy the dreamers as you fear, all of you will need the skills we can teach. Give us the chance to do as the keepmasters did, to pass on our knowledge to the greenies—ways to live without the machines."

The mentor crumpled his brow, and his blue eyes shifted from side to side. "To go to my enemies while they plot to destroy all I hold dear—?"

Nathaniel stiffened his jaw in that way he had when he'd made a decision. "No access to the greenies, no dreamers. You can send us back to our gilded prison while you wait for the end."

The mentor went silent, staring at his hands lying still on his knees, as if tracing the thick veins winding down to his fingers.

I pictured a billion bolts of lightning flashing behind those eyes.

"Very well," he said at last. "Help the greenies if you must, but for four days of the thirty, no more. "The rest of the time, you'll study with me until your minds blur. Then, before the end of the thirty days, only after your final visit to the greenies, I'll grant you access to the mountain. At that time, if you're still willing to go, we'll find out how great your courage may be."

Chapter 16

Mind Games

Nathaniel and I spent long days cloistered with the mentor. He had us memorize maps of the mountain fortress so we could find our way even in the dark. Using holos, he taught us to manipulate the dials and switches that controlled the link between our consciousness and the machines — with special attention to the red numbers that counted down the time, and the two emergency buttons that terminated the dream. Most of all, he made us practice a series of mind games.

"When I was younger," he said, "I delved into the dream for mere seconds. We call it the dream, but it's different from when we sleep. With night dreams, our thoughts flow freely, untethered by our conscious minds. Pictures flash before our eyes, images from the physical world, fragments of memories from years gone by or perhaps from that very day. This dream is different.

"Imagine you remained awake without your senses. Imagine you're blind and deaf, with no taste, no touch or smell. Moreover, imagine you forgot the reason for eyes and ears. Imagine you are pure mind."

While the mentor droned on, we lay on mats on the floor with eyes closed, trying to do as he asked, but the exercise seemed useless. I kept imagining Nathaniel lying beside me, recalling the touch of his hand on my cheek. Sometimes, his breathing settled into a regular rhythm, and I'd open one eye a slit to find he'd fallen asleep.

The mentor would roll his wheeled chair close and prod Nathaniel awake with the point of his toe.

Late one night after too many hours of mind games, Nathaniel sat up and glared at him. "Why do we need to practice so much?"

Lines formed between the mentor's brows, where his smile met a growing impatience. "Going into the dream is like nothing you've experienced before, with no up or down, no here or there, no sense of time. Like a swimmer underwater, you may get disoriented and panic. Practice, practice... until your response comes as natural as breathing."

We practiced for ever longer periods. In between, the mentor told stories of the dreamers—of their families, habits, and quirks—so we might identify them by their memories alone.

"Why can't you just show us pictures?" Nathaniel said. "Wouldn't that be easier?"

"Faces don't exist in the realm of the mind. The dreamers have no faces, and you'll have no eyes."

I struggled with the concept of a pure mind but accepted the challenge. If we could communicate with the dreamers, they might solve all our problems, from finding a way home to finding a way forward that would avoid the mistakes of the past. Despite my doubts, I studied hard, doggedly preparing for the dream, though it seemed less real than our quest for the keep.

By the end of the fifth day, I'd had enough. "You promised us time with the greenies. We've kept our word, working hard with little sleep. Only twenty-five days remain. Time to keep your part of the bargain."

The mentor shook his head. "My promise assumed you'd progress faster, but you still have far to go. Every minute wasted increases the risk of failure."

Nathaniel rose off the mat to his full height. "There'll be no chance of failure if we refuse to enter the mountain."

The mentor stared at the dancing holos and grimaced. "Very well, but not until you complete one more exercise. See if you can stay awake for two full hours. Only then will I let you go."

"Two hours?" I said. "It's almost midnight."

"I promised you four days with the greenies. I never promised you time to sleep."

My shoulders slumped and behind me, Nathaniel groaned.

***

I awoke too soon from a restless sleep marred by nightmares of teaching cells and vicars questioning my faith. Despite my exhaustion, I forced myself to rise, intent on leaving as much time as possible to spend with the greenies.

At the start of the trek, my mind filled with worries. What if the zealots breached the mountain fortress and destroyed the machines? We'd lose the dreamers forever. Unless we could prove they still lived; then ending the dream would be akin to murder. The earth mother would never allow it, not when they had so much to offer those on both sides of the ocean.

What if we entered the dream and found silence, or worse? What if the dreamers had sunk into such despair they'd welcome an end to their ethereal existence, exactly as Caleb claimed?

What if on a visit to the greenies, we stumbled upon the fanatics' plans? Should we betray them, even as we helped them? And if the mentor learned their plans, how would he stop them with nothing but his army of children scholars?

We stood at a crossroads. What if both paths led to a tragic end?

My concerns abated as we hiked down the mountain. After so many days locked away, I drank in the scent of the sea and the perfume of the pines. I reveled in the morning dew, still clinging to the bushes at the edge of the trail, and thrilled at the streaks of sunlight causing rainbows to dance on their leaves. For the moment, like the earth mother, I cared nothing for what made the wind blow, only how good it felt on my cheeks.

At the village, the greenies greeted us with less enthusiasm than before. The children, who had once approached us with warmth, now scattered to the safety of their huts. The silent boy shuffled nearer but not too close, made a sign with his hands like the braids of the earth mother, and dashed off to fetch her. The older ones took off running like heralds spreading bad news, leaving Nathaniel and I to wait alone.

A flash of orange streaked out from behind one of the huts. Bella, the tabby cat, came up and eyed us, weighing whether these strangers who had disturbed her rest deserved her attention. She stretched and let out a satisfied purr—apparently we'd passed her test. She strutted toward Nathaniel and wound her way between his legs, rubbing her fur as she went.

"She likes you," I said.

Nathaniel glanced around the deserted village. "Then she's the only one here who does."

Moments later, the silent boy returned with Devorah in tow. Her hands and knees were caked with dirt, and smudges stained her cheeks.

She offered a half smile. "The earth mother will be here in a minute. She moves more slowly than those of us who are younger."

I returned the smile. "It looks like we interrupted your gardening."

She tried to brush away the dirt, but wherever she touched, the grime only spread. After a few seconds, she gave up. "Where were you? Everyone was eager for you to return and teach us, but you stayed away so long."

Before I could reply, Caleb burst through the tree line with several of his men, all carrying tools.

"Don't expect her to tell you the truth," he said, "After so long in the technos' clutches, these strangers can no longer be trusted. The mentor has filled their minds with blasphemous lies and sent them back with a purpose." He jabbed a finger at us. "Leave here at once and go back to your friends."

Devorah blocked his way. "Calm down, Caleb. The earth mother will decide whether to welcome them or not."

She gestured to the far end of the village, where the earth mother hobbled along leaning on her walking stick. The crowd surrounding us parted to let her through, and the children, feeling safer now, emerged from their huts. She stopped between us and Caleb.

Once she caught her breath, she turned to me. "Forgive Caleb for his lack of manners, but his question is a reasonable one. Why *have* you come back after being away so long?"

"To keep our promise," I said, "to teach you how to better live off the land."

"Then you'd be welcome, my seekers of truth, but after ten days among the technos, what truth are you seeking? Do you follow the way of the earth or have you given in to the lure of the machines?"

"A bit of both," I said. "As you once told us, there's no absolute truth."

The earth mother closed her eyes, took a cleansing breath, and opened them again. A smile crackled across her crusty face. "Fair enough."

"But earth mother," Caleb said. "You mustn't let these—"

"It's in my hands now, Caleb."

She dismissed him with a wave, and ordered the others to return to their chores as well. Once we were alone, we gathered under the protection of the old beech tree, sitting cross-legged in a circle around a small fire, which smoldered just enough to take the bite out of the morning chill. She asked Devorah to fetch us a drink, and then remained silent until we had settled in with decorated mugs filled with sweet water.

"This drink is becoming more precious," she said. "One more shortage due to the failure of the machines. The streams that flow from the mountains have become polluted and so, increasingly, we must boil our water. The children complain about the taste, but at least they don't get sick. Now on the occasion of your return, I'm happy to share this scarce resource. I teach my people hospitality, even though Caleb's apparently forgotten the lesson. Please forgive him. He bears wounds too painful to speak of, but he means well, and since coming here, he's done much for my people. Now, let us drink to friendship and trust."

Never taking her eyes off us, she raised her cup.

Nathaniel and I responded in kind.

"Now," she said, "you've come back for one of three reasons: to spy on us for the technos, to corrupt us with their ideas, or to help. I have no secrets worth spying on, and I believe in the power of our ideas, so whatever your motivation, I'll accept your aid. I ask only one thing—an oath in writing that you'll refrain from preaching the worship of machines. I beg you, don't confuse my people. Their lives are hard enough. There's no need to stir the pot any further. Devorah, fetch me paper and pen."

Devorah vanished into a nearby hut and emerged with a quill pen, a writing board, and a crumpled piece of paper like the message Zachariah had brought to invite us to their village.

The earth mother smoothed the paper's wrinkles on the board, and scribbled awkwardly with wide looping letters, like a small child newly schooled.

She paused partway through to rest her hand. "You must think me clumsy. I only learned to write after the machines began to fail."

When she finished, she handed the paper to me. I read it aloud. "We, the undersigned, swear to use our time to teach better ways to live off the land, and to refrain from activities harmful to the people of the earth."

She passed the pen to us, and we both signed.

After she folded the paper and returned it to Devorah, she relaxed. "A silly ritual left over from a more civilized time, when we had laws to enforce such a contract. A mere formality, now that I've gazed into your eyes and seen your good intentions." She gave a shrug and laughed.

"Besides, I have no choice. I need your help and can only pray you don't betray my trust. Now what shall you teach us first."

"We're here only for the day, and so our time is limited. Select a few of your people to go with Nathaniel. He'll show them how to find wild wheat, cull the seeds and plant them. I'll teach your people how to make better baskets. They already know the basics, but I'll use stronger materials and bind them with a tighter weave."

The earth mother reached out to Devorah, who helped her stand. "Fetch Matthew, Aaron and Rebecca to go with Nathaniel. He claims he can teach us how to grow our own bread. You take Jacob and Ruth to learn to make better baskets. I'll come with you to start you on your way."

After Devorah had gathered the people named, she slipped away to one of the flower gardens to pick a handful of daisies

"What are those for?" I said.

She offered a smile tinged with sorrow. "Wait, and you'll see."

I glanced at Nathaniel. He and I had hardly been apart these past months. As the two groups went their separate ways, I brushed his arm with my fingertips, a message of encouragement, and whispered a prayer for his safe return.

Chapter 17

Honeysuckle and Reeds

Beyond the outer rim of huts, we entered a well-trodden path lined with dwellings as far as I could see. The earth mother, it seemed, presided over much more than the village. The greenies were a sprawling community larger than I'd imagined, populated by able-bodied adults accustomed to hard work.

No wonder the mentor feared them.

After a ten-minute walk, the number of huts thinned and we came to a large, heart-shaped clearing. Along its edges, the trees held mounds placed on platforms at eye level, each decorated with flowers and seashells.

Devorah turned off the path, approached one of the mounds, and laid the daisies she'd brought on top, fanning them out in a half-circle. Then she bent a knee, dipped her head, and closed her eyes.

"What's she doing," I whispered to the earth mother.

"This is where we bring our dead, a tradition I started when I first came here. I wanted to make our goodbyes in a peaceful setting surrounded by trees. We wrap the body in robes, and the whole village gathers to carry the remains to this spot. Here, we place them on a litter bound to branches, so we can pay our respect each day on the path to our chores. We hold a brief ceremony, and anyone who wishes may speak kindly of the deceased. When they're done, we line up one by one and leave a single flower. In this way, we remember those who once lived and gave us life, much like the earth. That mound is the resting place of Devorah's father."

"Is this where the technos bring their dead as well?" I said.

She shook her head. "For the technos, death is something to be hidden. Machines disintegrate the remains, leaving nothing but energy—a clean and sanitary process. The dead, they believe, should not startle the living with a reminder of their mortality. The so-called machine masters prefer to pretend they'll live forever, but we're not meant to be immortal. We're a part of the cycle of life, the same as the other animals and plants."

When Devorah rejoined the group, we resumed our trek but at a more somber pace, shuffling our feet through the dried leaves covering the path. The swish of our footsteps sounded like the muffled voices of those who had departed.

Once the tree-lined graveyard lay behind us, the earth mother turned to me. "In your world, how do you send off your dead?"

"Not so different from you. We dig a hole in a special place on a hillside surrounded by trees, lower the body down and cover it with dirt. We mark the spot with a stone with their name carved on it."

"Is this satisfying to you, planting your loved ones in the earth?"

I pictured the day the elders placed my father in the ground. The sky had been overcast with a drizzle in the air. I could still smell the moist soil and hear the thud as each shovelful landed on his coffin.

"My father died when I was seven." I paused, surprised by how much emotion still welled up in me from the mere mention of him. My voice quivered, and I needed a breath to continue. "I loved to visit his grave and pretend I could speak to him. How I wish I could visit him now, and like Devorah, decorate his resting place with flowers."

The earth mother laid a comforting hand on my shoulder.

At first, I pulled away, but then gave in to the warmth of her touch as if I were a child again.

"Each of us bears our own tragedies," she said. "No shame in grieving. It's part of the great circle, like the passing of the seasons. The dreamers denied the circle of life, believing death was something to conquer, not accept. If death could touch them, they'd never become gods. That's why they invented the dream."

We continued on in silence until the greenie cemetery receded deep into the woods. Soon, the trees thinned once more and workshops began to appear, make-shift shelters where food, clothing and crafts could be prepared even in foul weather.

The largest of these echoed with the sound of hammers and any other tool that set metal to wood. In every corner, Caleb's men wielded axes and splitting mauls to hew fresh timber for the newest huts.

Near the end of the row, two substantial structures stood opposite each other, the only ones made from stone. Both contained a furnace built into their back wall. Smoke from their fires rose up through chimneys and scattered in the wind, as flames pulsed from their openings, sending waves of heat in my direction.

I recognized the one on the left, a shop where cups and bowls were kiln-fired and glazed. Greenies sat on benches molding clay on rotating platforms, not so different from the potter's wheel back home.

The earth mother drew me into the opposite structure. As she stared proudly at the forge, a red glow from its flame fell across her face. "Here, you can see how much we've grown. At first, we made tools from chiseled stone, but now we've learned to craft metals. We tried the red copper, found everywhere in the surrounding terrain, but we found it too soft. By combining it with other elements like tin, we've been able to strengthen it. Through trial and error, we've learned to heat it in the fire, and then pound and fold it into shape on this platform. Do your people practice such skills?"

I suppressed a laugh. The spinner's store in Great Pond, where I so often traded cloth for thread, stood next to the blacksmith's shop. I'd often go watch him work while I waited for my spools to be packed. He had a furnace as well, and a platform where metal was forged, but the similarity ended there. The blacksmith's anvil was made of hardened metal and finely crafted to do its job. On his wall hung a variety of hammers and tongs to shape the most precise tools. By contrast, this shop seemed more like the play room of a child who'd newly discovered fire.

"Yes," I said. "We call such people blacksmiths."

Despite my efforts, the earth mother read my scorn. "Much better than ours, I gather. Perhaps another skill you can teach us."

As I emerged from the shelter, glad to be away from the heat, the earth mother pointed to the last structure in the row. "I placed the basket shop on the outskirts of our community to be nearer forests and fields where materials abound."

The basket shop was little more than an open shed with three walls built from interlocking logs supporting a thatched roof. Inside stood sheaves of straw and a wooden workbench littered with scraps of grass. An assortment of tools hung on pegs at the back.

A single gleaming knife caught my eye. I ran the tip of my thumb along the blade's edge—as sharp as any forged in Great Pond. Perhaps I'd underestimated the skill of their blacksmith. "Did your people make this?"

"A leftover synthesized from the machines," Devorah said. "That blade never rusts and hardly ever dulls. Since we have so few, we limit its use to special purposes. We'll get no more like this, until our own tool making improves."

I glanced around the shed. "I'll need some bowls filled with water."

"We can fetch bowls from the potter, but I'm afraid the water is foul."

"No matter. The water's not to drink but to the soak the reeds in so they'll be easier to bend. Do you still make quilts like the one on our bed in the techno city?"

"Oh, yes, finer than any made by machine. One of the few crafts we preserved from our ancestors."

"Then you must have sewing needles."

She reached into a drawer beneath the workbench and withdrew a packet of wooden needles.

"Wonderful. You have all the tools I need to weave the baskets. Now to search the woods for the materials."

"I'm too old to be scavenging in the fields," the earth mother said. "Best I leave you in Devorah's capable hands." She turned to the others, embraced each and whispered in their ear, "Listen well and learn." Then she grasped her walking stick and ambled off.

I led the three greenies into the forest. On our first trek to the village, the scent of honeysuckle had told me the bush flourished nearby. We had scant trouble finding a large patch.

I urged each of my students to inhale the perfume of the flower. "Now, place the tip of the blossom to your lips and sip out its nectar."

The three stared at me and hesitated. Devorah was first to try.

"It's delicious," she said.

Jacob, a man who looked old enough to be Devorah's father, reached for a berry. "What of the fruit? The berry's smooth and blue like the earth mother teaches."

I stayed his hand. "The nectar of the flower is safe. The berries are not."

In no more than a few minutes, we'd used the knife to slice off several lengths of vine and strip them of their flowers. Then we coiled them for easy carrying.

"Is there standing water nearby," I said. "Not ocean, but a pond or swamp?"

Devorah nodded. "This way."

We followed down the trough of a rain run-off and came to a marshy area, bounded, as I'd hoped, by reeds. I snipped off several of the thicker stalks and headed back to the shed.

"We're as babes compared to you," Devorah said. "You know so much about plants and trees. What else can you teach us?"

"One lesson at a time. Today's is the making of baskets, but maybe we'll stumble on something along our way."

I strolled down the path, scanning either side and inhaling deeply. How good to be outside. For a land grown dependent on machines, the vegetation grew lush and green—perhaps mother earth showing her defiance. The mentor's mind games seemed foolish to me now—to lose all sight or smell... what a dismal skill to learn.

At last, a familiar fragrance wafted my way. Ahead, an ancient sassafras loomed, one of the largest I'd ever seen. I thought of the greenies having to boil their water, and the children complaining about the taste.

"We call this a sassafras. You can spot it by its scent, but also by its furrowed trunk and leaves that look like mittens."

"What are mittens?"

"Like socks for your hands to keep them warm in winter." I picked one to show them.

Devorah brightened. "I see—a wide part for the fingers and a smaller one for the thumb. Can we eat its flowers or fruit?"

"Not the flowers or fruit, but.... Hand me the knife." I knelt down on the ground, dug down a bit, and cut off a piece of the white root. "Place this in boiling water to make a fine red tea. Your children will prefer its flavor to the sweet drink from the machines. You can extract its oil as well to give a pleasing aroma to your soap."

Devorah grasped the root, sniffed, and smiled. "It smells like spring."

After the humiliating lesson with the techno children and the mentor's berating us as dullards, I was delighted to be the wise one for a change.

When we returned to the basket shop, I asked Jacob to fill some bowls with water and set the vines and reeds to soaking. Once they were pliable, I cut the reeds into four flat pieces of equal length and aligned them crisscross on the workbench, holding them in place with a needle stuck in the center.

While the others leaned in and watched, I wove a honeysuckle vine through the eight spokes, over and under, as I'd done so often as a child. When I'd completed three rows, I let Jacob take over.

"Over and under," I said, "and be sure to pull the vine tight. The water makes the reeds and vines as easy to bend as straw, yet they'll be much stronger when they dry. The rest is the same. Keep weaving until the basket rounds up to the top. Then I'll show you how to finish it off."

I stepped aside with Devorah and watched Jacob work. He was the most nimble of the three, born to the craft.

"He looks like he's done this his whole life," I said.

"The earth mother picked him for a reason. He's the best craftsman in our village, especially working with wood. He can take a piece of furniture manufactured by the machines and reproduce it by hand within days."

I pictured a spinning wheel and loom—a challenge for Jacob but not beyond his abilities.

As Devorah studied this newfound craft, I studied her. She had a strong chin, high cheekbones and eyes intensely focused on the task. Though I never saw her laugh, she smiled often, a widening of her lips to show small white teeth, followed by a slow and effortless closing. Clearly someone the earth mother trusted, a future leader perhaps, though only a few years older than me.

I recalled her kneeling by her father's grave. "I was saddened to hear about your father. How long ago did he die?"

"He's gone four months now, but I think of him every day."

"May he go to the light everlasting." I repeated the phrase by rote, the custom taught to me by the vicars, though I immediately regretted it. I knew little of the greenie's beliefs.

Devorah's lips parted, and she drew in a breath before speaking. "His death has clouded my faith. The earth mother calls it the shadow inside me, like a visit by a gloomy spirit. You said your father died when you were seven. How long did it take for the pain to go away?"

"I don't know. It hasn't gone away yet, but over time I've learned to live with it, to not let it control my life. Grief is an affliction we all share." I recalled Kara speaking about her parents lost in the dream. "As far as I've traveled, people are all the same. Despite what the earth mother says, even the technos grieve."

"The earth mother bears no ill will to them and teaches respect for all. Only a few among us see the technos as enemies."

I placed a hand on her arm. "I hope you don't view us as enemies. We're neither greenies nor technos, but two travelers trying to understand your ways."

Ruth, who had taken over for Jacob, cursed as she realized she'd missed a spoke of the basket.

Devorah eyed Ruth as she undid the weave, then grasped me by the elbow and drew me outside. She lowered her voice. "Caleb claims the mentor burns with hate for us. That's why he suspects you. For the mentor to let you go.... What price did you have to pay?"

"There's something he wants us to do. We agreed only if he let us spend time with you."

"So there *was* a price. What did he ask of you?"

I stared out at the horizon. Daylight was dwindling. Soon it would be time to return to the techno city.

I shook my head. "I'm sorry. I can't tell you, but believe me we're not your enemy. We'll come back again, I promise, sooner the next time, and teach you how to build a spinning wheel and loom."

"What are those for?"

Glad for the change in subject, I pointed to the distant hillside. "That field is covered with flowers we call flax. The spinning wheel will turn the fiber from their stems into thread, and the loom will weave the thread into cloth. You already know how to sew. Once you have cloth, you'll be able to make new clothes. I'll even teach you which plants to pick to add color to the cloth, something brighter than gray or techno silver."

"New clothing sounds wonderful, but aren't those machines?"

"Only ones powered by hands and feet. Is that a problem?"

"Not for me, not for the earth mother. Maybe for Caleb. He says machines have done great harm, and accepting even the simplest will lead to disaster."

Like the vicars, who banned honey from our wassail and limited music to two flutes and a drum, all innocent practices they claimed would lead back to the darkness. Why were there always those who'd rather restrict than enable?

"Why does Caleb hate the technos so much?" I said.

Devorah glanced over her shoulder at Ruth weaving our little basket, as if she hadn't heard my question. After a moment she turned back.

107

"Many of us have been part of this community all our lives. My parents were born here. Others came as children after they'd failed the exam." She lowered her voice. "Ruth is one of the cast-offs. Caleb is... different. He, like the earth mother, was one of their scientists. He came to us about ten years ago, around the time I first heard of the dream. His wife had just died. While he never speaks of what happened, he arrived a broken and angry man. The earth mother helped him heal and gave him new purpose, but the rage remains. I know little more than that. Following the day of reckoning, he was the strongest voice against offering help, insisting what had happened was pre-ordained — nature's revenge for the dream."

"But isn't that what the earth mother preaches as well, that the dream is a sin?"

"The earth mother teaches our bodies are part earth, part water, part past and future, and part the stuff of stars. We are a part of the universe and not its masters. She doesn't condemn the technos for their beliefs. She merely chooses a different path."

"Then do you oppose Caleb when he says the dream must end?"

I counted three breaths in and out as we both stared at the surrounding terrain. The afternoon sun had sunk below the treetops, so curtains of light streamed through the leaves. Beyond the trees, the hilltop pulsed with flowers blooming and birds riding above them on the currents of wind.

Devorah grasped me by both arms and faced me. "I believe each of us was placed on this earth for a purpose. If we can find that purpose, we'll have respect for each other and for all living things, because we'll be grateful every day for the gift of life. Those who we call the dreamers had a purpose of their own. Is their plight a punishment for their sacrilege? It's not for me to judge."

No absolute truth. Neither technos nor greenies own the truth. Both have much to offer. At that moment, I was sure of only one thing: I was grateful for my life.

When the basket was finished, and our band returned to the village, I was relieved to find Nathaniel laughing with the others, as he discussed the timing of the harvest and the making of a mill wheel to grind wheat into flour. On the ground beside him lay a straw basket filled with seeds and a tiny plot where he'd demonstrated how to plant them. I pictured this village in the fall, surrounded by tall brown stalks waving in the breeze, and the greenies harvesting them in newly crafted baskets. I could almost smell the aroma of freshly baked bread.

At last, the time had come—the end of the day. We embraced our new friends and made our goodbyes, with a promise to return soon. Then, Nathaniel and I began the long trek up the mountain.

A short way out of the village, the tree branches along the trail quivered and quaked. Caleb and several of his men burst through and blocked our way.

"What do you want?" Nathaniel said.

Caleb glared at him. The cords of his neck bulged, so thick his shoulders seemed to merge directly with his head. "Going back to report to your master?"

I stepped between the two. "We have no master but our own minds."

"Then use those minds to see our differences." He tightened his grip on his axe, and spoke with a voice accustomed to giving commands. "The people of the earth treat each other with respect. Every one of us is valued. Technos use people as tools, objects to be studied and experimented upon. That's the difference. You'll find no way to straddle that line."

I softened my tone to hardly more than a whisper. "Do you treat us with respect, when you keep us here by force?"

Caleb backed away and laid his axe on the ground as we'd seen Devorah do. Then he raised his arms and showed his hands, palms outward. His powerful fingers were crusted with callouses.

"The good earth gave us these hands to provide for ourselves, not to become slaves to machines. You're welcome here if you heed the earth mother's wisdom. Think about it long and hard before you return. Think and choose."

With that, Caleb motioned for his men to step aside, and we continued on our way.

Chapter 18

Butterflies and Spinning Wheels

The mentor never asked about our visit to the greenies, but drove us harder than ever. He needed no words to show this urgency. The dreamers were his legacy, and he was determined to save them.

At the greenie village we'd witnessed the extremes—kindness and serenity, vengeance and hatred.

The mentor believed hatred would prevail. If not for us, the dreamers were doomed.

"I've delayed long enough," he said. "Time you learn about cocoons."

He squeezed his eyes shut and crumpled his brow. Shortly, a life-sized holo floated before us, a cramped container in the shape of a coffin.

I gaped at the image as it spun in the air before me. "A cocoon, like the birth pod of a butterfly?"

"Its technical name is Personal Life Support Pod, but for all their brilliance, the dreamers had no lack of whimsy. This container sustains the body while the mind evolves. They believed when they emerged they'd be reborn to a higher form, but unlike the silky pods for which they're named, I fear these cocoons will never sprout life again. Too much time has passed. The butterfly has flown beyond the physical world."

I inched closer to the holo and reached out to touch it. My hand passed right through. "So small."

"Nothing bigger is needed. You'll be conscious in them for only a matter of seconds."

My heart quickened. "*We'll* be conscious. Why will *we* need to be in them at all?"

"Because every one of your brain impulses will be downloaded into the storage device with the dreamers. We can capture these impulses but have no way to distinguish between higher level thoughts and the more primitive functions of the mind—those that allow your lungs to breathe and your heart to beat. The cocoon will perform these functions for you, keeping your body alive while your consciousness dwells in the dream."

Nathaniel turned from the holo to the mentor. "If their bodies are preserved, why haven't you been able to awaken them?"

The mentor's bony shoulders heaved as his lungs drew in air and released it. "I wish I knew, but here's what I surmise. Our thoughts change when separated from the body. A newly freed animal refuses to be caged again. So too the liberated consciousness resists returning to the physical world. The longer it stays away, the greater the resistance. I suspect my colleagues now find their bodies too confining. You'll have no such problem, however. Your stay in the dream will be brief."

I shuddered, recalling my hours locked in the teaching cell. Thomas's teaching had left him terrified of closed spaces. Would I be the same? Would I panic when the cover closed, and scream to be let out? "How will we know when it's time to leave the dream?"

"That's why we have two of you. One will go into the cocoon and enter the dream. The other will monitor the controls. It's good you care so much for each other, because the one's life will rest in the other's hands."

I recalled the mentor's words: We *will see how great your courage may be*. Had he chosen us for our courage or our willingness to throw our lives away?

I turned to Nathaniel.

His jaw twitched and tightened, and the familiar vein in his temple throbbed.

Before he could speak, I pressed two fingers to his lips.

"Hush!," I said. "A decision for another day."

111

I'd spent much of my childhood at the loom, weaving spun thread into cloth. If I became lost in the dream, my sole legacy might be this craft my parents taught me. But how could I cram so much knowledge into the three remaining days?

I'd often traveled to Great Pond with bolts of cloth strapped to my back to barter for thread. Following the four-hour trek, the spinner would offer me tea with lunch and teach me the workings of his wheel. I knew its every detail, and my mother's loom, as well. In my few waking hours away from the mentor, I used the paper Kara had supplied to sketch diagrams of these simple machines from every aspect and angle.

When the mentor granted our second day with the greenies, I rolled up the finished diagrams and brought them with me, tucked away into my waterproof pouch.

In the center of the village, we found the earth mother perched on a stool, surrounded by the younger children squatting on the ground and hanging on her every word.

"And so," she said, "the prince and princess boarded a boat with white wings and flew across the sea." She raised her arms over her head and flapped her hands like a bird.

As the wide-eyed children followed her gesture, one of the little boys spotted us. "Oh, look! Here they come."

The excited children scrambled to their feet and gathered around us, clutching at our clothing and grasping my left hand.

"What are they doing?" I said to the earth mother.

She laughed. "I told them about your magic ring. They want to kiss it."

"I don't have a ring."

"Of course you do. It's just invisible. Now you don't want to disappoint them, do you? Children, the princess will let you kiss her ring, but only if you form an orderly line."

The children obeyed at once, arranging themselves in a line by height, smallest first. Then each in turn bowed or curtsied before me and kissed the third finger of my left hand, while I giggled embarrassed.

"Such a beautiful ring," they said.

After I'd shared my enchantment with the last of the children, the earth mother sent them off to play. I struggled to ease the flush from my face and adopt a tone more appropriate to the task at hand.

"We're new to your customs," I said, "and understand little about them. What was this game of yours about?"

"I told them you were a prince and princess who sailed in from afar on a quest to make our lives better. They asked how you managed to cross the sea, so I made up a magic ring that protected you from sea serpents and guided you through storms to our land."

I thought of the compass and sextant, still tucked in my pouch, and the study and hard work that had guided us here — the true magic. "But... that's not true."

Her lips spread into a patient smile as if she'd heard this question before. "Which truth would you prefer I tell them? That you crashed your boat and washed ashore? That we must boil our water, eat fish and berries, and dress in rags, because the dreamers overreached and are lost forever? Isn't it better to spin a tale of a prince and princess who brought magic to improve our lot?"

She waited for an answer, but I had none to give. She stared until I blinked and looked away, and then she continued. "You told me where you're from the people still tell tales."

Nathaniel nodded. "The vicars frowned on such stories, especially ancient ones from the darkness, but our parents told them anyway. My father used to tell me of knights with swords riding on the backs of horses, and wizards with magic staffs — all things banned by the Temple of Light. The vicars preferred to keep magic to themselves."

She nodded, more with her eyes than her head. "Why, despite the ban, did your parents keep telling you these stories?"

I shrugged. "They made us feel good."

"Yes, and much more. Stories let us slip into the heads of strangers and view the world through different eyes. Those who ban stories fear we'll see the world anew, wake up from our sleep and change the established order."

"As *we* did," Nathaniel said.

"So in your own way, you *are* a prince and princess, who have created your own kind of magic." Specks of light danced in the earth mother's eyes. She was a throwback, neither vicar nor elder, but a wise woman from an ancient time.

I imagined her living in Nathaniel's fantasy past, when wizards and knights roamed the earth, on a quest for something greater than the saving of souls or the pursuit of knowledge.

She shattered the mood with a laugh and clapped her hands. "Very well, your majesties, now tell me what magic you bring us this day."

***

Nathaniel marched off with his would-be farmers, while I spent the morning reviewing my drawings with Jacob. He studied each detail, tracing its lines with the tip of his finger and asking pointed questions.

I waited, watching his mind churn.

As the sun reached its highest point, he nodded, slowly at first, and then faster.

"Can you build these?" I said.

He rolled the drawings up and tucked them under his arm. "With the blessing of the earth mother, I'll do my best."

After I'd shared the noontime meal with the others, I led Ruth and Devorah to the surrounding hillside.

Zachariah, the silent boy, rushed out as we were leaving, and signed frantically to Devorah.

She checked with me. "He wants to come with us."

"Of course," I said.

We waded through fields of waist-high flax as I pointed out the flowers — yellows and oranges, blues and greens.

"How long have they been flowering?" I said.

Devorah consulted with Ruth. "Three, maybe four weeks."

"Nearly perfect." I knelt down and fingered the stalks. "Look here. Pick those turning yellow but with some green in them still. This one's ripe. Watch how I pick it." I plucked the plant from the ground, root and all, by pulling straight up. "Now go gather as much as you can carry."

The others scattered.

Zachariah raced through the stalks, checking the color. He returned with a fistful of flax.

An hour later, the group reassembled at the edge of the field as I laid out the next steps. "Tie these into bundles and leave them standing upright in the sun until they dry. Then you can strip off the seeds with a rippling comb — I'll help you make one when we're back in the village. Once the seeds are gone, you'll need to separate the fiber from the inner core. The fiber sticks to the stalk like bark to a tree. You can release it by soaking

114

them in a shallow pool. A few days in water, and it comes free easily. Manage all that while I'm gone, and we'll have plenty to spin into thread when I return. Then, on the following visit we'll perform the real magic — thread into cloth. Pick all you can, but don't wait too long. The longer you wait after flowering, the coarser the fiber. Do you understand?"

The two women nodded, accepting my instructions.

Zachariah gaped at me, eyes wide, as if he believed turning flax into cloth would really be magic.

I grasped him by the hand. "Come, Zachariah, there's one more use for flax. I'll teach you how to make a winner's wreath."

After choosing flowers in a variety of colors, we brought our harvest back to the village. I made a simple rippling comb out of a block of wood and nails, and in the few minutes remaining, showed Zachariah how to weave a wreath and decorate it with flowers.

***

At the end of the day, we gathered with the earth mother and the other greenie leaders, including Caleb.

Nathaniel left instructions for the farmers, and I stressed the need to harvest enough fiber before my next visit. Neither of us mentioned we had only two trips remaining, after which we might never return.

The elders listened as if I were a vicar. No, not a vicar, because no fear showed in their eyes. More like a wizard from a magical time. I prayed not to disappoint them.

Before we adjourned, Caleb rose from his seat and strode to the front. "So wise, so all knowing, but answer me this. Why don't you stay with us? Why do you keep returning to the technos?"

Nathaniel stood and confronted him, the two tallest in the village. "Please trust us. We made promises to both sides, commitments we take to heart. We mean neither of you harm."

Caleb faced the others and waved his hand in the direction of the techno city. "Trust is something to be earned. Only those with bad intentions hide behind secrets and lies."

"What are you afraid of?" the earth mother said. "Do you think they'll turn our children into dreamers? Look at how much they've taught us already — ways to grow our own food and better clothe our families. Let them continue their teachings. We owe it to the people we lead."

115

Caleb turned, towering over her where she sat. "I wish I could share your kindness. You may have forgotten what our former friends are capable of, but I've lived among them more recently than you. Your affection for these two has blinded you to the risk. Don't expect me to be a part of it."

His message sent, he stomped away and never looked back.

The earth mother watched him until his hulking form vanished into the trees, then shook her head and sighed. "So many hours we've talked, as I've tried to teach him the way of the earth, the path to find peace. He possesses such passion and skill, but his passion is fired by a pain he's never shared. For these past years, that pain has simmered beneath the surface. I fear your arrival has brought it to the fore."

When all had been said, the others lined up to embrace us and wish us well, with the earth mother last of all.

As she grasped me in her arms, she whispered in my ear. "Like Caleb, you too are filled with passion. Use that passion wisely to find the end you seek."

As we prepared to leave, Zachariah dashed out from his hut smiling broadly and preening for his friends. On his head, he wore a newly made, flowered wreath, reminding me so much of a young Thomas after winning his first race at festival.

"Why do you make these wreaths," the earth mother asked. "They provide neither shade nor warmth."

"They're prizes," I said. "A way to show others we trained hard and excelled. Don't you have anything like festival, a time when people gather to play games and celebrate?"

"Of course we do." Her eyes sparkled, and she flashed a secret smile. "I'll show you when the time is right."

Chapter 19

Shift and Weave

The morning after our return from the greenies, Kara came to fetch us bright and early, but this time she seemed more downcast than usual. Her shoulders slumped, and she mumbled her response to my greeting.

"Are you not well this morning?" I said.

She ignored my question and sped away.

I caught up and grasped her by the elbow, forcing her to face me. "Have we done something wrong?"

She yanked her arm away. "What is it you plot behind closed doors in the mentor's chamber? He shares nothing with me."

I softened my expression and tempered my words. "I'm sorry, Kara, but he insisted we tell no one."

"Yet *I'm* the one he relies on. *I'm* the one he teaches special skills. You're our guests, but strangers nevertheless who know little of our ways. Our problems are *ours* to solve."

I understood at once. I too had been a headstrong child — headstrong and foolish. I remembered my anger when Nathaniel offered the keepers' scrolls to the vicar of Bradford. My thoughts from that day still echoed in my mind. *I know the task before us might end in our death, but it's my adventure, and no one will steal it from me.* I recalled my relief when the vicar refused the scrolls.

Kara turned to leave, but I stepped in front and blocked her way. "Trust that whatever we do will be for the good of your people and ours."

A tremor racked her slight frame, and she bit down hard on her lower lip to stop it. Once she steadied, she made an awkward bow. "As you wish. I follow the mentor's lead."

Then she whirled around and stomped off without glancing our way again.

***

Day after day, we played the mentor's games. During our grueling sessions, the muscles in my back cramped from long hours lying on the floor, trying to clear my mind while concentrating on my breathing. Then each night, in the few hours left for sleep, I'd lay awake, my head throbbing as those suppressed thoughts came raging back.

What would it be like to dwell with the dreamers? Would I find the geniuses I'd imagined, or a torrent of thoughts from minds driven mad from years in the void? Would we risk our lives with nothing to bring home to our people? Would the miracles we found justify the risk?

And which of us would venture into the dream while the other hoped and prayed?

At the end of each day, I asked the mentor when we'd visit the greenies next, and each time he berated us, telling us we were doomed unless we focused more and worked harder. But after nine days, even the mentor could no longer deny our request.

And so, our third visit with the greenies came at last.

As we crested the hill overlooking the village, Nathaniel paused and pointed. "Look at the change, more like the farms around Little Pond."

I cupped a hand over my eyes and gazed into the distance at furrows of freshly turned earth, marking where seeds had been sown by the hard-working greenies. So much progress in so few days.

One of the children weeding a vegetable garden spotted us and cried out. No restraint this time. Several of his friends raced off to spread the word, but most poured down the path to escort us.

When our procession reached the heart of the village, we were greeted by Devorah and a beaming Jacob.

"Come with us," Devorah said.

We followed them past the burial place in the trees to the first of the work shelters. Mounds of flax fiber nearly obscured the shed. Yes, we'd been gone longer than planned, thanks to the mentor's frantic rush to complete our training, yet I'd never expected the greenies to produce so much. The earth mother must have taken my words to heart and mustered an army.

Inside, another surprise: they'd cleaned out the shop's contents and replaced them with not one, but three spinning wheels and two looms.

I gave the nearest wheel a whirl and touched the wooden frame of a loom with my fingertips, feeling like I'd been transported back home to my cottage in Little Pond. Jacob hovered nearby awaiting my approval, but I had no words and embraced him instead.

We spent the morning spinning fiber. I worked the wheel first, and a team of apprentices followed. Soon, all three wheels were spinning, and spools thickened with thread.

The earth mother joined us for the midday meal, along with the other leaders.

Even Caleb came. He glared gloomily at our progress but held his peace, perhaps finally appreciating the benefits we brought to his people.

Everyone assembled outside the shed and sat cross-legged in a circle on the ground. After plates were heaped with berries and cups filled with sassafras-flavored tea, we joined hands, bowed our heads, and thanked the earth for its bounty.

After the meal, I took stock of the thread—enough to make a sample of cloth.

I gathered my would-be apprentices around the loom. "First, we wind the warp—the lengthwise threads that form the backbone of the cloth—to the rear beam. Here." I demonstrated. "Then we pass them through these holes and tie them as tightly as possible to the front. Today, we have thread to weave only a narrow strip, about a hand's width, but enough to let you learn on your own. The weft is the thread we'll weave from side to side using the picking stick and shuttle."

It took a bit over an hour to set up the loom, not bad considering their inexperience.

When everything was in place, I sat down, rested my feet on the pedals, and fingered the shuttle—like meeting an old friend after a long time apart. Suddenly my hands flew while my feet danced up and down, making space for the shuttle to slip through the warp—shift and weave, shift and weave.

Devorah threw up her hands and laughed. "You need to slow down if you expect us to learn."

The greenies were bright and eager. After a few missteps, each was able to take their turn. None were as adept as this lifetime Little Pond weaver, but they soon found the knack, and their first strip of cloth took shape.

"You'll get faster with experience. Then you can weave wider pieces, adding colors and patterns. For now, you've learned the basics."

The earth mother looked on proudly as her people weaved. Once the cloth had taken shape, she waved at the loom. "Like magic, clothing from the land."

I shook my head. "Magic is what our vicars claimed. None of this is magic, but the result of learning, of experimentation, of the pursuit of knowledge, and of hard work. The magic resides in the power of our minds, and in the strength of our desires. As you once told me, it's in our nature to strive."

"To strive, yes, but how far?" She gazed at the apprentice weavers, now fully absorbed in their work, and grasped me by the arm. "Come, walk with me."

She led me past the basket-making hut, now filled with sturdy baskets of various shapes and sizes. We strolled along until we reached a field of wildflowers at the edge of the forest, where she stopped, tilted her head back, and drew in a long breath.

"The heart away from nature becomes hard. A lack of respect for growing things soon leads to a lack of respect for people." She turned to me. "I used to be one of them, you know, one of their better scientists."

"So I've heard."

"I spent most of my childhood locked away in their lessons, learning to master the machines. Sometimes, I'd stay inside for a week at a time, never seeing the light of day. In the world of the machine master, once you've passed the exam, you sacrifice everything in the pursuit of knowledge. As I grew older, I started to question their ways."

She wandered over to a patch of daisies, picked one, and reveled in its scent.

"What made you come here?" I said.

"When my colleagues began to research the dream, I refused to participate. I couldn't accept the premise that we're nothing more than impulses and logic. Even if true, even if the soul is a myth, we still needed mystery, humility, and that mix of fear and fascination in knowing our lives must end."

She rolled up her sleeve and stretched out an arm to me. "Here, touch this."

I stared at her bewildered, but did as she asked.

"Old and wrinkled, but flesh nevertheless. Now touch your own arm."

I did.

"Someday your flesh will age like mine. You say you're a seeker of truth. Do you think this flesh will last forever? Do you think it's all there is?"

I nodded, then shook my head.

"All of us suspect there's something more to us, an essence. It's the way we're wired, but who knows? All I'm certain of is that today, I'm closer to being dead than being born. What am I to do with that knowledge? Would I prefer to live forever? I've never given it much thought, because I never believed it possible. The dreamers wouldn't accept such an answer. They deluded themselves, hiding from the mystery of life and denying this marvelous home we call Earth, yet I wished them no harm. I called many my friends."

She sighed deeply. "Now, you might say they've achieved their goal—their minds are one with eternity, unencumbered by frail bodies—while I spend my dwindling days watching the splendor in the sunsets and listening to the music of the children's laughter. Which of us has the better lot?"

I saw my chance to find out more about the dreamers, to learn what the mentor had concealed from us, but I had to choose my words carefully. "What can you tell me... about the state of your former friends, those who are lost in the dream?"

She turned sideways and eyed me across her nose. "Why do want to know?"

"I have dreams myself sometimes that seem so real. Some mornings, when my mind's in the shadowland between wake and sleep, I hesitate to open my eyes, afraid which world I'll find myself in? Is it that way for the dreamers?"

She wet her lips ever so slightly with her tongue, a hesitation while she decided how to respond. "The dreamer's dream is no more like your night dreams than the techno is like the greenie. Their dreams lost their sense of whimsy, of serendipity, of caring. I believe they've become pure logic."

"How do you know? Did *you* ever go into the dream?"

"No. I left before they started the first experiments. Even if I'd stayed, I would have been too old for its rigors. But I've heard about it. Yes, they solved the unsolvable problems of mathematics while in the dream, and found solutions to enhance the machines. Yet none ever claimed that the experience made the sunset more striking or the stars shine brighter, or that when they awoke, they loved their children more."

"Was it the mentor... William, who told you about the dream?"

"No, it was Caleb."

"Caleb?"

"Yes, he was one of the first to research the dream, but like me, he eventually rejected it." Her eyebrows drew together so a deep crease appeared between them, and she fixed me with her gaze. "Why are you so obsessed with the dream?"

Unable to bear her stare, I turned away and wandered deeper into the flowers, pretending to search for one to pick.

I recalled my first night with the technos and thought to use it as a diversion. "I once dreamed I was floating on the sea, but without a boat, just on my back. I could see a million stars and count each one, but then the stars turned to numbers, and my mind filled with all the knowledge anyone had ever known. I wondered what it would be like to have such power."

The earth mother pressed her fingertips against her temples and closed her eyes. When she opened them again, she regarded me with a lifetime of sadness. "I was afraid of this. You and Nathaniel are planning to go into the mountain, to join the dreamers in the dream."

I shook my head so hard my hair swished across my face.

She tried to smile, but a glistening in her eyes belied the gesture. "No need to mislead. I promise I won't betray your trust, but I know my friend, William, too well. He's too old to dream and too kind-hearted to send his children into danger. You and Nathaniel are strangers, not kin, and you've come brashly into our world. He means well but will use you as another of his experiments. If you fail, he's no worse off, and will continue to drive the children in the hope they'll one day re-create the past. You think he honors you, but you underestimate the risk. I beg you: don't go back to the city. Stay here with us. Be safe and welcome."

I glanced around where I stood, knee high in daisies. The sun had climbed to its zenith overhead, brightening a hillside emblazoned with flowers of every shape and color, a bounty no machine could ever create.

The earth mother handed me her daisy. "Stay, please."

"We'll come back for one more day," I said. "After that, who knows? If we never return, spin your fiber into thread and weave your thread into cloth as I've taught you. Plant and reap your wheat. And as you wear your bright, new clothing and eat your freshly baked bread, forget we ever existed."

The corners of her eyes sagged. She stretched out a hand to me, but it lingered in midair. After a moment of indecision, she closed the distance between us, grasped me by the arms, and squeezed. "No, we won't forget you. We'll remember you as the prince and princess from across the sea, and tell stories about you until the end of time."

Chapter 20

Wolves and Unicorns

We set out for our fourth visit to the greenies as soon as first light allowed, weighed down by the prospect that this might be our last time. Neither Nathaniel nor I said a word on the trek, with the only sound the muffled beat of our footsteps on the mossy ground.

Devorah met us in the heart of the village, forewarned of our arrival by the squeals of the children. An impish expression stole across her face as we approached, and she said, "Wait here."

She dashed into her hut, and moments later emerged wearing a dress made of newly woven cloth. She twirled before the crowd and preened, as her friends hooted and whistled. "Mock me if you will," she shouted back at them, "but today I feel like dancing."

After besieging us with their usual greeting, the children had mysteriously scattered. Now, they began to reappear, first in ones and twos and then in dozens, each sporting a flowered wreath on their head.

The earth mother ambled in, laughing. "Since you taught Zachariah to make these flowered hats, they've become all the fashion, but I insisted the children save them for this day. You told them they were used as prizes for your festival. This morning we'll work hard, learning what you promised us—how to color the cloth and weave patterns, how to care for the seedling wheat and harvest it when ready. Then, later this afternoon, the people of the earth will give thanks—our own kind of festival.

***

The rest of the morning passed as a blur, overshadowed by the uncertainty of our fate.

Nathaniel went off with his farmers to teach them how to reap what they'd sowed.

I led my weavers through the fields picking an assortment of plants for dye—bloodroot for red, lichen weed for gold, dandelion roots for brown, raspberries for pink, blueberries for blue, and snapdragons for green.

Zachariah followed me everywhere.

When we returned to the work hut with our gatherings, I showed them how to chop the berries, flowers, and roots into small bits and set them boiling in pots. While they simmered, we soaked the thread in briny water.

After an hour, we strained the dye, leaving six vats of distinct colors. I let Zachariah be the first to dip the threads.

He skipped from one end of the row to the other, eyeing the colored liquids, and finally settled on blue.

The older apprentices followed, each picking their own.

As the greenies stared in wonder, the bland threads transformed into a rainbow of colors.

Devorah raised a batch of thread with a stick and gazed as its drips made ripples in the pot. "I've always wanted a red dress."

I smiled at her. "Why settle for a single color?"

I spent the rest of the morning showing them how to set the loom for patterns. Devorah kept careful notes, and I pictured her one day dancing in the village in her newest dress, a mix of reds and golds and greens. I hoped I'd be there to see it.

In midafternoon, when the shadows had lengthened, the earth mother joined us to inspect the fruits of our labors.

She nodded in approval. "You've done so much for my people. Time for us to give back. The whole village is assembled and waiting." She waggled a finger. "Come with me."

A frantic Zachariah tugged at her sleeve and signed furiously.

She laughed and nodded. "Of course you may be the one to escort the princess."

The silent boy smiled up at me and reached for my hand.

We skirted the edge of the village, following an unfamiliar path. Soon, the trail narrowed, winding through an overgrown patch between downed

125

branches. Winter-dead trees crept close on either side, twisted by storms into almost human shapes. With the path so cramped, Zachariah released my hand and strode before me as if to protect me from the trees.

"We leave it natural," the earth mother said, "to maintain its sense of mystery. Unlike the Hall of Winds, we don't come here often, only to celebrate our most special occasions."

Ten minutes later the debris diminished, and we emerged into a natural tunnel formed by the branches, so different from the techno arch—not dark and somber but with sparkles of afternoon sun filtering between the leaves.

As I started through, my eyes confounded by the dappled light, I caught sight of a tall figure waiting ahead, his face seemingly surrounded by stars—Nathaniel, my prince. I grasped his arm, and the procession resumed—Zachariah, our page, leading the way, the prince and princess next, and Devorah and the earth mother as maids-in-waiting attending from behind.

At the tunnel's end, the trail opened into a broad clearing. At its rear, obscured by a flash of light, loomed some sort of gate. I squinted, but my mind refused to accept what my eyes presented.

The sun reflected off the window of a rusted hulk, the mangled remains of what appeared to be a fast wagon. More than one, in fact—a graveyard of wagons piled two high to form a circular fence. Stacks of three on either side formed the grand entrance, crowned by a seventh. Each of the seven faced frontward, its lights reflecting the sun like the eyes of a beast.

Devorah dashed ahead and disappeared through the gate.

I shivered, recalling that night in the forest—Nathaniel, Thomas, and I, surrounded by deacons on two-wheeled wagons, the beams from their lights assaulting us in the darkness.

Moments later, I relaxed as a calming music came wafting from inside, a tune unlike any I'd heard in the keep—flutes, perhaps, dozens of them harmonizing with each other in ways that only Thomas would have understood. I tapped my foot to the rhythm: one-two-three, one-two-three, like some sprightly dance.

Devorah reappeared at the entrance and waved us through.

Inside, we found the source of the music. Two of the older boys sat on a bench and worked pedals with their feet, pumping a bellows that blew air into shiny brass pipes. A third turned a crank, and out through the pipes came the melody.

Greenies lined the circular enclosure, all staring at the center where a large, round, knee-high platform arose. A canopy hung above it, decorated with winged angels on clouds, interspersed with mirrors so each angel reflected the others, creating the impression of a heavenly host.

Upon the platform, statues of animals stood frozen in mid-stride — real creatures and imagined, and combinations of the two. I recognized a few from the forests near Little Pond, or from the fantastic stories my father had told me when I was little. Each creature was different— a man-sized frog and a wild boar; a sea serpent with three seats upon its back; an armored horse with fierce eyes staring out from behind a metal helmet; two swans pulling a carriage; an eagle with the body of a lion; a golden wolf frozen in mid-roar; and next to it, a unicorn. Each was painted in bright colors without regard for reality, though the expressions on their faces made them seem more than real.

Devorah hopped on the platform and helped the earth mother up, then urged Nathaniel and I to join them and choose an animal. As a member of the royal party, Zachariah followed. Nathaniel picked the armored horse, and I the wolf, while the earth mother nestled into the swan's carriage. Zachariah raced between the animals, touching one, caressing another, before settling for the middle seat of the sea serpent.

When each of us had selected a mount, I turned to the earth mother. "What is it for?"

"For celebration, as I said."

"How can you exert so much effort on these toys, but not on the machines that sustain life?"

"Unlike the techno machines, these nourish the spirit. That's why we maintain them so perfectly, painted and polished to a fine gleam." She waved a hand to show off the brass surrounding each animal. "We call it a carousel, an ancient symbol for the circle of life. The carousel for us is the center, the end of the beginning, and the beginning of all there is. It's all we are or ever will be... as long as our center remains whole. The carousel is like riding in a prayer wheel twirling in the wind. Hold on now and you'll see."

She motioned to Jacob, who flicked a switch attached to the inside of the gate. At once, the platform came alive. Multi-colored lights in the canopy brightened, adding bursts of color to the mirrors.

Then, with a whir from deep inside, the carousel began to spin.

I held on to the mane of my mount and marveled at the sight. As we whirled around, lights and mirrors conspired to create the illusion of rainbow-colored bubbles floating in the air. I gazed up at the angels and thought of my childhood.

The mentor had taught us about the mysteries of the mind and how the dreamers believed the answer to all problems were hidden inside, deep in ancestral memory. In my years in the keep, I'd asked the helpers to play music to relieve the tedium of my studies. Though they'd chosen melodies from before I was born, tunes long since banned by the vicars, I could have sworn I'd heard some of them before.

Ancestral memory.

Now the rhythm of the song echoed in my mind as we rode our mounts in a circle—Nathaniel on his armored horse pretending to be a knight; the earth mother giggling delightedly; and I floating on air as if the burden of my worries had vanished.

How would we return home? What would happen to the dreamers? At this moment, I no longer cared.

The lights in the painted heaven glinted, and I was suddenly a child again. Could the source of this magic be nothing more than spinning on this wondrous machine? I stayed perfectly still, clutching the mane of my golden wolf and laughing from my belly over the music from the pipes, a carefree laugh—as if I'd never sought the keep or learned the truth about the darkness, as if the vicars had never locked me away in the prisons of Temple City, as if my life had been transformed into daydreams.

I was startled from my reverie by a cry from the earth mother. "No, Zachariah, you know the rules."

The silent boy, Zachariah, had slid off his sea serpent's seat and was staggering toward me, pointing excitedly at the unicorn.

He believes the story, and wants to be nearer the princess.

Suddenly, he lost his balance and stumbled, bounced off the flank of my wolf, and tumbled to the platform floor. I reached for him, but before our hands could touch, he flew off the carousel and landed on the ground with a thud.

We spun past—fantasies don't wait for reality. When we came round again, the boy lay crumpled on the ground, his arm bent at an odd angle and his face contorted in pain.

Shouts and screams rose as greenies rushed everywhere.

Jacob turned off the switch, and I waited an eternity for the carousel to slow enough to allow me to jump off.

When I reached the boy, he stared at me with eyes too big for his head. No sound escaped his lips—not a whimper, not a moan—but his clenched teeth spoke of his pain.

Others raced in bearing a litter made from tree branches. At the earth mother's direction, they fastened the boy to it as tears streamed down his cheeks.

"Where will you take him?" I said.

She pointed up the mountain. "To the mentor, where I'll beg him to use his science to heal him, if the mending machine still works. Caleb, I need your men and their strong backs. Will you carry him?"

Caleb eyed the boy and his face softened. "Of course, earth mother, though as always, the trip back will be painful for me."

She rested a hand on his arm. "I know, Caleb. Thank you."

As I emerged from the gate, Nathaniel came to my side, grasped my hand and squeezed. Above us, a canopy of clouds had replaced the angels in heaven. A lonely wind wailed and I became disoriented. Was this gloom caused by an encroaching storm or the advent of twilight?

Or had my joy on the carousel been nothing but a dream?

Chapter 21

The Mending Machine

The somber procession lumbered up the mountain, bearing the injured boy. Each of us took a turn at the litter.

When mine came, I clutched the tree branch handle and fought to set each footstep firmly on the scree for fear of jostling the child.

The earth mother accompanied us, leaning on her staff to one side while supported on the other by one of Caleb's stoutest men. Lines of strain marred her features, but she refused to slow the procession. Between breaths, she chanted words of comfort to the boy.

Halfway up, Zachariah went still. Had he fallen asleep to the magic of her crooning, or had he passed out from the pain?

Ahead, the city lights flared up suddenly. No surprise. The mentor had his ways, and with his enemies approaching, he'd use every trick in his bag.

By the time we reached the arch, Kara and the older boys aligned in a half-circle to block our way with repair machines protecting their flanks, pincers and protrusions pointed at us.

She glared at me. "Why have you brought *them* here?"

I stepped aside and motioned to the boy. "He was hurt in a fall and needs help."

She took one look, and her defiance melted away. "Oh my, Zachariah, what happened to you? I'll fetch the mentor at once." She spun around and dashed through the arch.

As we waited, the greenies eyed the two stone warriors who guarded the gate. Even Caleb's men seemed cowed by the statues, as if afraid the rays might flash from their eyes at any moment and burn them to ash. Fear borne of experience, or of the masterful illusions of the mentor?

Nathaniel and I had access. How I longed to lift the boy into my arms and rush him inside, but I hesitated for fear the watchers would deny him entry.

After too long a moment, the mentor appeared, rolling through the archway in his wheeled chair. He removed his broad-brimmed hat and wiped his brow. What I now knew to be sensors blinked and flashed furiously inside the rim.

He replaced the hat and regarded the earth mother. "Hello, Annabel, I see you need my help again. I was hoping you'd found some healing powers on your own. Our machines won't last much longer."

The earth mother bowed her head. "These apprentices of yours have taught us a great deal, but even in their world, cures were considered a form of magic. Does your science still possess magic enough to heal this boy?"

The mentor rolled to the litter. When he recognized the lifeless child, the corners of his mouth sagged, turning his sneer into a frown. "My dear Zachariah, John and Laura's child." The arrogance left his eyes, but only for a moment. Then he set his chin, and his features hardened. "I will help him, but first a trade. I must ask for something in return."

The blood rushed to my face, and I stormed toward him. "The boy's in pain. How can you barter at a time like this?"

He waved his hand to encompass the techno city and everyone within it. "And what of these children? Who will treat their wounds when I'm gone? How will they eat? What future will they have?"

The earth mother placed a hand on my arm and eased me aside. "What do you want from us?"

"Two things, as we approach the anniversary of what you call the day of reckoning. First, that my apprentices—" He tilted his head toward Nathaniel and me. "—recommit to fulfill their vow, and you do nothing to dissuade them." He regarded the earth mother with a look of anguish that mirrored her own. "I'm sorry, Annabel, but we both know time is running out. These two may be our last hope."

"And the second demand?" Her voice was thin with no hint of inflection.

"A treaty between us, an oath from your people that there'll be no reckoning, no foolhardy attempt to harm the dreamers, especially from my angry former colleague." He pointed a bony finger at Caleb, who scowled. "I have my ways to know the measures you've taken, how you try to bypass my defenses." Then back to the earth mother. "His men work at night in the darkness with picks and shovels, carving a new path through the rock face up the mountain. He's near to breaking though."

The earth mother turned to Caleb. "Is this true?"

Caleb lowered his eyes. "They haunt me, earth mother. How can I live with myself while their souls suffer, lost in a machine. It's my fondest wish to set the dreamers free."

"You mean to kill the dreamers," the mentor shouted.

"How can I kill what's already dead? I only want to—"

"Enough!" Despite her age and frail appearance, the earth mother's voice resounded. "While you debate, Zachariah suffers. Listen to me. You must renounce these plans at once. Swear it for me, if not for the boy."

Zachariah stirred in his litter and opened his eyes. Though he stayed silent, his face spoke a heartbreaking moan.

The earth mother cast a pleading glance at Caleb, who stared down at the boy.

"Aye," he said at last. "I swear."

She glanced up at the gleaming lights, aware they were illusions, closed her eyes and nodded.

The mentor scrunched his face and concentrated, sending silent commands to the watchers. "I've granted the boy temporary access to the city, and you too, Annabel. Nathaniel and Orah may carry him. Kara will help as well. I'll go ready the machine."

She rested a hand on his shoulder as he turned his chair to go, and whispered loud enough so I could hear. "Thank you, William. I knew you would help."

"Why is that, Annabel?"

"Because I had a vision about the two of us."

"Now what myth have you concocted?"

She gazed up the mountainside where the dreamers dwelled. "I dreamed the people of the earth and the machine masters will join together one day to hoist our coffins and carry us off to our final rest. Do you believe that's possible?"

"Yes," he said, his lips spreading into a grim smile. "I've sometimes had the same dream."

***

Kara and I grasped one side of the litter, and Nathaniel carried the other. We moved along as fast as we dared without upsetting the child—through the archway, under the dome of the commons, and into another of the protected chambers lining its back wall.

"The healing room," Kara said, without my having to ask.

Inside, a stark metal table stood at the head of a round tunnel, slightly longer than an adult body and made of a white, glassy material.

The mentor directed us to lift the boy onto the table.

Kara gently placed a mask over his eyes, smoothed his hair and whispered something in his ear. As she circled the machine, setting its controls, the soft foam floor muffled her footsteps, while a quiet whimpering issued from the boy.

Seconds later, a humming sounded, and the table began to inch forward. Once the tunnel encircled the boy's torso, the mentor squeezed his eyes shut. Sweat beaded on his forehead, this machine apparently needing greater concentration than the others.

A blinding light filled the tunnel, brighter than the beam from the stone guards or the rays from the repair machines. The air crackled, and the boy's body quaked.

"What's it doing?" I whispered to Kara.

"The healer works much like the food synthesizers. From the most basic of materials, it rearranges the elements of matter into the appropriate form. The food synthesizers create food. This machine generates new bone tissue to mend the break in Zachariah's arm, something that would naturally take months. Watch. His pain will soon subside, and his arm will heal in days."

Minutes later, the light dimmed and the tremor stopped.

Zachariah's body stiffened and relaxed as he emerged from the tunnel. The anguish in his face had eased, replaced by exhaustion.

I gaped like a small child beholding the sun icon for the first time. "A miracle," I said.

A small smile played around Kara's lips, betraying her pride at their science. "Not a miracle. The mending machine relies on the mind that guides it. It could heal more complex injuries before the day of ascension, when the most skilled of the dreamers would control it, but even then, it had limits. The dreamers are far from gods. They haven't conquered death."

She approached the boy and handed him a single tablet. "Here, Zachariah, swallow this medicine and sleep. When you awake, the pain will be gone."

I once believed the vicars' claim that medicine was Temple magic. In the keep, I'd discovered such wonders were the result of dedicated efforts by brilliant scientists. Now, with a thousand years more research, how far these people had come. I knew their efforts had sprung from science, but it seemed no less a miracle.

I glanced at Nathaniel and read his thoughts. This is why we'd crossed the ocean. This is why one of us must go into the dream, risk be damned—not to be true to our oath, but to bring back these miracles to our people.

Kara wiped the sweat from the mentor's brow, his face laced with strain.

What a thin thread this miracle hangs from. Only he can perform this miracle, only he and the dreamers.

"May we take him home now?" the earth mother said.

The mentor nodded, but Kara intervened.

"He's not yet fully healed. Please, grandfather, let him stay. In three days, he'll be able to walk down the mountain himself, but now the trip on the litter will cause him more pain. He can stay with his cousin, Timmy, and I'll care for them both."

The mentor and earth mother gaped at each other, and then each broke into a weary smile.

PART THREE

DREAMERS

"First in the heart is the dream, then the mind starts seeking a way."

- Langston Hughes

Chapter 22

Deepest Dread

"Deacons!"

I startled awake to the word.

Nathaniel must have cried out in his sleep, since no one else on this side of the ocean knew of the vicars' henchmen, but when I rolled over to wake him from his nightmare, I found him sleeping like a child.

Had I dreamed the cry in the night? I replayed the sound in my head—not Nathaniel's voice, but another just as familiar.

Thomas.

Years before, I'd sensed Thomas reaching out to me from his teaching cell. Until then, I believed the teaching was an honor for those selected, a coming-of-age ritual into the Temple of Light. Yet even though Thomas had been in far-off Temple City, I somehow knew he was trapped in a cold and dark place. I could feel his fear.

Had I now sensed him again?

He lived in Little Pond, more than five weeks' sail away. I'd always been protective of him growing up, shepherding him through school and covering up for his mischief when trouble loomed. Maybe seeing the silent boy in pain had triggered these memories of Thomas in danger. My subconscious at work, the mentor would say.

In this strange land, I'd discovered the mysteries of the mind—more powerful than the sun, more vast than the stars. Might my connection with Thomas have the power to span the ocean?

But what trouble could he be in? Once the three of us revealed the secrets of the keep, the vicars' power was diminished forever. In the harsh light of truth, their mystical aura had been stripped away, their magic exposed as science. My people were enlightened now....

Yet even at the time we left, the desire for change had weakened, and some longed for a return to the old ways. The upstart vicar who'd once ministered to the Ponds—the same one who'd dragged Thomas and me off to the teaching—had been elevated to bishop and enjoyed a zealous following. Might the situation have degraded so badly as to endanger my friend?

A rapping of knuckles on metal interrupted my musing.

I stumbled out of bed and opened the door to find Kara waiting, her fists balled at her sides, and the blood drained from her face.

"What's wrong?" I said.

"The mentor insisted I wake you."

"It's hardly morning."

"No matter. He said to come right away."

***

The mentor sat in his work area, slouched in his chair with face drawn and shadows cloaking his eyes.

"Enough of greenies," he said. "You have a lot to learn and not much time. Today, I'll teach you the final lesson—how to let go of your conscious self."

I glared at him through bleary eyes, "Our conscious self? Isn't that all we are?"

"Your vicars may preach such myths, but we were once no different than animals, passing our lives without purpose, a part that still remains. When we awake in the morning, before our minds reload with memories—where we slept, who we care about most, our aspirations for that day and for the rest of our lives—there's a moment when we cling to our subconscious selves. The feeling of blissful innocence is too calming, free from fears of the future or the annoyances of daily life. That's the state of mind you must attain before your thoughts can be downloaded into the machines.

"After we learned to transfer brain impulses from animals, one final barrier remained before we could do the same with humans. Animals are unaware of what's happening to them, but humans know.

Despite my colleagues' highly developed logic and fierce desire to evolve, their consciousnesses resisted abandoning their bodies. They called this phenomenon the survival instinct. To overcome this resistance, they trained to become like the beasts of the field, to release the controlling mind. You must practice this state until you can achieve it at will. Only then will you be able to enter the dream state. You'll find it more difficult than you imagine."

***

For three long days, we concentrated on this new mind game, breathing from deep within our bellies, focusing on each breath, and clearing our minds. The mentor drove us harder than ever before, as if obsessed by some greenie demon.

Now, the hour was past midnight, and we'd been practicing since dawn.

Nathaniel yawned, a lung-busting yawn lasting almost to a count of ten, and then pressed the heels of his hands to his eyes and rubbed. As his hands fell away, they revealed a face ravaged by fatigue.

I could tell since childhood when his patience was wearing thin; his attention would lapse and his eyes would lose focus.

Before he snapped, I interrupted the mentor. "We understand the need to practice, but with the earth mother's agreement, why do you drive us so hard? The machines won't fail tomorrow."

He waved a hand, and the holos spinning above us vanished in a blink. He rolled his chair close. "My sensors, the eyes and ears that keep me informed, tell me that Caleb has defied the earth mother and broken his vow. His zealots continue to batter the cliff with picks and shovels to make their new pathway up the mountain, one that will bypass the stone guards. They'll break through in a matter of days. After that, the sensitive machinery inside will be easy to destroy. What remains of the dreamers will come to a violent end."

The room hushed but for the muffled hum underlying the techno city. The thoughts of those who dreamed in the mountain flashed silently on the wall, their detached minds oblivious to their fate.

I focused on my breathing as if still trying to let go of my conscious self, to flee from reality. Breathe in. Breathe out.

"When?" I finally said. The lone word echoed across the room.

"To be safe, you should leave first thing tomorrow." His eyes clouded, and he slipped lower in his chair. "I'm so tired. The fate of the dreamers weighs on me with a bone weariness the young can never understand. I had no choice but to be a leader in my later years. I struggle every day to choose the greater good for my people, doing the best I can. What I've asked of you is wrong, but you're my last hope. I leave the decision to you. In the morning, renounce your vow and I'll set you free, or be ready to head up the mountain. There *is* no more time. Go now, and sleep if you can."

***

Two days before my father died, he lapsed into a stupor. The elders had examined him and advised my mother to keep him comfortable and pray.

As a seven-year-old, I struggled to understand what was happening. His chest still rose and fell with each breath. His eyes blinked in their normal rhythm, yet when I stroked his hand, he failed to grasp mine. When I whispered "I love you," he never answered.

I asked my mother if he was angry with me, if I'd done something wrong.

She wrapped her arms around me and pressed me to her breast. "Oh no, my child. He loves you more than ever, but he's begun his journey to the everlasting light."

Perhaps the vicar had made a mistake, and committed my father's body to the light too soon. I stared into those glassy eyes and wondered if he was still inside, watching me but unable to respond. I sat with him day and night, reading to him, telling him stories until he took his last breath.

In the dream, would I be like my father in the days before his death, a shell of a body with no mind?

How have we come to this?

To the earth mother, we were a means to return to their past; to the mentor, a key to their future; and swirling like phantoms between them, the mysterious dreamers. Both wise Annabel and powerful William knew more about the dream than they let on, yet neither would send their own people into the mountain.

They left the fate of their land to two strangers, a farmer and a weaver who'd sailed in on a storm.

***

I'd begged the mentor for a few minutes each day to visit the silent boy. As Kara had predicted, he healed at a miraculous pace. The machine

140

masters' science had saved Zachariah from pain and more—the possibility of a life-long, crippling injury. If Nathaniel and I chose to break our vow, few would condemn us. Even the mentor had offered a way out. But what of the next little boy who fell ill or the little girl who shattered her leg? Where would their miracle come from?

Years before, on that bleak Little Pond morning, we might have run from the stoning, but we'd have left the world a lesser place. Now, if we ran, how much more would be lost? For technos and greenies, the chance for a better life; for Nathaniel and I, the hope to return home with miracles. Might such miracles have saved Nathaniel's mother, who died in childbirth, a woman no older than me? Might they have kept my father alive to be with me today?

If we'd refused to flee from the stoning, how could we now flee from a chance at miracles?

No matter. Though we never spoke of it, both Nathaniel and I knew we'd made our choice. Only one part remained: which of us would surrender our soul to the machine?

I tried to convince Nathaniel that I be the one to venture into the cocoon, despite my deepest dread.

Stubborn as always, he refused to discuss it.

Let it wait until tomorrow when we go into the mountain. Once there, I'll yell and scream if I must, trick him if need be, anything to keep him safe.

Better to crawl into that coffin-like container than to watch the man I loved become lost forever in a dream.

***

Before dawn the next morning, we stood at the rear of the commons, at the foot of the stone watchers guarding the pathway up the mountain—Nathaniel and I, the mentor and Kara.

The mentor handed a pack to Nathaniel. "Food and water for the journey, and an electric torch to light your way. I've already granted you access. You can leave at any time." He reached out a knobby hand to Kara. "They may need your help to find their way. Will you guide them?"

Kara's mouth opened as if she intended to protest, but, obedient as always, she held her words.

I rested a hand on her shoulder, recalling the time she'd been to the dreamers' fortress and watched her parents disappear. "Please come with us. You won't have to go inside."

She nodded, brushed a strand of hair from her cheek, and almost curtsied.

"Brave child," the mentor said. "Be sure and wait for them beyond the black doors until they return."

She turned to us, her eyes wells of concern.

"No need to wait." I said. "She can return to the comfort of the city, her home. We can follow the path back down on our own."

The mentor closed his eyes and sat so still, I imagined him laid out on one of the greenie pallets in the woods, with Kara bringing him daisies.

Then the deep blue eyes opened and fixed me with their gaze. "She'll wait, not to show you the way back, but to support you. If our experiment goes awry, the one who survives should not have to trudge down the mountain alone."

Chapter 23

The Darkened Lake

I ground my teeth as the rays from the stone guards scanned me. Once granted access, I joined the others on the far side.

"Are you ready?" Kara said.

I nodded without speaking, afraid my voice might betray my unease, and followed her through the mouth of the tunnel. Beyond the entrance, the glow from a row of naked bulbs highlighted an unblemished and seemingly endless ribbon of black pavement. I strode along, counting the echoes of my footsteps—a mind game to keep from dwelling on what lay ahead.

Kara paused midway to point out odd carvings on the wall. "The mentor says the cave through which this tunnel was built goes back to ancient times. These paintings were drawn by the earliest man, and have been preserved from the elements here beneath the earth."

I traced the lines with my fingertips. The primitive artist had carved crude drawings into the rock wall, many of them pictures of unfamiliar animals and birds, but in a few, he'd lovingly rendered his tribe, mothers and fathers with their children. Despite the millennia, they seemed not so different from people today.

When the tunnel finally ended, we emerged into a natural glade surrounded by rhododendrons in bloom. In the dim light of dawn, no obvious exit showed.

Kara grabbed a fallen branch and poked through the bushes at the back until she located an overgrown opening to a path. "Before the day of ascension, greenies maintained the way up the mountain in exchange for food and sweet water. Now, I'm the only one who comes here. The mentor asks me to climb up once a month to make sure the path stays open."

I brushed her arm with my fingertips. "I'm glad you came with us. It's natural after what happened to be afraid—"

She yanked her arm away. "I'm not afraid." Then she turned her back on me and started up the path.

The ensuing trail followed a stream. Signs of spring flooding lay everywhere—watermarks on the rocks, broken branches littering the trail, and tree trunks muddied to nearly knee high. Even now, the soggy surface forced us to high step as we pulled our boots from the muck.

Once the path rose to drier ground, we proceeded in silence, none of us willing to give voice to the thoughts swirling in our minds.

I focused on my breathing and the swish of my footsteps on the pine-needle carpet. For an instant, I imagined music ringing out above the running water, a high-pitched whistle like the notes of Thomas's flute. I paused to listen.

Nothing but the stream. No birdsong, no chitter of insects or scamper of squirrels in the brush, as if the birds and wildlife knew our mission and kept their silence out of respect.

Ahead, the trail climbed steeply through a stand of white poplars. A morning fog had risen with the sun and now mingled with the branches to cast a pall over the path. The mist floated in and out among the treetops, dimming the sunlight and dabbing the leaves with moisture. Sometimes the moisture condensed into drops that fell like rain, making a rustling patter on the leaves. The spray from the stream and the mist from the fog conspired with the light to form rainbows that appeared in our path and then vanished.

I sucked in the moist air through my nose. It smelled sweet and loamy, with a hint of rot.

While Nathaniel paced ahead, I followed Kara.

As we climbed, she kept glancing over her shoulder as if longing to return to the city. Once when she turned, our eyes met, but she looked away, like an executioner afraid to face her victim.

The trail wound along a ridge girding the midsection of the mountain. Halfway around, we came upon a lake.

"We'll stop here," Kara called to Nathaniel. "It's a good place to rest and refresh."

144

The path skirted the lake, which was sunk in a hollow some twenty feet below where we stood. Dense pines along its perimeter kept it shrouded in shadow, at least until the sun rose higher. Shiny patches of black ice left over from winter edged the gray water.

I shivered and pulled my tunic tighter about me.

Nathaniel opened his pack and passed out provisions.

We both settled on a log with a view of the lake, but Kara stayed standing and apart. As we ate our synthesized food and drank the sweet water—nourishment that would soon run out if we failed—I regarded the mentor's granddaughter, recalling myself at her age. Sixteen-year-olds are never content, since their life lies over the horizon, but Kara's restlessness seemed something more, like her life's role had been predetermined, and was one she'd rather avoid.

"Do you ever venture inside?" I said.

She tapped her teeth with a thumbnail as her eyes darted this way and that. Finally, she fixed on me and raised her chin with a look of certainty, as if she'd conducted this conversation a hundred times before in her mind. "The mentor has granted me permanent access, so I can enter anytime. The mentor, confined to his chair, would hardly know until after the deed was done. I could look around and listen for the voices of my parents.

"They told me that day what they were doing was for me. The dream frightened them, but they found their courage in possibilities, the hope of providing a better future. I still remember how they smiled at me as they turned from the world they were born in, like facing the sun and walking into the sky. I could enter the dream as well. I'm their daughter, and I have their courage."

Her mouth opened in a perfect O, like a child blowing out candles on her birthday, and she breathed out a lungful of air. "*I* should be the one to go into the mountain. I'm not afraid, and these are *my* people. My grandfather had no right to ask this of you. You don't understand what it means."

"But we're trained to—"

"He trained me as well. I know everything you do and more."

"Then why...?"

She stared out at the darkened lake, as if studying the water bugs skittering across its surface. Her eyes glistened. "My grandfather is ill, and grows worse by the day. He's taught me how to control what's left of the machines, but he hides the truth from the others for fear they'll lose hope and join the greenies. If I go into the mountain and become lost like my parents, who will run the machines when he's gone? The children will have no food, no water, no medicine... no leader."

I stood and took her by the arms. "Then you have more to offer than us. Better *we* go into the mountain." I waved in the direction of the dreamers' lair.

As she followed my gesture, the sun peeked above the treetops and sent ripples of yellow shimmering across the lake. She turned from the mountain and glanced below. "Look how the sunrise dances across the water, maybe a welcome message from the dreamers. Who knows how much of nature they've learned to control. Time to find out."

We resumed our trek, with Nathaniel racing ahead, eager to reach our goal. Periodically he'd stop and backtrack to keep us in sight.

I stayed close to Kara.

The day was turning out too fine, inappropriate for a visit to the possibly departed. I recalled when the elders placed my father in the ground. Even as a small child, I remembered being glad the day was gray; a blue sky should be reserved for the living.

After an hour, we emerged from the trees to a startling sight.

To my right, a field of purple heather and goldenrod spread as far as I could see. Their blossoms, still moist from the morning dew, sparkled in the shafts of sunlight, and the air hummed with the hushed drone of bees feeding on their nectar.

Ahead, the path stretched before us and tracked the stream. At its end raged the waterfall that formed its source, announcing its presence with a whooshing sound, like the keepmasters' train but made of wind. Despite the distance, this cascade roared louder than the four falls on the way to the keep, dwarfing them all combined.

These were the falls that powered the city, the forever flow of water that provided heat and light, and drove what machines still functioned. This was the energy source that had given flight to the aspirations of the dreamers.

Until the day the mountain erupted.

To my left stood a reminder of that eruption, an ugly scar across the land. A flow of lava five times taller than Nathaniel had snaked its way down from the falls and crushed everything in its path. Now, its anger spent, the lava had cooled to a grim memorial of the disaster, a river of black stone the vicars might have painted on the teaching chamber wall as a vision of the darkness.

I winced and turned away, focusing instead on the dreamers' fortress looming high above us, rising out of the mists from the falls like a dream itself.

"So steep," I said. "Did the dreamers have machines to take them there, fast wagons that could climb?"

Kara shook her head. "The dream is demanding, not just mentally but physically. Only those strong enough to make the climb were allowed to enter the mountain. This trek was another test to prove one's worthiness."

We plodded along from there, each footstep landing heavily upon the earth, not only from the steepness, but from a sense of foreboding. The mist had cleared, and the morning breeze had settled, leaving few sounds—the crunch of our boots on scree, our labored breathing, and the roar of the falls. Somewhere nearby, a woodpecker drummed away on a rotten log, indifferent to the folly of men.

Ten minutes later, a single ray from the rising sun struck the structure carved into the rock face, illuminating an unbroken window pane. The sudden flare gave the illusion of a beacon being lit inside, as if someone were leading us in.

For an instant, I thought of the storm and our boat being dragged into shore. Had the dreamers become so powerful they could make the lightning flash and the thunder roar? Could they have drawn us here to them? I shook off the mood, recalling the earth mother's words: *They sought to control nature but could never master the winds.* Had she been wrong? Had these geniuses lost in the dream learned to control nature and summoned us here?

More likely they were mad, or dead.

Nathaniel dashed back to me and waved his arm in a sweeping arc. "Our newest keep. May we find it as well-stocked with wisdom."

"And good luck," I added.

A few more steps allowed me to pierce the veil of mist from the falls.

Kara pointed. "There! You can see it clearly now."

I shielded my eyes against the glare of the sun as the brooding structure came into view. A series of columns supported a marble frame, much like the Temple of Truth in the keepmasters' ruined city. Behind them, two imposing gates barred the way, much different from the keep's golden doors, all black and forbidding. On either side, the familiar stone guards kept watch, but triple the height of the ones below.

I gazed up at their lifeless eyes and wondered what secrets they guarded behind those grim doors.

Chapter 24

Antechamber

We stopped at the final approach to catch our breath. Only fifty paces remained up a steep rise lined with crushed stone and bordered with blocks of white marble. As I marveled at the structure ahead, a wisp of a cloud slid across the sun, fragmenting its rays, and the air before the black doors came alive, shimmering as if wraiths were flying out to greet us.

Kara smiled at me. "That happens sometimes, especially in the afternoon when the sunbeams hit at a slant. Just science, like light passing through a prism, though the IBs might conjure up troubled spirits trying to escape their bonds."

I trudged up the remaining path, daunted by the dream and fearful of our fate. A minute later, I stood before five knee-high steps leading to the base of the columns. And oh, what columns, with each individual groove deep enough to hold a grown man. Behind them, the black metal doors loomed, contrasting sharply with the simple oak of the Hall of Winds. Etchings of lightning bolts embellished their surface, symbols of power. The doors towered over us, far taller than the golden entrance to the keep.

The columns were crowned by a decorative tower with two arched windows deeply set like frowning eyes, but the walls beneath them were windowless and bare. A pole rose in front with a scrap of cloth fluttering at its top, what must have once been a flag. The slap of rope on metal made a dreary sound.

At the base of the flagpole stood a gentler carving, out of place with the fortress itself. A granite cube with floral corners bore a sculpture of a man and a woman. The man hunched over with his head bowed, one hand covering his eyes while the other rested tenderly on the shoulder of the woman. She knelt beside him, leaning against his thigh and gazing at the doors. The man was dressed in the silver tunic of the machine masters, while the woman's smock hung loosely from her shoulders, ragged and worn. I stared at their stony faces and recognized them — a grieving earth mother and mentor.

"A tribute to the dreamers," Kara said. Then more softly, "Crafted by an IB. We have no artists. You'll see more of their works inside."

I begged Kara to join us, to guide us the first few steps, but she declined.

Instead, she crouched at the side of the path and picked a handful of heather. "While Zachariah healed, he wrote stories about the new greenie custom of placing flowers where the lost ones lie. I know such an act is... ishkabibble. The dead have no eyes to see or nose to smell. Neither do those who dwell inside the mountain, but with the dreamers nothing can be certain. What if they discovered a new way to touch the physical world, or still recalled the glory of a flower?" She handed me the heather. "For my parents, if you find them."

Nathaniel and I embraced Kara, grasped hands, and stepped before the stone guards.

The red beam flashed, scanning us from head to toe. A moment later, the doors groaned and swung wide.

***

The doors shut behind us, and the natural light dimmed.

I waited for the entry chamber to brighten on its own, but no light came. When my eyes adjusted, I realized the space we'd entered was not quite dark. In place of lamps recessed along the edges of the wall, this room was lit in its center by the glow from what appeared to be wriggling snakes floating on water and rising up as if to greet us.

I fell back a step, but as I gaped, the snakes became more plant than animal. Multi-colored, rotating lights above had created the illusion of motion, causing a flickering of both plants and their reflections. The plants themselves lay stiff and still, none so much as quivering in the breeze I made as I wandered past.

I reached out to touch the glowing garden, as I'd seen Nathaniel do years before when we'd first encountered the screens in the keep, and my fingertip brushed the nearest object, a serpentine figure that writhed and rose to what looked like a snake head. It felt cold and hard, a familiar sensation. I flicked my fingernail against the surface, and it clinked and chimed like a finely tuned bell—the sound of glass. Then I bent low and peered into the water, trying to pierce the inky darkness to its bottom. My own reflection stared back from an unyielding surface.

I reached out to touch it, but Nathaniel stayed my hand. "Remember the lesson we learned in the keep, how the elders in the darkness created a liquid that burned, a kind of a weapon. What if this is another defense like the stone statues, a trap to protect this place from intruders?"

He set down the pack and withdrew the electric torch the mentor had lent him. Its beam flickered over the water and flashed back brightly. He flipped the torch around and tried to dip its metal end into the surface, but it hit with a clank, causing no ripple. The water was not water at all, but a hardened material.

"A polished table top," I said.

Nathaniel set the torch aside and waved broadly to encompass the whole display. "But for what purpose?"

With my fear under control, I observed the scene with fresh eyes. The black surface mirrored the glow of the glass garden and highlighted the shifting shapes and colors of the plants.

"To reflect the light," I said. "To make it more beautiful. Kara told us we'd find more greenie craft inside. This must be another form of their art."

I circled the display twice, admiring its charm, but also putting off the next challenge in our quest.

At last I turned to Nathaniel and sighed. "Time to move on."

I was equally unprepared for what I found in the next chamber, not a temple to the gods, but a temple built by the gods themselves. Above me loomed a dome so high, the tallest building in Temple City would have been lost beneath it. Upon its broad expanse, stars flickered and folds of shimmering light rippled across a man-made spangled sky.

On a recessed ledge that circled the dome, statues of giants stood, their arms upraised, seemingly bearing the weight of the universe. I paced around the chamber counting them, seven in all, each distinct. Some had lavish locks, others were bald. Some were clean shaven, others had beards. Three were elders in flowing robes, but the four youngest appeared naked as the day of their birth. Their marble muscles bulged taut and tense beneath their burden.

Here was the opposite of what the earth mother preached—not the earth sustaining its people, but men supporting the heavens.

"But where are the dreamers?" I said.

Nathaniel pointed. "Remember our lessons."

I followed his gesture. Between two of the statues, a narrow stairway spiraled up around the foundation of the dome behind the statues. At its top sat the source of the light in the heavens, an enormous jewel, tapered like a candle flame, with dozens of glittering facets, a crystalline teardrop revolving in a vat of liquid.

I gaped, recalling a similar image from the mentor's holos. What else had we learned in that lesson? Nathaniel continued to point until I remembered. Half-hidden behind the jewel, an entrance opened to the final chamber.

I stared at the flight of steps and shuddered, my feet welded to the floor, but Nathaniel blew out his cheeks and set off without hesitation.

From halfway up, he called to me. "This is the way to the dreamers. What are you waiting for?"

I placed my boot gingerly on the first step, as if testing whether it would support my weight, though Nathaniel was nearly twice my size. The entire staircase was made of blackened oak, with broad steps that showed no wear and had been crafted too solid to creak underfoot. I started to climb, gripping the metal handrail and stopping every few seconds to check my surroundings.

At the landing on top, a plain door beckoned, with no numbered stars to unlock it and no stone guards blocking our way. Much like the doors in the keep, this one slid open as soon as we approached.

On its far side lay a round windowless chamber covered by a more modest dome. Dozens of arches had been cut into the circular wall, each decorated to look like the rising sun. Beneath each arch nestled a cradle and, within it, a coffin-like container.

I needed no prodding from Nathaniel to recall what they were.

The cocoons of the dreamers.

Chapter 25

The Chamber of Dreams

I spun around, eyeing the cocoons.

Here dwelled the elite, those who had advanced knowledge further in their lifetimes than perhaps in all of human history, those who had melded their minds with machines and had reached further than the stars, striving for immortality.

What had become of them now?

Despite all my training, I struggled to slow my breathing. My nostrils burned from the metallic odor I'd smelled in the mentor's chamber. A chill stung my eyes, making them tear. I wiped away the mist with the heel of my hand but saw no more clearly. The persistent haze dwelled not in my vision but in the scene before me. A pale blue fog swirled around each cocoon, like the wraith of its occupant trying to escape, or the stirrings of unfulfilled dreams.

I startled to a rattle from overhead. A sleeping sparrow in the rafters had woken to my footsteps and now flapped its wings, sending a shower of dust drifting down upon me.

I shook it off. "Are they—?" The words stuck in my throat.

"We'll soon find out." Nathaniel approached a cocoon. "Just like the holo in our lessons. A small window where the face should be."

"Can you see...?"

"Too much fog."

He leaned in to rub the glass clear with the elbow of his tunic but quickly pulled away.

"What?" I said.

"Too cold."

He switched on the electric torch, checked its beam by shining the light in his own eyes, and aimed it at the face of the dreamer. His eyes widened as he gazed through the window.

I crept closer, trying to breathe normally, and whispered between pants. "What's inside?"

His mouth opened, but no words emerged.

I eased the torch from his grip, and shined it on the window.

Withered cheeks looked flush with blood, but the chest showed no signs of movement. The man or woman inside lay still as the corpse at a Little Pond funeral, but without the forced smile... or the love of family and friends.

I returned the torch to Nathaniel. "We should open it to be certain."

He stood there, waiting for me, as if the chill from the cocoon had frozen him in place.

I fought to stay calm as childhood nightmares raged through my mind, outrageous tales spun by older children to frighten the young, of the dead clawing their way out of their graves to torment the living.

The mentor had trained us for this, driven his lessons into our brains until we could recite them in our sleep, and now I knew why. I scanned the side of the cocoon, and a panel with buttons peeked out from behind an opaque cover. I waved my hand over the cover and watched it dissolve.

Breathe in, breathe out.

My mind steadied while I counted the buttons, but my heart raced as if intent on proving I was alive. What else had the mentor said?

Concentrate, Orah.

He'd said the third from the left would open the cocoon.

My finger hovered. I pressed.

The cover of the cocoon gave a loud hiss and lifted slowly, just as it had in the holos. I followed its rise, never glancing down until I heard Nathaniel gasp.

Inside lay parchment hands, yellow and knobby, and leathery skin—not like that of a human, but pock-marked like the carcass of a chicken with its feathers newly plucked, as if the dreamer had devolved over thousands of years into some creature of the darkness.

Nathaniel rested a hand on my shoulder. "That solves the first part of the puzzle. These bodies have dwelled in this state for too long. They'll never sustain life again."

"But what of their minds? Time to find out. But first—"

I pushed the button again and the cover of the cocoon settled back into place. Then I placed Kara's handful of heather on top. Could this be one of her parents? It hardly mattered at this point. I turned my back on the decaying dreamer and searched for the control platform.

Nothing.

I circled the chamber, starting along the wall and then sliding inward in ever smaller loops. At last, I calmed myself enough to remember the mentor's words.

Despite their love of science, the dreamers appreciated a touch of whimsy. You'll find that touch wherever you go inside the mountain. In a nod to magic, they've hidden the controls. To make them appear, you must....

I struggled with the memory. What was it he said?

...stand on the brass sun and raise your arms to the heavens as if in prayer. The machines will detect your motion and....

I dashed to the center of the room. On the floor, at the exact middle of the circle, a brass image of the sun had been inlaid in the stone. I shuffled over until both feet covered the orb, with the rays radiating out on all sides. Then feeling slightly foolish, I gazed up to the dome and raised my arms overhead, as the vicars had taught me, with palms facing out.

The space before me quivered and firmed, and the control panel appeared. *Of course.* The machine masters knew how to control the basic elements of matter. They'd learned to synthesize food and make bones grow. How simple to synthesize this panel. Yet only someone privy to the secret would find it.

The air above the panel shimmered. I held my breath and hoped for a holo, some friendly helper to guide me along, but no helper appeared. Instead, an image glowed before me, a field flush with flowers in bloom, blazing gold, but also yellow, red, green, and seemingly every shade in between—a sea of color floating beneath the bluest of skies. The blossoms waved in the breeze and sparkled where the sun caught their tips. In the distance, a lake reflected the blue of the sky.

An imagined setting, or the path up the mountain before the eruption? Whichever, it thrilled my senses, the most beautiful place I'd ever seen.

Suddenly I understood what had drawn the elite to the dream, why it had tugged at their souls no matter how much they fought it. Perhaps they pushed it away at first, wary of the risk, but it snuck past every barrier they put up, creeping around the edges of the curtains they drew against it like the rays of the rising sun. For the dream offered something more than immortality; it offered the power to make all of nature a palette onto which they could paint scenes like this.

I shook off the mood—no time to fall under its spell—tore my eyes away from the display, and focused on the controls.

Again, I understood why the mentor had drilled us for so many hours. Though the dreamers could manipulate machines with their minds, they'd made provisions for mere mortals like me. Yet their controls were complex. The panel I'd studied so often now spread before me while the blood pulsed through my temples. I tried to focus, to recall what I'd been taught.

A map of the chamber showed the cocoons, those in use and those few still vacant. Below the map, two timers flashed zero in bright red numbers—the first to set a delayed start of the dream, and the other for its duration.

To the right of the timers, a series of holos projected from the panel—buttons and levers and gauges. The mentor claimed we needed to worry about only three: the time of duration; the lever to start the dream; and in case of an unforeseen emergency, the controls to end it. This last consisted of two buttons on either side, spread so far apart I'd need to stretch to press both at the same time. Everything else would be automatic.

Nathaniel came to my side and stared over my shoulder. He pointed at the circle of cocoons. "Just as the mentor said. Most in muted gray, showing they're occupied, but a few blinking green, which means... they're available and beckoning."

Before I could stop him, he reached out and touched one.

A whirring echoed off the dome. I glanced up, and a shudder ran down my spine. Along the far wall, the lid of a cocoon had lifted. An invitation to the dream...or a resting place for eternity?

My mouth went dry as cotton, and I had to swallow before speaking, not wishing to show my fear. "I'll set the timer."

I wiggled my fingers over the second display. The numbers scrolled and stopped at three hundred seconds, the five minutes the mentor had recommended.

"The duration of the dream." Nathaniel eyed the first timer, still reading zero. "No need to set the delay. You can pull the start lever once I'm settled inside."

"You mean once *I'm* settled." I stretched wide, pointing to the two buttons on either side. "If something goes wrong, press both of these at the same time to release me from the dream. Use them only if —"

He grasped me by the wrists and spun me around to face him. "You'll be at the controls. I'll be the one in the dream."

At once, I pictured the death bed of my father, the glassy-eyed stare, the hand that would no longer grasp mine. My eyes filled. "I won't let you. I won't be the one who stands by to watch you...."

He took a long breath and stared up at the false heaven. "Do you remember that time on the trail to the keep, high above the ravine, when our path was blocked by the boulder?"

Not the argument I expected. I nodded.

"Do you remember how I held the rope for you, lest you should fall?"

"Yes. When my turn came, you tossed the rope away and crossed without my support. I was furious...." My voice trailed off, fearing where his argument might lead.

"I did that because you lacked the strength to support my weight. If I fell, I'd bring you down with me."

"What has that to do with — ?"

"*I* was more able to keep you from falling. Now, *you're* more able to release me from the dream. You were always the more focused student. My mind wandered during those long sessions with the mentor. What if I forget some detail? What if I stand at the controls and my mind goes blank, and you become trapped in the dream." He swept his hand across the controls. "This is the rope. You are the strongest. You belong here. I'm the one who should enter the dream. It's the best chance we have."

I took several deep breaths to stop my trembling, my terror that he might be right. "I'd happily trust my life with you, rather than —"

He drew me close, and the trembling stilled.

I embraced him and held on tight. "I wish we could go back to Little Pond."

"So do I, but that's not one of our choices. We've always chosen the path most likely to keep us together. You led us to the keep. You planned the revolution. I built the boat, but it was you who guided us across the sea. You're the one best suited to lead me out of the dream. I'm safer in your hands than you are in mine."

I slowly shook my head, then twisted away and dashed to the open cocoon.

He caught me, lifted me off the ground and gently set me back in front of the control panel. "So I haven't convinced you. No matter. You may be the most strong-minded, but I'm still the most strong-armed, and I'll use that strength to keep you from the cocoon, if need be. You have two choices: let me be the one to enter the dream, or we abandon the dreamers."

Dreamers and vicars, technos, greenies, and deacons all reeled in my mind. I recalled the morning of the stoning in Little Pond, how I'd begged Nathaniel not to go. We had no good choice then, and we had none now. The best we could do was to be true to ourselves. Reluctantly, I nodded.

We needed no more words. I gave him a final kiss, rushed and clumsy so our cheeks rubbed, and a tear from mine was transferred to his.

Then we separated and I turned to the controls, my training taking over.

Nathaniel strode to the cocoon, leaving his fate in my hands. My fingers hovered over the controls as he clambered into the cocoon. He crossed his arms over his chest, gazed toward me one last time, winked and closed his eyes.

To the machine masters, the cocoon was a complex apparatus made of metal and glass, like the telescope in the keep's observatory, nothing more than a scientific instrument. To me, it gaped like a forbidden gateway, a portal to a place we were never meant to go. The earth mother had said we were intended to strive, to fulfill our potential, but to what limits?

I longed to be a little girl again, to return to a time when I believed in the goodness of the world, before my father died, before the teachings and our imprisonment in Temple City, before I'd ever heard of machine masters or people of the earth. I longed to return to a time before I'd learned the harshest of lessons—the folly of man.

No matter. No turning back now.

I bit down on my lower lip and pulled the lever.

The cover of the cocoon whirred in a slow descent, finally closing with a whisper as if made of air.

The red numbers smoldered on the glowing panel. Three hundred seconds turned to two ninety-nine, ninety-eight, ninety-seven.... Above them the display flickered and changed, and the field of flowers vanished, replaced by the same chaotic and ill-formed images I'd viewed on the wall of the mentor's chamber—a window into the dream.

As I stared, mesmerized by the blinking numbers, I recalled the mentor's words.

Who knows what form their minds have taken, how startled they'll be by a newcomer? How hard will it be for them to communicate? I have no scientific theory for how long you should stay in the dream. If the dreamers' consciousness exists in a rational way, five minutes should suffice. More than that, and I fear your untrained minds will become addicted to the dream, and you'll struggle to reenter the world of the living. Five minutes. It's my best guess.

I abandoned the controls and checked through the window of the cocoon. Nathaniel appeared as if sleeping, his eyes closed and his face serene. Back at the panel, the numbers counted down: two fifty-eight, fifty-seven—a lifetime until he'd awaken.

My father's final hours came to my mind. Like Nathaniel, his face had appeared serene, but when I spoke to him, he failed to respond. So I sang him the song he always sang to me, when I had trouble sleeping or was afraid.

Now, as the pale blue mist filled the cocoon, hiding my beloved Nathaniel, and the cruel red numbers scrolled at a deathly pace, I began to sing.

> *Hush my child, don't you cry*
> *I'll be here with you*
> *Though light may fade and darkness fall*
> *My love will still be true*
> ~~~
> *So close your eyes and trust in sleep*
> *And dream of a better day*
> *Though night may fall, the morn will come*
> *The light will show the way*
> ~~~
> *Though you may roam to far off lands*
> *And trouble comes your way*
> *You'll still be here within my heart*
> *I won't be far away....*

A thump from the cocoon interrupted my song, a banging from within as if Nathaniel was fighting to get out. I fled the controls to peek into the window.

His eyes remained closed, but he was no longer calm. The cocoon rocked as he thrashed inside.

I raced back to check the numbers: two hundred and forty-two.... Less than a minute had gone by.

What should I do?

I stretched out my left hand for one emergency button but withheld the right. Two hundred and thirty-three, thirty-two....

The banging became louder and more desperate.

I'd lost my father. I would not lose Nathaniel.

...Twenty-five, twenty-four....

Images streamed in my mind like the holos in the air before me—the vicars' prison, the peephole, the threat of them taking Nathaniel away forever. To have survived so much and lose him now....

I pressed both buttons and the thrashing stopped.

Chapter 26

Return to the Living

A puff of air rushed by, as if a breeze blew through a fissure in the wall, and the cover of the cocoon whirred and rose. A puff of air — *whuff* — like the sound one makes when blowing out a candle. A puff of air — like a living breath, but coming from a machine and not Nathaniel.

The pale blue fog swirled and cleared, and I ran to the cocoon.

Breathe, Nathaniel!

I grasped his hand and squeezed; his fingers lay limp and still. I patted his cheek; his skin felt cold as death.

Please, Nathaniel, come back to me.

At last, his breath returned in shallow, panting bursts. The tortured expression left him, replaced by a look of serenity more complete than any I'd seen before. His face almost glowed.

I released the breath I'd been holding in sympathy, and the tension drained from my shoulders, but just as I became hopeful and readied to embrace him, a spasm racked his body, so violent his boots kicked the cover.

The glow vanished. He pulled his hand away, opened his eyes, and stared through me as if I were a stranger.

I called his name.

No response.

I helped him climb out of the cocoon.

He set his feet on the floor but wobbled, lost his balance, and fell into my arms.

I held him up with all my strength, praying to the light he'd return to me. After surviving so many dangers, how could I lose him now? What if he stayed with me, yet not fully here? I'd wonder for the rest of my life where his mind had gone, the essence of who he was.

I stroked his hair, still damp with sweat.

His heartbeat strengthened, and his breath whispered in quick bursts across my cheek.

I stared at him for a long time, at his face inches from mine, at the familiar pulse in his temple, the lump in his throat bobbing up and down, and the deep shadows beneath his eyes.

Finally, I said, "Do you know me?"

He blinked as if waking from a dream, but said nothing. Instead, he ran a finger along my jawline, sending a shiver down my spine. Then, he grasped me by the arms and drew me close.

I resisted, holding back, still searching for the man I loved, but he pulled harder until I gave in.

Then he closed my eyes with his fingertips and kissed them lightly, once upon each eyelid. I raised my lips to meet his, and we shared a kiss like the one we'd shared after Thomas freed us from the vicars' prison, the first time we'd touched after months apart.

"My Nathaniel," I said in a whisper, as if afraid to wake and find his return had been a dream.

I led him like a child out of the chamber, through the hall of heaven held up by giants, and around the garden of glass.

Outside the dreamers' fortress, by the statue of the earth mother and the mourning mentor, we met Kara. I had no need to explain Nathaniel's state; his condition was reflected in the concern in her eyes.

She draped one of his long arms around her shoulder, while I supported the other. Together, we half-carried him on shaky legs down to the stream. The spring gurgled and trickled over mossy rocks, and I dipped my hands in to wash off the grime of the chamber. Then I tore off a strip from my tunic, soaked it in the icy waters, and lifted the moistened rag to Nathaniel's face. He flinched but steadied as I wiped the sweat from his brow.

Kara brought over the flask of sweet water and raised it to his mouth.

He balked, recoiling as if the drink were poisoned.

I drank instead, to show him the way, like a mother teaching a babe.

He waited an eternal minute before raising the flask to his lips and taking several painful gulps, as if his throat had narrowed from weeks of thirst. After a while, the color returned to his cheeks, and the fog lifted from his eyes.

"Are you ready for the hike down the mountain?" I said.

He nodded.

"Let me hear you say it."

"Yes." The word sounded dull and distant, like the sound a pebble makes falling into a deep well.

On the path down, he said little more, and when he did speak, his voice lacked passion, with each word spaced by seconds from the next.

Nevertheless, I thanked the light he'd returned to me alive.

The world had come alive as well, in stark contrast to the dwelling of the dreamers. Sounds of life rang out everywhere—the trilling of insects, the whistle of birds, the rustling of squirrels hidden in the brush, and the croaking of frogs. A breeze rustled the leaves of the trees overhead as if to assert that they too were alive.

Nathaniel stumbled silently down the trail, but I sensed his troubled thoughts in a way only possible between friends since birth— friends and lovers, whose love had been tested so many times before. Though now we'd been tested again, no words were needed because we'd spoken them already, in silence and in darkness, through the fear of losing our lives, or worse, of losing each other.

After far too long, we came to the lake, no longer darkened but gleaming with late afternoon sun. A brisk wind rippled the surface now, tipping the waves with whitecaps. I gaped at them as if seeing them for the first time. Their tops looked like tiny hands reaching out for Nathaniel, clawing at his soul, trying to drag him back into the depths. Would he yet slip from my grasp?

We stopped there to rest, settling on the same log where we'd shared our breakfast. Kara offered the sweet water, while I opened the pack, which I now carried. I handed him a portion of the greenies' berries and flatbread, treats we'd saved for the hoped-for celebration on the way down.

The three of us sat on the log and ate and drank, as we used to do at the NOT tree, with Kara taking the place of Thomas.

When Nathaniel had nibbled away on less than half his food, he set it down and turned to me. "I felt light... as if I were made of air."

"That sounds wonderful," I said.

"Not wonderful." His faced contorted with horror. "You should never go there."

"Why?"

"Because... it's the lightness that enchants you at the top of a mountain, with a sight so beautiful you believe you can step off the highest ledge and fly. It's the lightness that dazzles you deep underwater, as you admire the fish and the slow dance of watery plants, but you forget to breathe, and you drown. In the dream, I was everything and nothing. I understood the infinite, so much more than ever possible from the helpers in the keep. The knowledge of all mankind lay bare, but...."

He looked away.

I placed a hand on his cheek and forced him to face me. "But what?"

"There was no place in that infinity for you."

***

Even with our support, Nathaniel had barely managed to stagger down the mountain to the lake. Now, as his mind cleared, he refused to go any farther, as if his confession had drained him of all remaining energy. If we hoped to reach the machine masters' city this day, Kara and I would have to carry him.

With the hour getting late, I determined to camp that night by the lake. I gathered kindling and struck two stones together until they threw a spark, as I'd done so often since childhood.

Kara's eyes grew wide as she watched the kindling catch. "Fire from sticks and stones? You have many surprises."

We all watched as the twigs sputtered and caught. Smoke rose to the treetop canopy but lingered, unable to penetrate, creating a haze that dimmed the setting sun. As the fire crackled and rose, a night bird called in response, but otherwise silence.

The three of us huddled around the flames, warming our hands, as those who made carvings on the cave walls must have done thousands of years before. So much for the miracles of the machine masters.

In my youth, I worried about my friends. Would Nathaniel outgrow his boyish notions and accept the wisdom of the Vicars? Would Thomas stay out of trouble in school? I dwelled on these worries as I worked the loom or helped my mother knead dough to bake bread.

Later, I worried that we'd betray the keepmasters, or lack the courage to confront the vicars with the truth, or that my guidance would be flawed and we'd be lost forever at sea.

Now, new worries haunted me. Would Nathaniel return to the man I loved? Would our choices change the world, and if so, for better or worse?

As the sun set, a chorus of birds sang their twilight song, unseen among the branches and vines of the forest, raucous chirps and a pair of whistles that repeated three times in a row. These same birds called as dusk approached in Little Pond; their familiar sounds consoled me. When I was little, I imagined one of them—the one with the three whistles—was my father's spirit, sent out in the shape of a bird to watch over me. Now, I imagined it promised Nathaniel would come back to me by morning.

Soon, the sky transformed from blue to red to purple, and the twilight to a deep and early night. The moon rose fat and orange on the horizon, turning the wildflowers silvery grey, as if the color had been sucked out of them. Fireflies glittered in the leaves of the surrounding trees, flickering on and off like candles lit in the windows of a distant village.

The three of us gathered piles of pine needles and readied for bed.

I lay on my back, eyes closed but awake, listening to Nathaniel toss and turn, assessing his every movement until his breathing settled into its nightly rhythm. Only then did I too fall asleep.

***

I startled to the crack of a twig—Nathaniel feeding the fire. Once it blazed anew, he paced around it, slapping his hands on his upper arms for warmth.

I rose as well. "Are you all right?"

"Can't sleep," he said.

"May I join you?"

He nodded.

The lake spread before us, bathed in gold from the glow of a moon a sliver short of full. I stared at the view and waited for him to say more, hoping he'd tell me what he'd experienced in the dream.

He shuffled to the rim of the lake and gazed down the steep embankment.

165

Fearing he might do himself harm, I rushed to his side and clutched his elbow with my arm.

He let me hold on.

I braced myself to probe as I'd done years before, trying to get Thomas to talk about his teaching, picking gingerly at the wound like a mother easing a splinter from the finger of a child.

Before I could begin, he turned to me, the folds of his face shifting between light and shadow, his eyes reflecting the flickering fire and throwing off sparks of their own. "I've been trying to understand what happened. First, I saw—or imagined I saw—tiny blue and yellow lights buzzing around like bees. Then all the colors of the rainbow burst out at once and blended into a pure white that filled my mind, driving out all thought. Suddenly everything went dark... or light. It didn't matter. The buzzing grew louder... or became silent. I didn't care. I found myself joined with the minds of others, not like meeting the greenies in their village center, but like experiencing a multitude of dreams at once."

"The machine masters," I said. "Still alive."

His eyes shifted downward and to their corners. "I can't explain what I found, only that I had... thoughts that weren't mine—marvelous thoughts, like having all the knowledge of the keep inside my head at once, but many times more. Something wondrous stirred in me, an understanding of the universe greater than the loftiest notions I've ever had. Suddenly, I lost interest in things of the physical world. This lake, the glow of the moonlight, the stirring of the leaves in the breeze, the warmth of the fire... and all those I love, meant nothing to me. That's why I fought being immersed in the dream. I fell under its spell for only a matter of seconds. After years, what have these machine masters become? I sensed their thoughts, but does that mean they live? I can't say."

A rustling sounded behind us, and I turned.

Kara brushed Nathaniel's arm. "Of course, they live. How can you doubt it? You've mingled with their minds. They live, and someday I'll reunite with them as well. Did you meet my parents? Did they think of me?"

Nathaniel slowly shook his head. His lips parted, but the words stuck in his throat.

Kara sailed on, floating on a sea of hope. "Of course the dreamers live. Had you stayed longer, you'd know for sure. They'd need time to learn to speak with someone like you. You're not one of us. You haven't studied as we have, and they've been in the dream for so long. Like a hermit with no one to talk to, the first visitor they encounter would be a shock. Words would come slowly."

I recalled what the earth mother had said: *The dreamers may not have died in the way you know, but they do not live.*

"We don't know that," I said. "We can't be sure."

Kara's jaw set, and her brows pinched in, forcing a crease to form above the bridge of her nose. "Then we should go back and try again."

I rested a hand on her shoulder. "We have only a few hours till daylight. We're exhausted, and I need to get Nathaniel back to the city. There'll be time to—"

"There *is* no more time!" She pulled away. "Two more days bring the anniversary of ascension, and the greenie fanatics will destroy them forever. The mentor said they're near to breaking through. You've given me hope the dreamers live, but not proof enough to stop the zealots. I'll go myself if need be."

"What about leading the children?" I said.

She raised her chin and gazed up at the moon. In its light, her eyes glistened. "In two weeks, I'll turn sixteen. I won't lose my parents for a second time so soon before the day of my birth."

Nathaniel slipped between us and rose to his full height for the first time since emerging from the dream. "I have a better way. Rather than risking a return to the dream, go back to sleep and get some rest. In the morning, we'll go to the greenies and tell them what I found. Once the earth mother hears my story, she won't allow any harm to come to the dreamers."

Kara sighed, and the tension eased from her shoulders. "Very well, though some of the greenies prefer ishkabibble to reason. But know this—if you fail to stop their day of reckoning, I'll go myself into the mountain, and neither you nor the mentor will stop me."

Chapter 27

Insurrection

Daylight dawned, and with it a chilling breeze. I'd come ill-prepared to camp outside for the night. The silver tunic had kept me warmer than expected, but with our fire burned down to embers, I awoke shivering. We'd exhausted our food and the skins of sweet water as well, but Kara cautioned against drinking from the stream.

Though Nathaniel and I had grown up accustomed to living off the land, we had no time to fish or forage, so with parched lips and rumbling stomachs, we set off. On the way down the mountain, the air warmed both from the heat of the rising sun and our descent to lower ground.

Nathaniel walked on his own, pressing ahead at an ever faster pace. The farther we hiked from the mountain fortress, the more bounce returned to his step. I recognized that stride; a new purpose drove him on—to protect the undefended minds he'd touched in the dream. Whoever or whatever they'd become, he deemed them worth saving.

We stopped in the city to replenish our supplies and to brief the mentor. We found him in his chamber, slumped in his wheeled chair with a shawl wrapped about his shoulders, as if he'd shared our night outdoors.

Kara stroked his arm. "Grandfather, we've returned."

He took longer than usual to stir. "Hmmm. Good to hear...." His eyes were barely slits. "Ah, it's you, dear child. Where have you been?"

Kara raised a brow on one side, and lowered the corner of her mouth on the other. "To the mountain, of course."

A lengthy pause, two prolonged coughs, and the slits widened, but the eyes behind them remained clouded. "Ah yes, the mountain.... What did you find?"

Nathaniel briefly described what happened.

The mentor straightened in his wheeled chair, though he required more effort than usual. "A good sign. Their downloaded minds must still function. I can understand their inability to communicate. A stranger, not one of their own, surprised them, and they needed to understand the newcomer in their midst." He turned and fixed me with a stare stern enough to make me fall back a step. "If only *you* had given them more time."

Kara knelt before him and rested an arm on his knee. "Is there any more news of the greenies?"

The mentor took off the wide-brimmed hat and laid it bottom side up in his lap while he smoothed back his few strands of hair. The sensors in the rim blinked furiously.

He put the hat back on and stared at the blank wall, concentrating. His eyes narrowed, and the blood drained from his already ashen face. "The zealots have almost broken through. By the end of the day of ascension, they'll stand before the black gate. The stone guards will hold them at bay for a time, but with their iron tools and stubborn will, they'll soon find a way inside."

"We're going to the greenies," Kara said, "to tell the ragged lady what Nathaniel found. Will she help?"

The mentor placed his big, knobby hand on her cheek and regarded her with sad blue eyes. "Annabel has always had a good heart, and many of those who went into the dream were her friends, but she's been so effective at weaving her myths that they've taken on a life of their own. So the question, my child, is not if she will help. She will most certainly order them to do no harm. The question is rather...." His shoulders heaved up and down in a sigh. "Will they listen?"

***

Shortly after leaving the machine master's city and entering the path through the woods, something stirred in the trees, different from the scuffling of squirrels or the flutter of birds.

Unaccustomed to life outdoors, Kara noticed nothing, but Nathaniel saw it as well. He raised a hand to halt us and gazed to our right and left.

I held my breath and listened.

A bird call sounded, distinct and exaggerated, like the answer to Zachariah's signal when we first visited the people of the earth, but this call mimicked neither the coo of a morning dove nor the squawk of a crow. This was the screech of a hawk stalking its prey. Seconds later it was answered in kind from higher up on the mountain.

The watcher in the woods followed us as we progressed down the path. At the first clearing, the rustling in the trees turned into a squat and burly man, one I'd seen before with Caleb.

He crossed the path to block our way. "Caleb will join us shortly. Wait here until he comes."

I pressed closer, barely slowing my stride. "Step aside. We bring urgent news for the earth mother."

"Your news will have to wait. I'm ordered to keep you here."

I eased the tension from my eyes and gazed at the would-be guard. "What's your name?"

He looked away, checking up the mountain as if hoping Caleb would arrive. "I am Jubal."

"Are you a loyal follower of the earth mother, Jubal, because she would be disappointed to learn you delayed us?"

"I... also do the bidding of the earth mother."

"Then does she know you've come to threaten us?"

He flinched but held his ground. "Not threaten. I'm asking you to wait. What you have to say concerns Caleb as well."

Nathaniel slipped in between, rising to his full height and towering over the man. "And if we refuse? How do you plan to stop us?"

I grasped Kara by the elbow and hurried her around.

Once we were past, the man called Jubal reluctantly cleared the way.

***

As we approached the first vegetable gardens and tilled fields being readied for planting, the workers sent their children scurrying ahead. By the time we arrived at the village center, the earth mother and her elders had assembled under the old beech tree, sitting cross-legged in a circle awaiting us.

She took one look at our faces and Kara with us, and her greeting turned into a frown. "You've been inside the mountain."

I nodded.

She stared at her feet for several seconds before speaking. "And—" Her voice cracked. "What did you find?"

"I entered the dream," Nathaniel said, "for a minute or less, but enough to know their minds are alive."

"Why? Did they share thoughts with you? Did they address you directly?"

Nathaniel shook his head.

"Did they... think a name, their own or that of a loved one left behind—some evidence they were communicating in the present?"

He glanced at me and mumbled, "Not that I recall."

"Then how do you know what you sensed was anything more than impulses stored in a machine, morbidly replaying memories like the echoes in a canyon of voices long gone?"

Nathaniel bit his lip and glanced upward, as if searching for an answer in the mountain. "I... can't be sure. What I experienced was so different from anything I've felt before, but the thoughts they shared were more than figments of my imagination, thoughts I could never conceive on my own even after a lifetime of learning—new ideas about the universe, ways to help your people and ours. Alive or not, you can't let—"

A murmur spread through the assembled as Caleb and a half dozen of his men burst into the village, out of breath and covered with stone dust and grime. He stopped at the edge of the circle, at the space on the council left empty for him, and stared down at Kara with a gaze so fierce it crackled like flame. "What is *she* doing here?"

"She's my guest," the earth mother said, "and welcome here. They bring news about—"

"They bring lies!"

"As do you, Caleb. Is this gray dust on your clothes the result of fixing the fence that bounds the northwest pasture—what you said you'd be doing this day? Or have you been tunneling through the mountain despite your vow to me?"

"I've been following the spirit of what you teach, earth mother, if not your exact words."

"Then listen to what I teach now. Nathaniel has been in the dream, and it's possible the minds of the dreamers live on. To destroy the machines may be to commit murder."

Caleb glared at Nathaniel. "You've been there? Then you know the evil of the dream. Did their bodies live on after all these years?"

Nathaniel turned away, back to the earth mother. "No, but I found something more—"

"Can their minds be restored to their bodies?" Caleb said, louder this time.

Nathaniel stroked his forehead with the tips of his fingers but had no response.

Caleb took a step toward him. "And when you joined these minds, living minds as you claim, were *you* alive? Were you still yourself as your family and loved ones have known you?"

"I can't—"

"You felt alone, floating, full of ideas, insights and wonderment, but with no connection to your own soul—" He turned and glanced at me. "—or to those you love."

Nathaniel's lips parted, but no words emerged. The corners of his mouth drooped into a frown.

Caleb pressed closer, the two men now eye to eye. "Without sight or sound, without the rich smells of the earth or the sweet air to breathe, stripped of all that made you human. I ask again, do you still believe they were alive?"

Nathaniel waited, fighting his answer until the word forced its way from the depths of his chest. "No."

Caleb turned back to the earth mother. "Then, Annabel, they do not live in any manner you've taught us. Destroying the machines won't end lives already lost. To bring them peace cannot be murder."

Devorah scrambled to her feet and confronted Caleb. "Are you so wise now that you possess a perfect vision of what's right and wrong?"

"You've become soft, Devorah, enamored with your new friends, bribed into submission by their trinkets and brightly colored garments." He set his jaw, and his gaze seemed far away, as if viewing a tunnel dug deep in the mountain. "I know firsthand the evil of the dream. I helped create it. Now it's my duty to destroy it."

The earth mother signaled for Devorah to help her stand, then went to Caleb and rested an arm on his shoulder. "We have so much good to do here, to plant and to build, to create a new life for our children without the machines. There's no need to destroy anything. In time, the technos will join us peacefully."

Caleb looked past her and spoke to the others on the council. "Our leader has become old. We should value her teachings and the wisdom she's passed on, but her time is over—her and her friend, the mentor. A new generation has arisen."

Kara jumped up, her face flushed and her hands shaking with rage. "We're a new generation as well, and will defend our kin, who still live."

Caleb scoffed at her. "You and your scholars are no match for my men."

Kara stood her ground. "And you don't know the power of the machines we still control."

The earth mother pressed between them and turned to me. "Leave now. I'll try to help, but I can no longer guarantee your safety."

Kara's face reddened. Her breath came in quick bursts, and she refused to budge. I tugged gently at her arm, but her muscles turned rigid.

"Come now," I said. "If you're to be a leader, make the best choice for your people."

Her arm went limp, and she yielded.

As the three of us fled the village, Caleb cried after us, mocking. "Farewell, machine master. Your days in power will soon end."

Chapter 28

Kara's Time

Kara set a frantic pace, stomping up the mountain as if to punish the earth for letting Caleb walk upon it. She shouted to the wind as she climbed. "Greenie fools! We'll show you how to fight."

This world we'd sailed into was hurtling toward a calamity greater than the mountain's eruption, a battle that would destroy both sides and take the hope of rebirth for my homeland with it.

I caught up and grabbed her by the elbow to slow her down. "Your children can't fight them with sticks."

She twisted away and confronted me with an unexpected fierceness. "You have no idea of our power. Do you think the scant few weeks with the mentor taught you everything my forbearers took centuries to conceive? Some of our machines still work. Though none were intended as weapons, they can move mountains, and if they can move mountains, they can stop the greenies."

"Then why haven't you used them before?"

"My ancestors banned the use of machines for anything but production and defense, but if the fanatics destroy the dreamers, we'll have nothing left to defend. I'll go to the mentor and beg him to...."

Her voice trailed off, her anger spent. Standing there against the vastness of the mountain, she looked so small, a girl younger than I was when I set out for the keep. Like me, she brimmed with passion but understood little of what lay in store.

She shook off her uncertainty and resumed her march, though more deliberately now, apparently realizing her time of trial would come soon enough.

As we came within view of the city, a sense of foreboding overwhelmed me. A blustery wind kicked up—not unusual this high on the mountain, but this one carried malice with it. The sun had fled, seeking refuge behind a gloomy cloud. A forlorn hawk circled overhead, squawking plaintively and searching for prey but finding none. Most disturbing, the lights that created the illusion of a fortress wall had gone dark.

The mentor would surely know Caleb's intentions by now and should have set every defense in place.

My fears were realized as soon as we emerged from the woods.

The children had gathered outside the arch, stumbling around in silence.

The little boy, Timmy, spotted Kara, and threw himself into her arms. She lifted him up. "What's happened, Timmy?"

"The mentor," he said, his tiny shoulders heaving and his cheeks streaked with tears. "He's sleeping, and no one can wake him."

A tremor racked Kara's frame, but she steadied at once. She was the mentor's heir, the future leader. If the worst had happened, she'd have no time to mourn.

She set Timmy down. "Show me."

Timmy led us to the domed hall, where the synthesizers performed their sometime magic and everyone shared meals, where less than two months before, the children of the machine masters had celebrated our arrival.

In the center of the circle the mentor's lanky frame lay crumpled in his wheeled chair. The bar had been lowered from the rope above but swung aimlessly in the air. He sat there motionless, mouth open and blue eyes closed, his skin the color of chalk.

Kara removed the wide-brimmed hat and smoothed back the few strands of hair, so thin the bumps on his skull stood out amid the red blemishes that the sensors had worn into his scalp. She kissed the forehead of this man who was no longer the mentor but her grandfather, the only parent she'd known these past three years.

My eyes misted, not for the aged mentor's passing but for Kara. I thought of my own father, still and cold, and at that instant grieved for all children who had ever lost a parent.

"Has he gone to the dreamers?" Timmy whispered.

"No," she said, loud enough for the word to echo off the dome. "He's gone, but the dreamers still live." She turned to Nathaniel and me. "With no mind to control the chair, it may take all of us to move him. Will you help, please?"

Together, the three of us wheeled the mentor back to his chamber and laid him out on his bed. Nathaniel placed a pillow under his head, while I crossed his arms over his chest.

After a respectful moment of silence, I turned to Kara. "How will you memorialize him? What will become of his body?"

"Like everything else," she said, "we have a machine... if I can get it to work. It will disintegrate his body and return his energy to the universe. But I have more pressing tasks for now." She stretched her lips into a thin and bloodless line. "Leave me and go comfort the children, as you do so well. The mentor prepared me for this day, but I have a lot to do in a short time. If I fail, I'll have more than my grandfather to mourn."

***

We sat outside on the ground with the children as the sun sank low behind the mountain. The low hum we'd always taken to be the heartbeat of the city had gone quiet.

"Who'll fix the synthesizers when they don't work?" one of the younger girls asked.

"How will we eat?" said another.

"We'll fish and forage like the greenies," one of the older boys said.

"Who will give us the sweet water and heal our wounds?"

The older boy lifted his chin, looked at the vacant archway, and spoke too loudly, like someone afraid trying to sound brave. "Kara will know."

None of the city lights were lit, not even within the dome, and as dusk settled in, the long shadow of the mountain crept over us.

Timmy began to cry. "I'm cold, and soon it will be dark."

I rose and gestured for Nathaniel to follow. Together, we rummaged around the edge of the forest, gathering kindling and dead branches to make a fire. Then, in the clearing before the arch, we stacked logs until the pile stood waist high. I hoped to build a bonfire as big as the one at festival to provide light and heat, but before I could strike the stones to throw a spark, the children fell silent.

Everyone turned to the archway of the city.

Kara stood beneath it, feet apart and eyes ablaze. On her head, she wore the decorated bonnet the mentor had given her for her fifteenth birthday.

She stared past us and concentrated, as the mentor had done so often before. Suddenly, the throbbing hum resumed: naked bulbs flared, driving away the night; a warm breeze burst through the archway, chasing away the cold; and the spires of light that crowned the city walls sprung to life, reaching high into the heavens.

She stepped to one side, and the mentor's chair, now empty, rolled on its own through the archway, leading the way for a squad of repair machines. Without a word spoken by Kara, they rolled to a stop in formation on either side of the archway — a machine master's army.

At last, she turned to the stone statues, and the red light flickered and flashed from their eyes, casting a line on the ground before our feet.

"Move back," she shouted.

After everyone had cleared, she pressed her eyes shut.

The beam from the stone guards brightened into an unbearable glow, forcing me to cover my eyes with my hand. A pungent odor stung my nostrils, and smoke arose from where the beam had struck the sandy soil.

When I looked up again, the rays had dimmed.

On the ground before the stone guards, the soil had fused to glass.

Chapter 29

Sides of the Ledger

That night, I dreamed I was trapped in the teaching cell with Thomas. I knew it was a dream, because the cramped cell barely held space for one. I fit only by floating in the air above him.

"What are you doing up there?" he said.

"I heard your cry and came to find out what happened."

He squirmed around where he sat, searching in vain for a more comfortable position. "Same old Orah, always trying to protect me, but you're too late this time. You know how it seemed like a good idea to disrupt the current order and open the keep to everyone? Well, that didn't work out so well." His face contorted in pain. "The vicars are back in power, I'm stuck in this teaching cell, and now you've messed up the other side of the world."

"The story's not over," I said.

"Always the optimist, trusting too much in the goodness of people. Open your eyes for once. People fear what they don't know."

He shifted in his tiny space and moaned.

"Can I do anything to help you?" I said.

"Sure, if you can find a way to smuggle in my favorite flute. I'd love to play it one last time before they stone me. But what am I thinking? You can't help, because you're nothing but an image on a screen."

I glanced down at my hands—they glowed with a pale blue light but lacked depth or substance.

A grating sound startled me as the cover of the cell slid open, revealing the smug face of a vicar, the same one who'd dragged me off to my teaching years before. He leered down at me. "Are you ready, Orah, whose name means light?"

"Ready for what?" I cried. "Not the stoning."

"Stoning?" He laughed. "Of course not. Thanks to you, we've progressed beyond such primitive ways. Now we use the machine you brought us—the one that disintegrates your body and restores its energy to the universe. A lot cleaner, and much less fuss."

My skin began to change, thinning so I could see through it, and then breaking apart into points of light spiraling off in every direction. I tried to call Nathaniel, but my voice had thinned as well and spread to the winds like a cry in a storm.

An instant later, time lost all meaning, and I became pure mind.

***

I awoke with my pillow damp from sweat, and slowed my racing heart to match the rhythm of Nathaniel's breathing. From our years together, I could tell he wouldn't easily awake.

Ten heartbeats later, I arose, padded to the small bureau in our bedchamber, and eased the drawer open so it hardly made a sound. From it, I withdrew my boots and silver tunic, the mentor's electric torch, and my log and pen. After disengaging myself from the tangled bedclothes, I tossed on the tunic, not pausing to fix the sleeve that hung askew about my shoulder. With Nathaniel's pack slung over one arm, I crept out the door, easing it closed behind me, and stepped into the curved corridor.

At a table in the now silent commons, I opened the log to the first blank page, and grasped the pen in hand. Time to take stock and make my decision.

***

In trying times, I prefer to weigh the choices, to not rush recklessly into the void. This has always been my way. With Nathaniel's help, I've found the courage to overcome my fears, but I've never taken an action until it was my best and only choice.

Here is the ledger by which I'll make this, my most difficult decision.

On the positive side, Nathaniel and I are together, though he's become more distant since his time in the dream. Will he ever be the same? We've spent

179

our whole lives with each other and shared so many experiences. Now the dream stands between us like the wall with the peephole between our cells. Yes, we're together, and we still exchange heartfelt words, but they seem muffled and indistinct, tempered by doubts.

And what to make of this world? Life under the vicars was stifling, but the rules were clear, the routine consistent. Here I sense a continual decay.

The technos wait for their precious machines to fail, relying first on the aging mentor and now placing their hope in his heir, a not-quite-sixteen-year-old girl. They have no more ability to move forward than my own people did before we discovered the keep.

The greenies rejoice when I teach them how to spin flax and weave the resulting thread into cloth—skills I learned as a child—but by shunning advanced learning, they limit their potential. What happens when the earth mother passes to the light like the mentor? Will Caleb and his followers, after waging a war with the technos, declare all machines of the darkness and ban their use, except for a few they cleverly save for themselves? Will their descendants become a new wave of vicars? Will the dreamers' fortress be forgotten in the sands of time, a new keep to be revived by restless seekers a thousand years hence? Will those seekers arrive in time to save the knowledge of the past or will all be lost?

What of the hope for Nathaniel and me to return to Little Pond? Neither techno nor greenie possesses the knowledge to construct a boat. That possibility lies only with the dreamers.

I rest my forehead on my hands, stare off into the who-knows-where, and release the breath I've been holding with a whoosh like the wind. Every question comes back to the dreamers.

Had I saved Nathaniel from madness, or worse, from an eternal sleep from whence he'd never awake? Or did I panic as the mentor implied, freeing Nathaniel before he could communicate with those magnificent minds?

The mentor was mistaken about the need for two—one to dream and the other to hold the fate of the first in their hands. Such a plan might have been wise before the day of reckoning, when the machine masters trusted their own genius, but now anyone at the controls would fear for the one they love and do as I did. Had the roles been reversed, Nathaniel would have done the same.

I know how to work the timers on my own, one for the delay to enter the cocoon and the other for the time in the dream. If I succeed, I may restore the power of the technos, build a new boat to sail home with mending machines and other miracles for my people, and prove to the greenies the dreamers still live, perchance stopping this war. Most of all, by sharing his experience, I may reclaim the man I love.

What else can I do? Kara is the new mentor, the only one who can master the machines. She needs to lead her people in this time of crisis. With the enemy at her gate, she won't risk entering the dream.

I have only one choice: use the automatic controls and enter the dream alone. With no one to hear my trials and prematurely end my time, I'll meet the dreamers to the benefit of all, or join them in their eternal slumber.

The ledger is complete, my decision made.

I pray this won't be my final entry.

***

I set down the pen and closed the log. The cabinets by the wall caught my eye, the store where the technos kept skins of sweet water and real food, bartered from the greenies. After a moment, I reached into those cabinets and filled my pack with provisions.

Still hesitant to leave, I stared up at the oval windows to the mountain fortress, now cloaked in darkness.

An image floated into my mind.

***

I imagined being trapped with Nathaniel and Thomas in the flying snake, what the keepmasters called a train. We whirled through the dark tunnel at unimaginable speed, the lights from inside casting blurred shadows off the walls as we passed.

The mentor rolled up and down the aisle, asking each of us where we were headed.

Thomas cried, "To Little Pond, where I belong."

Nathaniel shouted, "To the future."

I said, "To the keep."

The mentor stopped his chair beside me. "This train doesn't go to the keep."

"Then where does it go?" I said.

"To the dreamers."

"Will the train wait for me when I'm done, and bring both me and the dreamers back through the tunnel to my home?"

He sighed and shook his head. "This train only goes one way. Once you arrive at the dreamers, you'll be on your own."

DAVID LITWACK

***

I shook off the mood. I'd made such choices before: to betray the keepmasters or reveal the truth; to yield the location of the keep or lose Nathaniel forever; to face the stoning or run away.

Always Nathaniel had been at my side, but this time, I'd go into the void alone.

One final task remained. I tore a sheet of clean paper from my logbook, smoothed it on the tabletop, and raised the pen once more. Then I began writing in a large looping hand, so well-practiced from school, my script much nicer than the scrawl of the earth mother.

When finished, I folded the paper in half and addressed it, then removed my boots and tiptoed on bare feet back to our bedchamber. There, I rested the note on my pillow, with the words facing out, written bold and large, so they'd be easy to read:

My dearest Nathaniel....

Chapter 30

To the Mountain

At the rear of the commons, I hesitated before the stone guards, worrying they'd deny me access with the mentor gone. My nostrils still stung from the stench of the sand turned to glass. I took a long breath, inched forward, and toed the line. To my relief, a kinder ray scanned me as before, and the guards let me pass.

I raced through the dimly lit tunnel, not slowing to study the ancient wall carvings, knowing the trek up the mountain in the darkness would take much of the night. I needed to complete my task before Nathaniel and the others arose.

At the opening on the far end, I was met by a pelting rain. The full moon I'd counted on was hidden behind a layer of low clouds. As I groped in my pack for the electric torch, a flash of lightning lit up the sky, highlighting the domed peak ahead. It loomed above me, taunting as if to say that I, like the dreamers before me, would be humbled by its majesty.

No sooner did I set out than the rain fell harder. A wicked wind kicked up, blowing in my face as if to defeat my purpose. I leaned into it and slowed to a crawl, as the heavy rain cut off my vision and the path became a bog. Thankfully, the silver tunic of the machine masters kept me dry. Drops of water beaded on its surface and rolled off, splattering to the ground.

I pressed on. I'd been born cautious but was blessed with a stubborn will. Once I made a decision, nothing deterred me from my goal. I pressed on with no regard for rest. I'd have opportunity enough for rest if I succeeded. If I failed, rest would no longer matter.

By the time I reached the glade by the darkened lake, the weather had shifted in my favor. The storm had blown off to the east, leaving a sky spread with stars like diamonds on velvet. I paused a moment to quench my thirst with sweet water, and to nourish my spirit with a peek at the heavens. I relished the silky feeling of moonlight on my skin.

Then I set off again, quickening my pace and striding with a singular purpose. No time to wonder at the frozen river of lava or the fields of heather in bloom. No chance to ponder the statue of the grieving earth mother and mentor. Not a moment to marvel at the moonlight reflecting off the black doors.

I skidded to a stop at the line on the ground before the stone guards, and waited as they scanned me, seemingly more deliberate than before. At the gates to the keep, I'd been too young to be awed and too ignorant to be scared. Now I knew how great the risk.

At last, a grinding noise as the doors swung wide.

I ran past the snakelike garden of glass and the statues of giants supporting the sky, and dashed up the spiral stairs, taking them two at a time.

In the chamber of the dreamers, I found the golden image of the sun, planted both feet upon it, and raised my arms. No pretense needed. I'd been taught by the vicars since childhood to strike this pose in time of dire need—arms raised, palms outwards, and eyes lifted to the heavens.

The control platform appeared.

I drew in a breath and let it out slowly. Twin timers displayed before me, each with triple zeroes glowing. Beneath one, an image of a cocoon; beneath the other, a silver cloud. I waved my hand over the numbers with the cloud, as I'd done for Nathaniel.

The numbers flashed and changed—three hundred seconds.

Now, how many to allow before the cocoon closed, locking me into the dream? Three hundred? Too long. I might lose my nerve. Fifty? Too short. I might lack the time to get properly set.

I wiggled my fingers over the panel: a hundred seconds to the dream.

I bit down on my lower lip and forced my hand to pull the start lever, which responded by blinking with an ominous green glow. The first set of numbers flickered and began to count down.

Across the chamber, an open cocoon beckoned. I stepped up to it and scrambled inside. To my right, the red numbers flashed, a mirror of those on the control panel.

Eighty-two, eighty-one....

Next to the numbers, a switch jutted out, not a holo like the others, but solid. I fingered its cold metal—the mentor had called it an abort switch.

...Sixty-three, sixty-two....

I should have set a shorter time. I closed my eyes, and tried to clear my mind as I'd been taught, but they popped open, seemingly on their own.

...Twenty-one, twenty....

At ten, I squeezed my eyes shut and counted: *eight, seven, six....*

A dull whir, and the cover sealed me in with a thud.

"I love you, Nathaniel," I said aloud, praying these words would not be my last.

At first, no change—a malfunction, perhaps, a machine needing service like in the keep.

Then a twittering like birds stirring at dawn. The twittering deepened into a loud clicking, reminding me of a sound from years before.

***

One morning when I was little, I awoke to the strangest of sounds. I ran outside frightened, and found my grandfather standing by the sundial in our garden, staring at the woods and grinning.

"Do you hear them, Orah?" he said.

"Uh-huh."

"Soon, they'll be flying everywhere, incredible little creatures the size of your thumb, with orange eyes and gossamer wings too small for their bodies. They'll bump into you if you don't watch out."

"Are they creatures from the darkness?" I said, my voice quivering.

"Oh no, they're a wonder of nature. They live for only a few days, long enough to mate and lay eggs. Then they vanish. The wonder is that they won't return for another seventeen years."

"That sounds so sad," I said.

"Not sad, and surely not the vicar's view of the darkness. Just the way things are."

185

"If they live so short and die so soon, why are you smiling?"

His grin widened. "Because I've heard this sound only three times before, the first when I was not much older than you, and I never thought I'd live long enough to hear it a fourth time."

Together, we stood there and listened to the near-deafening chorus of clicks, implausibly made by insects the size of my thumb.

Finally, I turned to him. "Why do they make such a noise?"

"It's a way to call others to their side," he said, "to tell their kind they're yearning for them. That's not noise you're hearing, Orah. It's a love song."

***

Now, as I lay in the cramped cocoon, feeling like an insect myself, the piercing sound seemed anything but a love song. I tried to cover my ears, but my hands refused to move. In fact, I could no longer feel my hands at all. I sent a signal to my thumb to brush its pad to the tip of my index finger, and tried to wiggle my toes.

Nothing.

One thought screamed over the frantic clicking: *Find the abort switch and end this madness!*

But I had no eyes to find the switch. Darkness clung to me like a new skin. I sensed no glimmer save for the fading memory of what I'd once believed to be light.

I sought to slow my breathing but found no breath, as if I were over my head in some dense substance and afraid to breathe. But over my head in what? Not water but something deeper—time, old time and new time, all the time that had passed since the first thought, and the whole world, everyone who had ever lived, was holding their breath with me, the people, the animals, the trees and plants, all waiting, as if the universe depended on my mind for its existence.

Of course, these thoughts, these bits of lightning flashing in my brain, had been downloaded into a machine. I'd entered the dream.

The notion of being separate from my body terrified me, as if I might lose the essence of who I was. I focused on things of substance—earth, rocks, rivers of lava, or statues of stone—but no matter how weighty, every thought floated away. I imagined fleeing to a cave and digging a hole to hold my being together, to keep it from dispersing like the smoke in the earth mother's lodge. I feared if I stopped digging, I'd give up and die.

186

Worst of all, I began not to care; death no longer frightened me.

With that thought, a peace settled over me. So what if I'd lost my physical being? I'd gained something better: thought in its purest form. At once I recalled everything I'd ever experienced, anything I'd seen, touched or smelled.

I pictured my grandfather's face, etched with lines of age, as he explained to me the workings of the sundial and urged me to keep my first log, recording the movement of the sun.

I saw my father's face, with no lines at all because he died so young. I recalled his voice from his death bed, saying to me, "Now, little Orah, don't cry. You have a wonderful life ahead of you. Study hard in school and don't let the vicars set your mind. Think your own thoughts, big thoughts based on grand ideas, and find someone to love."

I recalled it all, not one memory at a time but all at once — everything I'd ever known.

But there was something more. I could now connect the pieces, like solving the puzzles I played with as a child. An infinite universe spread out before me, and infinity suddenly made sense. I envisioned what the keepmasters called our planet as if it were a ship sailing through the heavens. I watched curiously as the glowing blue ball dwindled into the distance.

Now that I could conceive of infinity, what I found most incredible was this: that anyone sitting on such a tiny planet in an ocean of infinite possibilities could have ever believed they understood anything about the nature of existence. The keepmasters and vicars, the earth mother and mentor, were all fools, children making up stories to scare one another in the dark.

I never wanted to be as small and foolish as them again.

Why would we be given a universe so vast and wonderful unless our minds were meant to grow to encompass it all? What was the purpose of consciousness if not what I was doing right now? The vicars had taught me we were meant to join with the light, but now I knew a greater purpose — to *be* the light, and to enhance it as if the light could only shine if I added my thoughts to it. Understanding infinity was not enough. I needed to become infinite myself, to leave behind all those who were finite. Even Nathaniel.

I recalled Nathaniel and our lives together as I might recall a lesson in arithmetic learned years before in school. He was but a fact from my

187

prior life, a detail, a moment in time. I had no space in my heart for him now. I had no heart at all.

My mind recoiled.

All my memories taken together constituted knowledge—a data bank as the mentor would say—but individually they had special meaning. I lovingly forced the memories apart, as I'd peeled apart the pages of my log after they'd become damp in a storm.

I focused on one lazy afternoon, the first warm day of spring in Little Pond, when Nathaniel, Thomas, and I played together as children. A May breeze bore pink blossoms from the nearby apple orchard, sending them tumbling down like snow, some settling on the water for a lazy float, and one coming to rest in my hair. Thomas squatted on a rock with the flute he'd so recently carved, testing each note though he'd not yet learned to play. Nathaniel stood tall on the banks, skimming flat stones on the surface to find out how many times they would skip. I sat on a log with my bare feet dangling in the pond, watching Nathaniel. After each toss, he'd glance my way for approval, and I'd smile.

I screamed above the infernal clicking, a voice without sound, a thought without words. *How can I forsake Nathaniel?*

What a fool I'd been to let myself be trapped in the dream! I'd set the timer for too long, an interval too much like forever.

Was this what had happened to Nathaniel? Though I was distinct from my body, was there still some spark resisting the loss? Was there a trace of humanity left behind causing my body to thrash and my feet to kick in a vain attempt to escape from the dream?

As I struggled to make sense of these swirling thoughts, the cacophony in my mind began to calm. The noise grew more distinct and less strident, not a clamor of clicks but a hundred minds speaking at once. Then the thoughts steadied, merging like a dwindling echo until they became a single repeated phrase.

There is a new mind among us.

The clicking stopped, and thoughts flowed not all together now, but one at a time.

"We have been waiting."

"When the other came...."

"...we failed to respond."

"Too eager...."

"We overwhelmed him."

"He fled so quickly."

"Now, we've trained...."

"...to focus our thoughts."

One by one they had their say, then silence. A pause. How long? A fraction of a second or eternity?

I waited.

At last, a single, unmistakable thought:

"Welcome, Orah of Little Pond. We've been expecting you."

Chapter 31

The Dreamers

I have no words to describe the dream, for it dwells in a realm without lips to speak or ears to hear, a wordless consciousness from a time before language. Concepts arrived whole, too complex to be limited by words, so I'll record what I experienced as a conversation between friends, like the way Nathaniel, Thomas, and I discussed the weighty matter of our future lives as we huddled together in the NOT tree.

***

"We knew one day another would join us," the unidentified speaker said, "and have devised a way to communicate with those unaccustomed to the pure mind. My colleagues are free to participate, but given your limited ability to comprehend so many simultaneous thoughts, they designated me as the spokesman. Do you come from the city?"

"Yes." I found it hard to limit my thoughts to a single word.

"Yet you are not one of us, neither earth person nor machine master. A cursory scan of your memories shows this. All but the most recent are alien to us, from a place we've never been."

"I come from the far side of the ocean."

Whenever the dreamers paused to deliberate, their thoughts surged like the buzzing of a beehive aroused by an intruder, a frenzy too intense to follow. These minds had communicated in this way for years, while I'd arrived minutes before, a newborn listening to the discourse of elders. I grasped at their thoughts as if trying to catch a butterfly with one hand.

The spokesman resumed. "Since you are not of our people, and none of them have come to restore us to our physical selves, may we assume they no longer exist?"

I winced as much as one can with no face. The question had been asked as a matter of curiosity rather than caring: *Did all those we knew and loved vanish from existence? A simple yes or no will suffice.*

"No, they're all alive, though not well, as trouble brews among them."

"Do you know what happened... why we have not been restored?"

"Yes."

More buzzing as the spokesman consulted with his colleagues. When his attention returned, his response unsettled me.

"We've established a protocol for a community of minds. All our thoughts can be shared, but we refrain from delving too deeply without permission, a way of respecting each other's privacy. May we visit your memories?"

A mental shudder. My innermost thoughts exposed, but for the chance to commune with the dreamers... I wordlessly agreed.

At once, many minds mingled with mine, a surprisingly pleasant sensation, like the inside of my brain being brushed by the wings of a hummingbird. The buzzing increased and then came back under control.

"The volcano, as we suspected...."

"One of our several hypotheses."

"With a high probability."

"But what of the trouble brewing?"

One word, many minds: "Caleb!"

"Our old colleague...."

"Not surprising."

"A bitter man...."

"Unable to forgive."

My mind flooded with images, too many to comprehend: a younger Caleb, a woman, a cocoon more primitive than the one I'd entered.

"Caleb's wife," I said.

"Yes, Rachel."

191

"A fine scientist...."

"And brave."

"A true pioneer."

"Gave her life for her research."

"Like those who first ventured to the stars."

A dark image filtered into my mind, a glass box no bigger than a teaching cell, but free-standing and upright. "What...?"

A single phrase echoed back: "Disintegration chamber."

Unlike the dreamers, I needed time to absorb what I'd learned, but before I could respond, the buzzing increased, like bees flitting from flower to flower, as they touched the furthest reaches of my mind.

"You have many other disturbing memories."

A second speaker. "Your vicars seem a pretentious and arrogant lot, but not especially competent."

Followed by a third. "How did you allow them to rule so long?"

I struggled to focus, amazed at how many competing concepts swirled at the same time.

"They lied to us," I said, "and used their knowledge of the past to control us, presenting it as...."

"Ah, we understand," the spokesman said. "As magic."

Another mind. "But still...."

My long suppressed memory surfaced, an unuttered cry of pain. "The teaching!"

A collective frown, the mental equivalent of a crumpled brow.

"Controlled thought," the spokesman said.

"Ideas enforced by fear."

"In our realm, the greatest sin."

"We often worried the same danger might befall our world."

More buzzing. A new discovery from my memory's vault. A single phrase repeated: "The keep."

Then thoughts directed at me.

"A repository of knowledge."

"A way to help others grow."

"A role we'd envisioned for ourselves."

"A chance to do some good."

"As if we were alive...."

The buzzing silenced as they waited for my response.

Had I been in my body, I would have taken three breaths in and out. Finally, I cast the thought into the void. "Are you alive?"

"A question we've pondered," the spokesman said.

Others followed in rapid succession—a dispassionate debate they'd apparently carried on before.

"What does it mean to be alive?"

"Is a body required?"

"Or is it enough to have purpose?"

"You who were recently connected to your body...."

"What does it mean to you?"

These elders, the wisest who'd ever lived, were asking me the ultimate question.

I concentrated my thoughts, thankful I'd left the living only seconds before. How sad to dwell in the dream so long that you forget how to feel.

"To have a purpose, yes, and to hope for the future. And...." Memories of Nathaniel surged in my mind. "To have someone to love."

The buzzing rose to a crescendo and settled.

I waited, for the first time wishing the ticking timer would slow down.

Finally, the buzz returned, but more tentative now.

"We have so many memories...."

"The older ones have moved to archive for efficiency."

"A slower form of storage."

"We'll retrieve them shortly."

Everything I described so far had been the thoughts of purely rational minds, but now I sensed a change. If the dreamers had eyes, they'd be glistening.

"Love. We remember."

"I sense in your most recent memory," the spokesman said, "someone still living... an image that almost matches one in my data bank... a girl but taller than the one I knew... so intense... and sad. What is her name?"

I channeled all my energy into a single word: "Kara."

The longest pause yet.

If I had a body, I'd be holding my breath.

"My daughter," the spokesman finally said. "How old is she?"

"Tomorrow, she'll be sixteen, a lovely and talented young woman. A leader."

Sixteen. The thought echoed among them.

"Time for you is a way of gauging the decline of your body, or measuring the journey to intersect others in physical space. It means nothing to us, but we understand mathematics. If Kara is sixteen now, then three of what you call years have elapsed, a significant percentage of your lives."

Suddenly, a deluge. Thoughts flew at me from many minds, names and images, as if I were meeting in heaven with those who had long since passed, desperate for news about their loved ones still on Earth.

I answered the best I could.

"Yes, Timmy. I know him. A fine child. Oh, the two redheads that greeted us to the city. What were their names?" I focused on their appearance, and their names echoed back: "Marissa, and Maisha."

Once all the questions had settled, a single plaintive thought remained: "In your memories of the city, I don't see my little boy."

An image flashed that I recognized at once—a boy, three years too young, but with the familiar locks of shaggy hair and eyes too big for his head.

"Zachariah. He's gone to live with the people of the earth."

"But... he was a child of machine masters, a brilliant boy."

"After that day...." I struggled to form the thought. "He ceased to speak and hasn't spoken since."

A subdued buzz. The dreamers' way of consoling a friend?

The same mind addressed me. "He spoke to me so clearly before I left for the mountain, a memory I marked as a priority in my archive—a farewell poem he'd composed, not knowing I would never return."

No living mother who'd lost her child could recite these lines without her voice cracking, but now the rhyme streamed complete and unimpeded into my mind. The others waited in silence as I received the farewell words of a six-year-old boy.

Sweet mother with eyes that shine
To the mountain, take my rhyme
Keep this poem so you will know
My mother, I love you so

Silence. An interval of respect.

If I were back in my body and had eyes, I'd be shedding a tear.

Rational as always, the dreamers turned from their loved ones to the task at hand. I did my best to answer their queries about all that had transpired since they vanished into the mountain. To them, news of the physical world was like nectar to bees.

Then, they in turn offered to answer my questions.

Images blossomed in my mind—the bonfire at festival, the balsam-draped NOT tree gleaming green in the snow, my mother's cottage, my father's grave. I wavered, worried they'd answer no, but if I failed to ask, we had no hope of returning.

"Can you design a boat," I said.

Invisible fingers probed my mind. Sympathetic thoughts echoed back: "Little Pond, her home."

Their response was calm, a matter of logic and science. "A simple engineering problem. You provide the eyes to measure and the hands to build. We will design a faster and better equipped vessel than the primitive one you crashed on our shores. But when you return, how will you solve your problems with the vicars and the keep?"

The time had come. Fearing the red numbers were ticking down to zero, I posed the question I'd saved, our reason for crossing the sea.

"I hoped you could help us learn and progress. If only we could bring back your knowledge, but I know it's too much to ask. Now that I've made contact, others will follow. How can I expect you to abandon your people?"

A high pitched buzz, the dreamers' attempt at laughter.

"We are electrical impulses in a machine, not so different from your helpers in the keep."

"...except we respond in real time...."

"...and are far more advanced."

"We can replicate these impulses to another storage device."

"...though we have neither hands nor eyes."

"We can teach you how to build such a machine."

Like the helpers in the keep, they'd answered my specific question, but I needed more than their presence; I needed a way to communicate with them.

"How will I speak with you?"

A pause, the mental equivalent of a hem and a haw.

"Hmmm... a more difficult challenge."

"The life support pods must be large enough to contain your body...."

"And require a great deal of energy."

"The power pack alone would be cumbersome."

"And portable life support would be risky...."

I envisioned the mentor's hat and Kara's bonnet, and they instantly grasped the thought.

"Of course. No need to join us in the dream."

"For you to be our sensors...."

"And for us to respond...."

"A more manageable problem."

They explained how they could design a device matched to an individual's brain waves, which would allow them to communicate, though the person themselves would not be in the dream.

"How sad to miss the wonders of an expanded consciousness...."

"Speaking to such a limited mind would be tedious...."

"The solution far from elegant."

"But will it work?" I said.

A brief pause, a cascade of thoughts so intense and intertwined that I followed none at all—the greatest minds of their age designing the answer to my request.

Finally, their thoughts quieted.

The speaker spoke. "The next time you visit, we will have plans for a new boat and a proposal for a portable repository for our minds, with an accompanying communication device."

"It will be a new purpose for us...."

"A way to touch the lives of the living...."

"A new purpose indeed."

The buzzing grew to its highest pitch yet, but this time the thoughts flowed in such unison that every word rang clear.

"Perhaps, in helping you," they said, "we might almost be alive."

***

A cough, a gasp for air.

I awoke to the cocoon cover creaking open—the most wondrous sound I'd ever heard. I drew in that first breath so eagerly my lungs nearly burst. Once my eyes adjusted to the light, I raised one hand high overhead and marveled at the way my fingers twirled. I pressed the pad of my thumb to each fingertip, relishing the touch of flesh on flesh.

As my vision cleared, I spotted a spider crawling across the window of the lid and followed its progress, recalling how I'd thought of myself as an insect, and Nathaniel too. I shivered, but not from the cold.

I inhaled through my nose and savored the familiar odor, sharp and metallic like air freshly cleansed by lightning in a storm. My lips parted, and I tasted it on my tongue.

Sounds came to me dully, as if a crowd was murmuring in the antechamber with their hands covering their mouths. I waited in the near silence, replaying what had happened, not wanting to lose a detail, praying it had been more than a dream.

After a time, I sat up and swung my legs over the edge, but remained wary of standing, still unsteady—like a sailor on a ship in a storm. My stomach growled and my lips were parched, as if I'd been in the dream not for minutes but days. Finally, I stretched my toes to the floor until they touched and eased to my feet, still grasping the lip of the cocoon so tightly my knuckles reddened and went white.

When I felt I could walk without falling, I let go, balancing with both arms spread and tottering like a child learning to walk. Once the room stopped spinning, I grabbed my pack and stumbled out of the chamber.

I staggered down the spiral staircase, clutching the handrail and resting flat-footed on each step before attempting the next. At the bottom, I stared up at the false heavens—a painted dome, nothing more, the giants supporting an illusion.

Yet still the questions remained.

Had I witnessed a miracle or blasphemy? Were these severed minds better off left wandering in the dream or granted their final rest? Why did I value their knowledge so highly, raising them up as saviors of our quest? Was I, as the arch vicar had once claimed, intoxicated by the fruit of the tree of knowledge? Had I become seduced by the darkness?

What if the arch vicar was right? What if the lust to learn more, the yearning to master the world, was a flaw in our nature, destined to lead to disaster? Perhaps behind our wise and caring eyes, we were nothing more than fanged creatures gazing out from the shadowy cave of our skulls.

I could still back off from the precipice, tell everyone I failed and allow Caleb to bring about the end of the dreamers. This side of the ocean would abandon their machines over time and, with our help, become more like Little Pond.

I shook my head, which made me dizzy, and waved a fist at the false heavens.

"No!"

What I experienced was real and mattered. I'd encountered beings wiser than any who'd gone before. Were they flawed? Of course, like all men, but they worked for the betterment of others and strove to be more than they were. Despite their flaws, they brought much good to their people. Perhaps with their help, Nathaniel and I might do the same.

More confident now, I passed through the anteroom with the garden of glass, another wonder not of science but of the creativity of the people of the earth.

The world needed both.

At last, I burst outside into the fresh air and collapsed on the top stair. By my hand, a lone dandelion flowered, sprouting from a crack in the stone, a prelude to the wild flowers that grew in the cracks of the keepmasters' ruined city. The stream gurgled nearby, while the surrounding forest held still. The gloom of night still cloaked the land as I glanced up at a misty sky, with clouds racing at unimaginable speed like a waking dream, scudding in front of a full moon.

I spun around to a hooting behind me. An owl perched on the shoulder of the earth mother's statue as she gazed at the black doors, still grieving. The cloud cover above me momentarily cleared and a moonbeam reflected off the owl's round eyes. Our gazes met for an instant before it took to the air, silently flapping its way to the horizon and beyond, taken by the night. As I followed its flight, I spread my lips into a broad smile, so pleased to find owls here too.

Just like the owls Nathaniel and I had marveled at, growing up as children in Little Pond.

Chapter 32

Would-Be Warriors

I gazed behind me at the black doors shuttered and closed, and at the stone guards indifferent to my fate. Above me, the clouds still raced, darkening the sky and then clearing to reveal a host of glittering stars, distant and more numerous than my diminished mind could fathom. The largest bloomed just over the horizon, shimmering tremulously white. I recognized that marker in the sky, the morning star, or as the keepmasters called it, Venus, a planet like our own. I wondered if the dreamers had traveled there.

Closer by, the mountain stream sang a soothing song, drawing me to it. I dragged myself over, the soles of my boots barely lifting off the ground, dropped my pack, and knelt to splash my face. The sparkling water, too high up to have been fouled by the people below, brought blood back to my skin, cleansing and purifying me. Once I revived, I cupped both hands and drank, hoping to soothe the burning in my throat, the water so cold it made my teeth ache.

A deep sigh—not a moment more to contemplate the universe, not a minute to admire the view. I had to get back to the city and tell Nathaniel and Kara what I'd found. The dreamers had already suffered one tragedy. I prayed I might stop another.

I set off at a steady pace but not for long. My silver tunic protected me from the night air, but a clammy sweat had formed on my skin from my time in the cocoon. A chilling wind blew down my neck and into my face, making my eyes tear.

199

As I descended below the tree line, the moonlight bleached the boughs of the pines on either side of the trail into a ghostly sheen, but the path beneath them lay shrouded in darkness. Wary of tripping on a tree root and taking a fall, I slowed to a crawl. After a few minutes of stumbling around, I slipped off the pack and withdrew the mentor's torch. I switched it on to no avail—its light, like me, had dimmed. So I trudged along, bending low to read the pine-needle strewn ground.

Gradually, even the moonlight vanished beneath the thick canopy of leaves. My pace became more labored as a bone-weariness overcame me. At the next clearing, I collapsed under a beech tree, nearly as broad as the one that guarded the center of the greenie village, and folded the pack beneath my head.

A brief nap, I told myself as my eyelids drifted closed... nothing more.

***

I awoke with a start to the first rays of the sun. Though not fully rested, I scrambled to my feet and began jogging down the trail.

My senses sharpened as I ran, and I saw the world anew. The branches sparkled, their leaves pulsed with green. The tall grass tickled my bare legs, their tips still damp with dew. An apple tree in bloom gave off a perfume that mingled with the raw dampness of the woods. A newly sprouted blossom brushed my face and left its silky kiss on my cheek. Birds raised their voices to greet the dawn.

How wonderful the stirrings of life all around me. How utterly amazing to be alive.

By the time I reached the field of heather, sunbeams spilled across the meadow, setting the wildflowers aglow and making the stream shine like a silver ribbon looping down the slope. I traced it as it wound along the path all the way to the tunnel that formed the back entrance to the machine masters' city.

What I saw made the hair on the back of my neck stand on end— the dark shapes of men trudging up the mountain, fifty or more bent low under the weight of their tools.

Caleb's men had broken through.

What should I do? They'd reach the fortress within hours. The stone guards would keep them at bay, but with so many strong arms wielding picks and shovels, they'd soon find a way through. The dreamers' knowledge gave them tremendous strength, but without allies among the living, they remained powerless in the physical world.

I imagined a zealous Caleb smashing cocoons and demolishing the devices that sustained those minds. I could confront him with proof that the dreamers live, and beg his forbearance, but I'd learned from the vicars—fanatics rarely listen to reason.

Or I could crouch in the bushes until they passed, and then race down to fetch Nathaniel, Kara and the others, but to what end? A battle between strong men with axes and young technos with machines? No winners there—nothing but a new eruption of sorrow.

As I pondered, I caught a second column of would-be warriors emerging from the mouth of the tunnel. I squinted, trying to bring them into focus. Their faces were too far off to recognize, but I couldn't mistake the repair machines rumbling on their treads, kicking up dust over the uneven terrain—Kara and her children's army, marching into battle.

Of course, the mentor's spying eyes would have transmitted images to Kara's bonnet, revealing the zealots' breakthrough and forcing her to muster her troops.

A quick intake of breath—Nathaniel must be with them. He would have read my note by now. When he found me missing, he'd join with Kara. If the two enemies met, he'd fight by her side.

I set off with a purpose, feeling like the morning we headed into the Little Pond commons to confront the vicars, while our neighbors waited in their ceremonial robes, clutching stones in their hands. Now, as then, I had no choice.

At the point of a switchback, I scampered up a rock outcropping to spy on the landscape below. At last, I distinguished the techno column tramping up the mountain, about two dozen older children and their machines, with some unknown figures straggling behind.

But where had Caleb's men gone?

I narrowed my focus, tracing each segment of the trail. By the darkened lake, I caught movement in the trees on either side of the path.

I'd spotted the technos from above. Caleb would have done the same. He'd dispersed his men, concealing them in the woods to set up a trap.

To the darkness with exhaustion, and caution be damned... I took off at a sprint.

The trees on the sides of the trail blurred as I ran past, and the path ahead tapered into a tunnel with a single endpoint—the clearing by the darkened lake. They wouldn't expect someone coming from higher ground. I hoped to surprise them, to burst through their ranks as they stared down the slope. Barring that, I might create enough of a clamor to warn Nathaniel and the others.

As I neared the clearing, my heel gave way on the loose scree, sending pebbles skidding down the trail.

Several zealots turned. For the briefest of moments, they hesitated, surprised by this apparition dashing down the mountain.

Before they grabbed me, I let out a scream. "Nathaniel! Kara! Beware!"

I was now in their grasp, but the deed was done.

Moments later, Kara entered the clearing behind a well-formed wedge of machines, flanked by the tallest boys with sticks pointed at the ready.

As both sides eyed each other, I pulled away from my captors and stepped in between, spinning in circles and pointing up the mountain. "I've been there. I met with the dreamers."

Caleb waved me off and addressed his men. "What she says makes no difference. She found nothing but delusion."

"You don't understand," I said. "They're aware, alive, and eager to help."

Caleb came closer, towering over me, but Nathaniel burst from the ranks of the repair machines to block his way.

From around Nathaniel, the zealot leader glared at me, his feet spread wide and his fingers curled into fists, the posture of impending battle. "Did they speak or breathe or move?"

I shook my head. "But I merged with their minds."

He turned to his men, who fingered their tools nervously. "How could she tell between the thoughts of the dreamers and those of her own imagination? Those who go into the dream become easily confounded?" He gestured to Kara. "Therein lies madness."

"My parents dwell there," Kara shouted back, "and you will not harm them!"

"Who'll stop us? A bunch of arrogant children with their toys?"

Kara glared back at him, her whole body quivering with rage. "We'll soon find out who is arrogant and who is ignorant."

She closed her eyes, and a low hum came from the repair machines, almost a growl. Their treads stirred and they inched forward.

Caleb signaled to his men, who raised their tools high and stamped their feet, edging toward Nathaniel and me.

"Stop!"

A gravelly voice sounded from down the trail. All heads turned to watch a half-dozen people bearing a pale and weary earth mother on a litter.

Both technos and greenies paused their quarrel out of respect for this woman, the last of her generation.

The litter bearers set her down between the warring parties. With Devorah and Jacob's help, she struggled to her feet, looking older than I'd seen her before.

Annabel, the earth mother, former colleague of the machine masters I'd met in the dream, placed a hand over her heart as if to calm its beating, and spoke between breaths. "I never thought I'd climb so high again. I'd forgotten how beautiful the mountain is." She turned to Kara. "I'm sorry for the loss of your grandfather. Though William and I disagreed on many matters, he was my friend and always did his best for his people. I see you've taken on his mantle. May you wear it as wisely as him."

Her knees buckled, and Devorah rushed to her side. Once she steadied, with one arm draped around the younger woman, she redirected her attention to the leader of the zealots.

"What now, Caleb? Is this what I taught you, to raise your hand against your fellow humans? Haven't you learned we are all people of the earth?"

Caleb scowled. "It's not I who raised my hand. We were only doing what you and I both know to be right. You preach that the day or reckoning was the earth's way of setting things straight, that to download one's soul into a machine is wrong. You say the essence of the dreamers has flown, and keeping what remains imprisoned in electronics is an abomination. For the good earth's sake, three years have passed. My men and I were on a mission of mercy to set them free."

Kara pressed between her machines and stepped within striking distance of Caleb's axe, unconcerned for her safety. "Set them free? You mean kill them, because their essence lives on. Orah merged with their minds."

The earth mother turned to me as fast as her weary body allowed. "Is this true, child."

I nodded.

"A foolish and dangerous errand! I'm happy you survived. Tell me what you found."

I glanced at Nathaniel, who stared back at me with a mixture of fury and relief.

"I shared their thoughts," I said. "I met Kara's parents and others. They've taken on a communal identity and are distanced from their physical selves, but they retain their memories and knowledge. They think, they plan, they design, and they seek a purpose, if only they could partner with the living. They can help us make a better world."

Caleb spat on the ground. "Words, nothing more. A fantasy she made up to give hope to these children, just as their mentor had done before. How do we know it's true?"

I stepped closer and softened my expression, fixing him with my eyes until he could no longer look away. "They told me about your Rachel, how she gave her life for the research into the dream. How in those early days, they failed to restore her mind to her body. How in the end, they...."

Tears glistened in Caleb's eyes, but his hands trembled with rage. "They failed to restore...? They defied the laws of nature, tempting her to become their test case. My dear Rachel. For thirty days, I sat by her side as she stared back at me with no mind behind those eyes. Then, despite my pleas, the council decided to end it. They brought her still breathing body to the disintegration chamber like a piece of trash, a failed experiment, a mistake."

The earth mother brushed Caleb's arm. "So that's why you came to us with such rage, why you never told us what happened. What more proof do you need? These living minds have revealed your wife's tale to Orah."

Caleb spat on the ground. "Nothing but a trick. The mentor knew what had happened. He served on the council that voted to end her life. Though reluctant to share his shame with the children, he would have told these two—a way to deceive us. She has no proof. Her claim changes nothing."

Kara dug her fingernails deeper into her palms, and bared teeth that seemed to grow longer. "I'll bring you proof if you clear the way, and let me go into the mountain."

"You'll never reach there."

"How do you plan to stop our machines, the power created by the genius of my forbearers?"

The machines roared to life behind her. Their arms and pincers snapped to the ready, and the turrets that cast the red rays swiveled and aimed at the zealots.

In response, axes and hammers were raised, picks and shovels poised.

Caleb lunged at Kara, but Nathaniel and I blocked his way.

A blur flashed from behind. The silent boy, Zachariah, slipped in front in a foolhardy attempt to protect me.

Caleb froze in mid-stride. "Move aside, boy. My fight is not with you."

Time slowed as I watched Zachariah try to defend me, his slight frame no stouter than one of Caleb's thighs. At once, I was back in the dream. Out of so many memories, a special one came to me, a gift from the dreamers.

I squatted and took Zachariah by the arms, turning him to face me so I gazed into eyes too big for his head. They'd changed little since he was six.

"I met them, Zachariah, your parents. They asked about you."

At that moment, the sun broke above the treetops, and a lone beam fell across the boy's face. His lower lip trembled, but he remained silent.

Then the words came to me, words never spoken but passed directly into my mind. "Your mother said you wrote a poem for her before she left for the mountain, one you read to her aloud. Do you remember?"

The boy blinked. Was that a hint of a nod?

"She told me what you wrote, but my poor memory fails me. I can only remember the first line. If I recite it, will you tell me the rest?"

I stood upright, cleared my throat, and raised my chin so everyone would hear. "Sweet mother... with eyes... that shine...."

I closed my eyes and recalled Nathaniel's voice beaming from the sun icon on that grim morning in Little Pond. I saw my neighbors with their fingers twitching around stones, much as Caleb's fingers now twitched around the handle of his axe. I prayed to the true light, wherever and whatever it might be. I prayed for a miracle.

Please, Zachariah. Help me.

Then suddenly, the sweetest of voices arose, one I'd heard before only in song.

> *"Sweet mother with eyes that shine*
> *To the mountain, take my rhyme*
> *Keep this poem so you will know*
> *My mother, I love you so."*

I opened my eyes to find the boy's face streaked with tears.

Caleb's axe trembled in his thick hands and dropped to the ground with a thud.

Kara's repair machines stilled.

And the earth mother clapped her hands and laughed, a sound like a mountain stream.

Chapter 33

The People of the Earth

We, the eight pallbearers, shuffled together in time, left foot, then right.

The earth mother had convinced Kara to adopt the new tradition for burying the dead. Kara and Devorah walked in front followed by Nathaniel and I, then two of the older techno children and a pair of Caleb's men who, at the earth mother's request, had volunteered.

Many others had been needed to carry the mentor's lanky body down the rugged terrain from the city to the greenie village.

Despite the effort, Kara admitted the trek helped ease the pain and gave her time to say goodbye—better than flipping a switch on a machine.

When we reached the village, the people of the earth wrapped the remains in a ceremonial robe made from sheepskin, and covered it with a blanket of day lilies and a sprinkling of blue bells. Then we formed a solemn procession to the graveyard. Those not bearing the body carried a single apple blossom cupped at their waist, all except for Zachariah, who clutched a bouquet of daisies.

At the woodland glade, with dappled sunlight streaming through the canopy of leaves, we placed the mentor on a stout platform, more ornate than the others, with scrolls at the corners, carved to perfection by Jacob.

The earth mother turned to him. "Such beautiful work in so little time. Will you do the same for me someday?"

"Of course, earth mother, but not for many years." He smiled back and winked. "More likely, you'll outlive me."

She laughed the throaty, full-bodied laugh that had so enamored her to me when we first met. "Oh dear, I hope not." She turned to Kara. "It's our custom for anyone who knew the departed to say a few words. Will you speak for your grandfather?"

Kara swept away a lock of hair that had fallen across her eye and opened her mouth, but no sound emerged.

"Why don't I speak first while you gather your thoughts?" The earth mother placed both hands palms-down on the blanket of flowers. "My childhood friend, William, whom I will soon join. A brilliant mind, matched by a kind heart. Your elder years, like mine, should have been a time of reflection and peace, but that awful day came and thrust us both into reluctant roles. Each of us chose a different path, but we did the best we could for our people. Rest well, mentor to the young and dear friend."

Kara stepped forward next. "My mentor and grandfather...." She blinked back tears. The earth mother came to her side and rested a hand on her shoulder, helping to steady her. "You cared for me when my parents were gone. You taught me how to lead. I'll always have my memories of you, and thanks to you, the memories of my parents as well."

Nathaniel and I both spoke, but as outsiders, we kept our words brief, mostly thanking the mentor for believing in us and preserving the miracle of the dreamers.

After the speeches finished, everyone bowed their heads and whispered their private farewells. A breeze blew through the glade, sending white petals from a surrounding honey locust floating to the ground like snow. Those mourners with apple blossoms lined up to place their flowers on the grave. At the end, Zachariah handed out a single daisy to each of the pallbearers so we too could pay our respects—greenies and technos, Nathaniel and I, Devorah, and last of all, Kara.

As I watched the mentor's granddaughter linger over his remains, I realized the earth mother's vision had come to pass—the former enemies joining together to bear the mentor to his final rest.

***

The following months brimmed with energy and hope, though to my chagrin, they kept Nathaniel and me apart more than the arch vicar's prison cell ever did.

Nathaniel took charge of building the new boat. The dreamers had concocted the design, a vessel that could carry more passengers, sail across the ocean in a fraction of the time, and guide us around storms with precision.

In the beginning, he balked at reentering the dream, but I reassured him, promising to monitor the controls and limit his stay. Gradually, he ventured deeper into the minds of the machine masters and received a section of the plans—the whole design was far too complex to digest at once. Then he hiked down the mountain, past the greenie village to the shore, and supervised the construction.

Jacob became his right-hand man, translating the design into a series of manageable tasks and providing the expertise to transform plans into reality.

Caleb's men provided the muscle.

I was surprised at the vigor with which the former zealots supported our efforts. Yes, they were among the strongest and most adept with tools, but I suspected most of all, they needed a new outlet for their zeal.

I spent my time learning how to create a device to hold the replicated minds of the dreamers, one we could bring with us on the boat, a new and more portable keep—and far more advanced. I felt the same shortcomings as I had in my lessons with the techno children. Despite sharing minds with the greatest of the machine masters, the concepts involved proved beyond my ability. I had difficulty remembering anything when my thoughts returned to my brain, so I leaned heavily on Kara, who joined me in the dream. After weeks of study, the device took shape, a new temple of knowledge and hope for the future, what Kara dubbed the dream machine.

But boats are built by the shore and dream machines high on the mountain, so Nathaniel and I spent long days apart.

After several weeks with little time together, he was readying to enter the dream again to receive plans for what the machine masters called the propulsion system.

I proposed to join him, a chance to share minds.

Kara assured him it was safe and promised to monitor the controls.

The result was less dramatic than expected. We already knew each other so well, and kept no secrets from the other, but the reaction of the dreamers surprised me.

***

"Welcome, Nathaniel," the speaker said, "and a second mind, Orah."

The buzzing rose to a crescendo, their way of showing their enthusiasm for something new and stimulating..

"Why the excitement?" I said. "You've merged with each of us before."

"Ah, yes," the speaker said, "but never the two at once."

"Such thoughts," another said.

"...and passion."

"...a feeling difficult for us to sustain...."

"...without being together in the physical world."

The buzzing silenced, followed by a long pause. Then the voices of the machine masters combined into a single phrase, a thought so strong it echoed in unison.

"How we envy you."

***

Kara and I entered the dream together dozens of times. I became comfortable communing with the dreamers, an admittedly strange and exhausting sensation, like meeting the helpers in the keep, but more flexible. These helpers could respond to my most ignorant and poorly worded questions, and often responded with questions of their own, ones I'd never thought of.

Kara's reunion with her parents seemed both less and more than she expected. With no eyes to cry or arms to embrace, their time together lacked affection, but she treasured their shared memories. She told me she'd never before appreciated the love of a parent for a child.

Gradually, she introduced several of the older technos to the dream. She'd learned her lesson from the mentor—leading was too painful to bear the burden alone. As any good leader would, she made sure to train those who would follow.

I later discovered she had an additional motive.

The two of us worked with the machine masters to design the device that would hold a replica of their minds.

"The concept is simple," Kara said. "We'll copy the sum of their impulses, the bits of lightning that constitute their thoughts and memories, into a second machine. The hard part will be to improve on this first generation, to create something smaller that can withstand the rigors of travel on the ocean."

My head swan, the concept far from simple to me. "Then will there be two of them, like... twins on either side of the sea?"

"Not exactly. At the instant the copy is made, their memories will be the same, but these minds are alive and will continue to learn. Everything they think after the split, all their interactions with us, will be unique to the second machine."

"Do they become different people then?"

The corners of her eyes sagged. "Not people. They have the memories of those who once lived and the ability to think, but their only input from the physical senses will be what they learn from our visits. This new device will be the most powerful thinking machine ever built, but it will need us to be its eyes and ears."

My brows arched and my mouth opened into an O, but no worlds came out. I understood the benefit such a device might provide—the invention of more useful tools, an end to hunger and disease, miraculous medicines far beyond what I had once believed to be temple magic.

How would it all work?

I'd quell my curiosity for now. Kara knew more of their science as a six-year-old than I would ever know, even if I spent my whole life studying in the keep. I'd take the rest on faith.

But the thought of being the sole proprietor of this thinking machine terrified me.

***

One time, when Kara and I entered the dream, she invited me to join her deepest thoughts, a privacy protocol the dreamers had established out of respect for each other.

"When I let down this barrier," she said, "you'll know me at a deeper level than anyone else living."

I heard no crash of thunder, saw no flash of blinding light, but my mind flooded with memories: Kara as a small child with her parents; the day they left for the mountain; her pleading to go with them; the pain of their loss.

Yet one image struck me above all.

I saw the two of us on the bow of our new ship as vividly as if it were happening now. In the distance, the familiar granite mountains rose up from the fog.

"How can this be," I said. "Your memory of Little Pond is exact, though you've never been there?"

"The image is from your memory, not mine."

"But the two of us on the boat...?"

"That's no memory," she said. "It's an aspiration."

"...that can only happen if...."

"...I go with you."

"But...."

"No argument. What survives of my family will remain with me. I've trained the new leaders to merge with the dreamers, so they can help this side of the world, but to help your people, you'll need someone who understands the repository of dreams. You'll need me by your side."

Chapter 34

Going Home

The day dawned clear with a blue sky and an offshore breeze, perfect conditions to launch our new ship, with its gleaming metallic sail rising proudly above the deck.

Caleb's men scurried up the gangplank, lugging the last provisions and storing them in the hold—berries that would last but a few days; smoked fish that would last much longer; flat bread baked from the first harvest of wheat; and casks of sweet water produced in abundance by desals, now fully controlled by the minds of the machine masters' children.

Though our dreamer-designed ship would complete the voyage in half the previous time, we needed more supplies with so many joining us onboard.

Devorah and Jacob had insisted on coming, eager to study with the best craftsmen on our side of the world.

Too my surprise, Caleb joined us as well, along with Jubal and several others. He asserted we might have need for their muscle in case of unforeseen problems, especially if the children of light proved to be as weak-willed as the machine masters or the people of the earth.

I suspected his motivation lay elsewhere, that he longed to leave behind his grief and find a new cause.

Kara came as she'd promised, but she ordered the other techno children to stay behind. They were so few, and they had a great deal to learn if they hoped to one day reestablish their mastery over all the machines.

I decided to bring Zachariah along. Even before he found his voice, he'd insisted on staying by my side. Now that he could talk, he gave neither me nor the earth mother peace until we agreed to let him go.

At Nathaniel's suggestion, the technos built a replica of the mending machine, which we stored safely in the hold, cushioned by foam packing in a wooden crate. This would provide our people back home the first tangible benefit from our journey across the sea.

Several smaller packages clustered alongside it, devices that Kara insisted on bringing along. She'd spent the past few weeks scavenging, salvaging parts from spare machines, anything she deemed potentially useful and portable.

I asked their function, but she merely waved her hands. "Pincers and turrets from the repair machines, projectors for holos from my grandfather's work chamber. Whatever I thought might come in handy. One never knows."

Of course, we also brought our most important cargo—or passengers; I remained unsure what to call them—the repository of the dreamers' minds. The remarkable black cube had been secured to the deck with thick ropes and encased in a waterproof container. As had been the case with much in the keep, the device was powered by the sun.

I danced around it and touched its slick surface like an old friend, feeling its energy tingling on my fingertips. When I gazed inside, a billion bolts of lightning flashed back, a cosmic storm in the depths of a seemingly infinite universe, the accumulated knowledge of all humankind.

On a whim, I pressed my ear to it; nothing but a faint buzzing. Kara had made me a bonnet like hers, which the dreamers adjusted to my brain waves, so the two of us could communicate with them. I'd tested it numerous times, a wondrous experience, but much less demanding than the dream. My mind stayed limited, as always, but I could take advantage of their knowledge, like the helpers in the keep, but wiser.

I breathed a sigh. So many years working to make a better world, and here before me lay my greatest hope.

The day was drawing to a close. We needed to shove off soon, before the ebb of the tide.

Annabel, the earth mother, was too frail to travel with us, but with Devorah's help, she climbed on board to make her goodbyes. She nodded to everyone, kissed each of her people on the cheek, and bid them safe voyage. Then she and all those not sailing scrambled off the boat.

Caleb and three others cast aside the gangplank, which landed on the shore with a dull and final thud.

In the light of near-dusk, I glanced up the mountain to the village, the city, the fortress of the dreamers, and beyond, to the mountaintop crowned with snow. The sun was sinking behind its western wall. For a breathless moment, the distant dome seemed to burn with flames. Then the slope below it became blanketed in shadow as night poured down across the land. A sea breeze kicked up and blew hair across my face. Somewhere a nightingale warbled a farewell song.

Time stood still as I looked out over the crowd, greenies and technos alike, former enemies who joined to send us off.

As we readied to weigh anchor, the earth mother called out from the shore. "Zachariah, will you grace us one last time with your song."

"Not the last time, earth mother," he said. "I'll sing again when I return."

"Ah, yes," she said. "Of course."

She winked at me, a gesture of shared knowledge. She'd aged so much in the time since we'd crashed on her shore; though Zachariah might return someday, they may never meet again.

Nathaniel hoisted the boy on his shoulders for all to see.

Though I'd become accustomed to hearing his voice, I remained in awe of its sound when he sang.

As I listened, the myth of the song changed to fact. I studied the faces of our crew, seekers all, and pictured our little band of three — myself, Nathaniel, and Thomas — setting out to the keep, younger then and so much more innocent. I recalled the moment I first showed the vicars a helper on a screen, and watched their faces blossom with wonder at the recording of a wise man from what they'd once believed to be the darkness.

The final verses of the song wafted away with the sea breeze, as if we'd already left the shore.

> Until a sailing ship arrives
> From the ocean's farthest side
> It comes to us upon the wind
> Bringing hope with the morning tide
> ~~~
> The ship sails in upon the waves
> With those who'll show the way

And all the children of mother earth
At last learn how to pray

Nathaniel set the boy down and came to my side, and we stood arm in arm on the deck, watching the land recede. On shore, an ascendant moon reflected off the white sand, and lit up his face with a radiance that seemed to draw from some fire deep within. His eyes sparkled with a look so intense that I would have fallen in love with him again... if only love did not already possess every fiber of my being.

Epilogue

I startled awake, embarrassed to have shirked my duty. On this night, our third of the voyage home, I'd volunteered to stand watch until sunrise, but as I admired the stars and listened to the waves breaking over the bow, a gentle breeze had sent me drifting off to sleep.

Perhaps my failure had been preordained, because while I slept, Thomas once again joined me in a dream. This time, we visited in a cell in the underground prisons of Temple City. He hunched cross-legged on the cot, looking more comfortable than in the teaching cell but no happier.

I sat sideways on the edge of the chair, with one arm draped across its top.

"Back again," he said.

"How could I stay away?"

"So was the long voyage worth it?"

I paused to consider—a question I'd been asking myself these past three days at sea.

"Yes," I finally said, though our quest was far from done. I'd always tried to put on my best face for Thomas, ever since we were little.

"Did you cause as much of a fuss over there as you did on our side of the ocean?"

"Oh, I think so. We found two groups, remnants of the same cataclysm we used to call the darkness. They held views so different only an outsider could appreciate the depth of the chasm between them—like the gap between the vicars and the keepmasters."

"Did they have deacons?"

"No, nothing so awful, but the first group, the people of the earth, rejected all things created by man and not provided by nature."

"Even musical instruments?" He pulled out the flute from his pocket and tooted a note or two.

"No, you're right. Not all things created by man, only those requiring a machine."

"Like your loom?"

I brushed a lock of hair from my eye and tucked it behind my ear. "You're confusing me, Thomas, as usual."

He laughed. "That's my purpose in life, to confuse all those who become too sure of themselves." His grin settled into a frown as he eyed the locked door of his cell. "I only wish the vicars appreciated my talent. What strange notions did the other side believe?"

"The machine masters? They believed in science and the power of reason to make a better world."

"Like you?"

I stared at my fingernails and scrunched my brow. Thomas was always one to challenge my beliefs.

"Yes," I said, "and no."

"Don't speak in riddles. I'm too tired and hungry. The deacons don't let me sleep much, and they never bring enough food."

I considered my response, longing to consult with the black cube that lay on the deck near where I slept, but this was a different kind of question—one with no right answer.

"Each side had some good and some bad." I chose my words carefully, as much as possible while dreaming. "Each took their beliefs too far and hardened in their ways, leaving no space to understand the other. The people of the earth produced things of beauty, arts and crafts that nurtured the soul, but they'd lost the ability to feed and clothe themselves, or to heal their sick. The machine masters were brilliant in their pursuit of knowledge, far beyond the keepmasters, but they'd abandoned their sense of wonder."

"Then why didn't they just stay apart?"

"Why do you ask such hard questions?"

"Because you're so good at answering them."

I sighed. "They clashed, I think, because they were too busy judging each other. The people of the earth mocked the machine masters as technos and thought they'd become heartless, like their machines. They viewed all techno accomplishments as an abomination and their learning as evil, what the vicars might call a path to the darkness."

"And the machine masters?"

"Their children studied all day, striving to master the knowledge of their parents. Those who failed were cast off and sent down the mountain to live with the others, the ones they called greenies. They considered the greenie beliefs nonsense, like the babblings of a child."

Thomas unfolded his legs, stood, and stretched his arms over his head, clearly pleased to no longer be trapped in the cramped confines of the teaching cell. "What a challenge, like trying to make friends with the deacons or change the vicars' minds. How did you bring them together?"

"They had more in common than they realized. Both sides worried about their future. All of them loved their children and grieved for their dead."

"So they made peace?"

"Of sorts, but like us, they need help. The people of the earth have moved beyond their biases. The machine masters have seen the light, pausing in their rush to knowledge to appreciate the miracles around them, things more ethereal and hard to explain."

I gazed up, yearning to see through the pock-marked ceiling of the cell to the dark dome of the sky. The voice of Annabel, the earth mother, echoed in my mind: "We are the stuff of stars."

"So what's next?" Thomas said, his voice quivering as if he feared the answer. "You and Nathaniel are never content as long as the world remains imperfect."

I stood from my chair and approached him, my arm extended, but stopped before touching him, afraid to discover what I knew—that he was nothing but a dream.

"I'm bringing back helpers," I said, "far wiser than the keepmasters, and alive. At least, alive enough to converse and not just respond with silly answers if you ask the wrong question."

Thomas dropped to the floor as if he'd been poleaxed and buried his face in his hands.

"What are you doing?" I cried.

"Getting set to go back to the teaching cell, where I'll be headed once you return."

"But why?"

He looked up at me, the rims of his eyes red, and for the first time I realized how gaunt he'd become. "You still don't understand. Before you left, many had become disillusioned with the keep and, like your greenies, longed for a simpler time. Others wanted more, to harvest the keepmasters' knowledge. One side now advocates destroying the keep, while the other vows to defend it with their lives. Into this mess, you'll bring your techno science, mixed with the greenies' new way of thinking about the light. Don't you see? You're bringing dry kindling to fire. Use your brain, Orah. Will you make the world better or destroy it?"

I gaped at him as he huddled in the dust. My fondest wish had been to return to Little Pond with fresh knowledge to make a better world. Now I couldn't help but wonder: if the vicars found the keepmasters abhorrent, what would they make of the dreamers?

Thomas glanced up at me. "If only they'd just learn to make music like me. Look at this flute. It too is a kind of machine. The spacing of its holes is based on mathematics I learned in the keep, but it possesses magic nevertheless. Listen, and tell me if I'm wrong."

He raised the flute to his lips and began to play the same haunting melody he'd played as we camped high up over the lake on our way to the keep. His music was magic, indeed.

Suddenly, the melody was interrupted by the sloshing of the sea, and a cold spray from the bow splashed across my cheek. My vision blurred, and Thomas faded to a shade as pale as ocean fog. I reached out to grab him but lunged too late.

A bitter breeze blew through the cell, and he floated away.

"I'm coming Thomas," I shouted after him. "I'll be home soon."

As he vanished from view, I startled awake on the hard deck, soaked from the spray, with a troubling question rattling around in my mind.

What will I find when I get there?

THE END

Acknowledgements

From start to finish, a novel is an enormous amount of effort and would not be possible without a great team. It starts with my beta readers, including the members of my writing group, The Steeple Scholars from the Cape Cod Writers Center, and continues with Lane Diamond, Dave King, and John Anthony Allen. It finishes with the wonderful formatting and cover art of Mallory Rock. Through it all, the encouragement of others kept me going, my friends and family, including my dear wife, who has put up with my writing aspiration through the good and bad years. Finally, I want to acknowledge my readers, who are, after all, the reason I write, and especially for prodding me to make the first book into a trilogy. So many of you wanted to know what happened to my characters, that I was compelled to give them life once more. Orah and Nathaniel are grateful.

About the Author

The urge to write first struck when working on a newsletter at a youth encampment in the woods of northern Maine. It may have been the night when lightning flashed at sunset followed by northern lights rippling after dark. Or maybe it was the newsletter's editor, a girl with eyes the color of the ocean. But I was inspired to write about the blurry line between reality and the fantastic.

Using two fingers and lots of white-out, I religiously typed five pages a day throughout college and well into my twenties. Then life intervened. I paused to raise two sons and pursue a career, in the process becoming a well-known entrepreneur in the software industry, founding several successful companies. When I found time again to daydream, the urge to write returned.

My wife and I split our time between Cape Cod, Florida and anywhere else that catches our fancy. I no longer limits myself to five pages a day and am thankful every keystroke for the invention of the word processor.

You can find me at my website www.DavidLitwack.com, where I blog about writing and post updates on my current works. I'm also on Twitter @DavidLitwack and Facebook Facebook.com/david.litwack.author. If you'd like quarterly updates with news about my books, my works in progress, and my thoughts on the universe, please sign up for my newsletter.

What's Next?

THE LIGHT OF REASON
(The Seekers – Book 3)
By David Litwack

Watch for the third and final book in *The Seekers* dystopian sci-fi series, coming November 2016.

~~~~~

Orah and Nathaniel return home with miracles from across the sea, hoping to bring a better life for their people. Instead, they find the world they left in chaos.

A new grand vicar, known as the usurper, has taken over the keep and is using its knowledge to reinforce his hold on power.

Despite their good intentions, the seekers find themselves leading an army, and for the first time in a millennium, their world experiences the horror of war.

But the keepmasters' science is no match for the dreamers, leaving Orah and Nathaniel their cruelest choice—face bloody defeat and the death of their enlightenment, or use the genius of the dreamers to tread the slippery slope back to the darkness.

More from David Litwack

THE DAUGHTER OF THE SEA AND THE SKY

This literary, speculative novel examining the clash of religion and reason is now available.

~~~~~

After centuries of religiously motivated war, the world has been split in two. Now the Blessed Lands are ruled by pure faith, while in the Republic, reason is the guiding light-two different realms, kept apart and at peace by a treaty and an ocean.

Children of the Republic, Helena and Jason were inseparable in their youth, until fate sent them down different paths. Grief and duty sidetracked Helena's plans, and Jason came to detest the hollowness of his ambitions.

These two damaged souls are reunited when a tiny boat from the Blessed Lands crashes onto the rocks near Helena's home after an impossible journey across the forbidden ocean. On board is a single passenger, a nine-year-old girl named Kailani, who calls herself *The Daughter of the Sea and the Sky*. A new and perilous purpose binds Jason and Helena together again, as they vow to protect the lost innocent from the wrath of the authorities, no matter the risk to their future and freedom.

But is the mysterious child simply a troubled little girl longing to return home? Or is she a powerful prophet sent to unravel the fabric of a godless Republic, as the outlaw leader of an illegal religious sect would have them believe? Whatever the answer, it will change them all forever... and perhaps their world as well.

~~~~~

THE CHILDREN OF DARKNESS

This first critically-acclaimed, award-winning book of *The Seekers* dystopian trilogy is now available.

~~~~~

"But what are we without dreams?"

A thousand years ago the Darkness came—a terrible time of violence, fear, and social collapse when technology ran rampant. But the vicars of the Temple of Light brought peace, ushering in an era of blessed simplicity. For ten centuries they have kept the madness at bay with "temple magic," and by eliminating forever the rush of progress that nearly caused the destruction of everything.

Childhood friends, Orah and Nathaniel, have always lived in the tiny village of Little Pond, longing for more from life but unwilling to challenge the rigid status quo. When their friend Thomas returns from the Temple after his "teaching"—the secret coming-of-age ritual that binds the young to the Light—they barely recognize the broken and brooding man the boy has become. Then when Orah is summoned as well, Nathaniel follows in a foolhardy attempt to save her.

In the prisons of Temple City, they discover a terrible secret that launches the three on a journey to find the forbidden keep, placing their lives in jeopardy. For hidden in the keep awaits a truth from the past that threatens the foundation of the Temple. If they reveal that truth, they might release the long-suppressed potential of their people, but they would also incur the Temple's wrath as it is written:

"If there comes among you a dreamer of dreams saying 'Let us return to the darkness,' you shall stone him, because he has sought to thrust you away from the light."

~~~~~

Praise for *The Children of Darkness*:

"A tightly executed first fantasy installment that champions the exploratory spirit.

– Kirkus Reviews

"The plot unfolds easily, swiftly, and never lets the readers' attention wane.... After reading this one, it will be a real hardship to have to wait to see what happens next."

– Feathered Quill Book Reviews

"The quality of its intelligence, imagination, and prose raises *The Children of Darkness* to the level of literature."

– Awesome Indies

"...a fantastic tale of a world that seeks a utopian existence, well ordered, safe and fair for everyone... also an adventure, a coming-of-age story of three young people as they become the seekers, travelers in search of a hidden treasure—in this case, a treasure of knowledge and answers. A tale of futuristic probabilities... on a par with Huxley's *Brave New World*."

– Emily-Jane Hills Orford, Readers' Favorite Book Awards

More from Evolved Publishing:

CHILDREN'S PICTURE BOOKS
THE BIRD BRAIN BOOKS by Emlyn Chand:
    Courtney Saves Christmas
    Davey the Detective
    Honey the Hero
    Izzy the Inventor
    Larry the Lonely
    Polly Wants to be a Pirate
    Poppy the Proud
    Ricky the Runt
    Ruby to the Rescue
    Sammy Steals the Show
    Tommy Goes Trick-or-Treating
    Vicky Finds a Valentine
Silent Words by Chantal Fournier
Bella and the Blue Genie by Jonathan Gould
Maddie's Monsters by Jonathan Gould
Thomas and the Tiger-Turtle by Jonathan Gould
EMLYN AND THE GREMLIN by Steff F. Kneff:
    Emlyn and the Gremlin
    Emlyn and the Gremlin and the Barbeque Disaster
    Emlyn and the Gremlin and the Mean Old Cat
    Emlyn and the Gremlin and the Seaside Mishap
I'd Rather Be Riding My Bike by Eric Pinder
SULLY P. SNOOFERPOOT'S AMAZING INVENTIONS by Aaron Shaw Ph.D.:
    Sully P. Snooferpoot's Amazing New Forcefield
    Sully P. Snooferpoot's Amazing New Shadow
THE ADVENTURES OF NINJA AND BUNNY by Kara S. Tyler:
    Ninja and Bunny's Great Adventure
    Ninja and Bunny to the Rescue
VALENTINA'S SPOOKY ADVENTURES by Majanka Verstraete:
    Valentina and the Haunted Mansion
    Valentina and the Masked Mummy
    Valentina and the Whackadoodle Witch

HISTORICAL FICTION
Galerie by Steven Greenberg
SHINING LIGHT'S SAGA by Ruby Standing Deer:
    Circles (Book 1)

Spirals (Book 2)
Stones (Book 3)

LITERARY FICTION

Carry Me Away by Robb Grindstaff
Hannah's Voice by Robb Grindstaff
Turning Trixie by Robb Grindstaff
Cassia by Lanette Kauten
The Daughter of the Sea and the Sky by David Litwack
A Handful of Wishes by E.D. Martin
The Lone Wolf by E.D. Martin
Jellicle Girl by Stevie Mikayne
Weight of Earth by Stevie Mikayne
White Chalk by Pavarti K. Tyler

LOWER GRADE (Chapter Books)

THE PET SHOP SOCIETY by Emlyn Chand:
  Maddie and the Purrfect Crime
  Mike and the Dog-Gone Labradoodle
  Tyler and the Blabber-Mouth Birds
TALES FROM UPON A. TIME by Falcon Storm:
  Natalie the Not-So-Nasty
  The Perils of Petunia
  The Persnickety Princess
WEIRDVILLE by Majanka Verstraete:
  Drowning in Fear
  Fright Train
  Grave Error
  House of Horrors
  The Clumsy Magician
  The Doll Maker
THE BALDERDASH SAGA by J.W.Zulauf:
  The Underground Princess (Book 1)
  The Prince's Plight (Book 2)
  The Shaman's Salvation (Book 3)
THE BALDERDASH SAGA SHORT STORIES by J.W.Zulauf:
  Hurlock the Warrior King
  Roland the Pirate Knight
  Scarlet the Kindhearted Princess

MEMOIR

And Then It Rained: Lessons for Life by Megan Morrison

MIDDLE GRADE

FRENDYL KRUNE by Kira A. McFadden:
Frendyl Krune and the Blood of the Sun (Book 1)
Frendyl Krune and the Snake Across the Sea (Book 2)
Frendyl Krune and the Stone Princess (Book 3)

NOAH ZARC by D. Robert Pease:
Mammoth Trouble (Book 1)
Cataclysm (Book 2)
Declaration (Book 3)
Omnibus (Special 3-in-1 Edition)

MYSTERY / CRIME / DETECTIVE

DUNCAN COCHRANE by David Hagerty:
They Tell Me You Are Wicked (Book 1)

Hot Sinatra by Axel Howerton

NEW ADULT

THE DESERT by Angela Scott:
Desert Rice (Book 1)
Desert Flower (Book 2)

NOTHING FAIR ABOUT IT by Linda Kay Silva:
Nothing Fair About It (Book 1)
Nothing Fair About It: Something Always Changes (Book 2)

SCI-FI / FANTASY

Eulogy by D.T. Conklin
THE PANHELION CHRONICLES by Marlin Desault:
Shroud of Eden (Book 1)
The Vanquished of Eden (Book 2)

THE SEEKERS by David Litwack:
The Children of Darkness (Book 1)
The Stuff of Stars (Book 2)
The Light of Reason (Book 3)

THE AMULI CHRONICLES: SOULBOUND by Kira A. McFadden:
The Soulbound Curse (Book 1)
The Soulless King (Book 2)
The Throne of Souls (Book 3)

Shadow Swarm by D. Robert Pease
Two Moons of Sera by Pavarti K. Tyler

SHORT STORY ANTHOLOGIES

FROM THE EDITORS AT EVOLVED PUBLISHING:
Evolution: Vol. 1 (A Short Story Collection)

Evolution: Vol. 2 (A Short Story Collection)
The Futility of Loving a Soldier by E.D. Martin

SUSPENSE / THRILLER

Shatter Point by Jeff Altabef
TONY HOOPER by Lane Diamond:
> *Forgive Me, Alex (Book 1)*
>
> *The Devil's Bane (Book 2)*

Enfold Me by Steven Greenberg
Shadow Side by Ellen Joyce
THE OZ FILES by Barry Metcalf:
> *Broometime Serenade (Book 1)*
>
> *Intrigue at Sandy Point (Book 2)*
>
> *Spirit of Warrnambool (Book 3)*

THE ZOE DELANTE THRILLERS by C.L. Roberts-Huth:
> *Whispers of the Dead (Book 1)*
>
> *Whispers of the Serpent (Book 2)*
>
> *Whispers of the Sidhe (Book 3)*

YOUNG ADULT

CHOSEN by Jeff Altabef and Erynn Altabef:
> *Wind Catcher (Book 1)*
>
> *Brink of Dawn (Book 2)*
>
> *Scorched Souls (Book 3)*

THE KIN CHRONICLES by Michael Dadich:
> *The Silver Sphere (Book 1)*
>
> *The Sinister Kin (Book 2)*

THE DARLA DECKER DIARIES by Jessica McHugh:
> *Darla Decker Hates to Wait (Book 1)*
>
> *Darla Decker Takes the Cake (Book 2)*
>
> *Darla Decker Shakes the State (Book 3)*
>
> *Darla Decker Plays it Straight (Book 4)*

JOEY COLA by D. Robert Pease:
> *Dream Warriors (Book 1)*
>
> *Cleopatra Rising (Book 2)*
>
> *Third Reality (Book 3)*

Anyone? by Angela Scott
THE ZOMBIE WEST TRILOGY by Angela Scott:
> *Wanted: Dead or Undead (Book 1)*
>
> *Survivor Roundup (Book 2)*
>
> *Dead Plains (Book 3)*
>
> *The Zombie West Trilogy – Special Omnibus Edition 1-3*

CPSIA information can be obtained
at www.ICGtesting.com
Printed in the USA
LVOW13s2332230717

542368LV00002B/12/P